PROGRESSION

Other titles by Aaron T. Brownell

Reflection
Contention
The Long Path

PROGRESSION
A SARA GREY TALE

A Novel

Aaron T. Brownell

PROGRESSION
A SARA GREY TALE

iUniverse books may be ordered through booksellers or by contacting:

iUniverse LLC
1663 Liberty Drive
Bloomington, IN 47403
www.iuniverse.com
1-800-Authors (1-800-288-4677)

ISBN: 978-1-4917-4456-7 (sc)
ISBN: 978-1-4917-4457-4 (e)

Library of Congress Control Number: 2014915071

Printed in the United States of America.

iUniverse rev. date: 09/10/2014

Once again, I would like to thank Jeff for editing the manuscript. He does a masterful job of suffering through the horrendous beating I give the English language.

The third journal chronicling
the life of
Lady Sara Anne Grey

Born: London, England
June 21, 1633

Died: London, England
July 2, 1651

Current age: 380 years

Penned in New York, USA
September 2013

CHAPTER 1

To be perfectly plain, I'm not opposed to killing. I rather enjoy it. The ending of a life, the cessation of the heartbeat, life pulling itself back into the void from whence it came, slowing to a beat and gone, all preceding a long pause before the calm. It's a powerful and awe-inspiring thing. Spilling someone's blood and watching it drain away as their time quietly goes with it is a profoundly terrifying, yet highly attractive, scene.

That being said, there is a time and place for all things. One in my position needs to be practical about killing. Killing takes planning and practice. I learned long, long ago that if the bodies started to pile up, you were going to draw attention. So I tend to plan—not a sociopathic type of scheming, as that would be entirely too human. My planning is purely practical. I research areas where people are not likely to be missed and where there are good places to dispose of bodies. For a dead body lying in an alley, the smell both drawing and repelling passersby, rodents probing it for a potential meal, calls humans to action faster than any invading army. Trust me—it's true. Today, the killing has become a matter of choice: to remove someone from my path or to find victory in the conquering of an adversary. It wasn't some uncontrollable need to embrace taboos. That specific desire does consume others of my kind, though I have never found the need to embrace its demonic undertones. It's simply one choice of several, an option, as it were.

Now, back in the times just preceding 1865, where this story begins, it was more a matter of lifestyle. I used to kill people and drain their blood on a fairly regular basis. It wasn't really a need, just a desire.

There were plenty of outlets for blood in the New York City of the 1860s. Surviving, low impact as it were, was an easy enough thing to accomplish. Many of my kind stayed quite anonymous in those days by proficient use of contacts at the local slaughterhouse. I did the same myself.

That method worked fine most days, but not some days. Let's just say that—some days a lady needs the true adrenaline surge that pulses through the body by drinking several pints of blood drawn from a completely terrified human being. The killing, the person knowing they are about to die, makes blood potent. That potent fluid is really what every vampire is seeking. I mean, why just live when you can live well?

Wow, this is really beginning to sound like a manifesto. I guess it is, in a sense, since it is the story of me: why I am the way I am and why I do what I do.

To answer quickly, my name is Lady Sara Anne Grey. I was born in London in 1633 and died in London in 1651. And I am a vampire. I was made this way by another vampire, a man named Antonio Boca. Why I was made to be a creature outside the rules of God is a long story that has already filled two journals preceding this one. Why I do what I do is simple: I do it because I can. It took me a long time to realize that there is a place for everything in nature, including me. I exist and prolong my existence by utilizing the same base rules as any other creature. I move about society in the same fashion as any other individual, though be it with better success. I run a business, hold title, and freely move about society. And yes, I kill. I kill as I see fit, which is where this story begins.

I had been living in New York City again for some decades. It was the year 1865. New York City had always been a good home to me. It wasn't North London or the fields of Bristol in the United Kingdom, but it was a good third home—well, up until recent years.

The killing from America's Civil War was literally everywhere. It was so prevalent that I stopped viewing myself as a menace. My killing went as unnoticed as everyone else's. So many people were killing so many other people that it eventually turned my stomach. I just didn't want to be adding to the pile of death anymore.

The pall that the war put over the country left me out of sorts for a time. The whole affair made me long for my English homeland. I tried to put it from my mind and pulled energy to survive from the magick in the amulet that I wear.

The amulet is made up of a shiny jewel comprised of two fused stones, etched on every side with mystical symbols, all collected on a long, golden chain. The amulet itself is a vessel. It holds a life force that funnels and controls the primal powers that keep the universe in sway. The controller of the Void, She is my constant and long-standing friend. We have had our differences over the years, as she has a greater hatred of mankind than I, but we look after each other as best we can.

On an everyday level, Effie (as she is known) releases a sliver of her limitless power into me. That power supply relaxes and replaces my blood urge. She extends my need to feed from days to months or more, which helps me to blend into society at large. Not needing to feed makes me look and, oddly enough, act much more human than others of my kind.

In the fall of 1865, I was feeding on humans at a rate of maybe one every six weeks or so. The remainder of the time the amulet would pull energy from the sun and infuse me with it. It helped me along. Effie sustained and comforted me, and I protected her and allowed her back into the world. We were great friends.

Now the opportunities to kill humans were much better than when I had first come to New York City many years before. By 1865, the city had swelled to some 860,000 souls. People were, quite literally, everywhere. One simply needed to pick a person off the street and feed. It was fabulous for the predators, since the majority of these souls were immigrating to the country. They were just not going to be missed when they were gone.

The boom in population was also a good sign on other fronts. Business for Grey Cargo was particularly outstanding. The completion of the Erie Canal around 1825 helped to draw freight out of the harbor and into the Great Lakes. The pull of goods into the landlocked interior and the transportation of salt out of the Great Lake's mines helped to make New York City the harbor of choice. By 1840, the harbor saw more freight and passenger ships than any other large port in America. An early and prominent location on the docks helped propel Grey Cargo into a major mover of freight. Even though the main corporate offices were still in London, the office in New York City conducted the majority of the Atlantic business. It was windfall profits all around. For a girl who had grown up on the sketchy docks of the Thames, it was a justification of skills.

The corporation ran along nicely under the Wyndell stewardship. I stayed mostly out of the way and did what vampires do. This is the way things went for some time. We made the rules as we went along. We made the rules, and by proxy, a ridiculous sum of money. Business was so good that it seemed to run itself. Yet, at the same time, it was an albatross around my neck. I had not been born to be a businesswoman. It had been forced upon me by my father and the vampire named Antonio Boca. They apparently knew what they were doing, because since shortly after my eighteen-year-old human life ended, I had been doing it to the sum of millions of pounds.

I embraced the business because it allowed me to focus my will on something. I could use my excess energy to get what I wanted out of people. From a business point of view, you couldn't beat it. But it wasn't the ideal life for a young lady, not even a young lady raised on the docks of the Thames by a father who owned a shipping company. It had always been an adventure when I was a human girl and the thing that had set my personality. That exasperated my nanny, Ms. Palmer, to no end. She had tried to make me a proper lady, but the docks had beaten her out.

All I had ever really wanted to do was marry a gentleman of some good station and have a family like every other girl I knew. But that was before I was killed, turned into a vampire, informed I had a noble title, pushed into unrealistic responsibility, and forced to survive at the cost of man. We really never are what we intend.

Over the passage of time, life has adjusted. The business has helped me live the life of a wealthy, independent lady. It has also clung to me like the marks left from a good bout of plague. You know—ring around the rosie, a pocket full of posies.

My once manly confidants, the Wyndell men, were allowed to slowly take over the daily wheel of the corporation. It worked, since their family had a natural aptitude for business. They received more power as I slowly faded from the spotlight of the business world. It had started with Charles Wyndell, back in 1651, when he became my first human confidant. He had taught me many lessons about being both a vampire and a human being. He was my first true friend. His son took his place, by choice, and so started a long line of men standing by and helping me out.

I had done my best over the years to make sure that the Wyndell family was exposed to optimum chances to promote their own wealth. In so doing, the Wyndell family had gone from nothing to being one of the wealthiest families in England. If you added in the fact that they looked after my extravagant fortune, they were unmatched in most of Europe. The family really did have a knack for it all, which was why I let them do it. They wanted power and I wanted anonymity. It all just worked well.

At the present moment, Fletcher Wyndell ran the corporation from the main office on the Thames, London, England. His brother, Charles Wyndell, was my confidant and friend and lived in New York City. There Charles oversaw the New York office for Fletcher. They both knew I was a vampire and knew full well how I lived. All men who moved into the levels of business manager or confidant were well educated in the ways of my kind. Some of them took quickly to the occult, and some did not. But all had gone too far to think about turning back, so they continued on.

Though Charles was still in the mix at this point, it was much more a tea-and-afternoon-talks relationship. He was getting on in years, and his son, Charles Brian Wyndell, had basically taken over the heavy lifting part of the confidant duties. Spending time with a vampire really is a game for the young. The knowledge gained often tends to take a toll on individuals. As a matter of course, these individuals don't tend to go into their later years. I don't hold it against them. They do what they can, and then the next one takes over. Brian, as most knew him, took to it all with the same gusto that the rest of his clan had. His father was also happy to pass the torch.

I think it was the watching of it all that made the business an albatross. They came and they went, yet my business and I remained. Thinking about it made me melancholy. Many things over the years made me melancholy, but this one definitely did so.

Normally when melancholy, I went home to London. The Grey Estate could always pull me back to the bright side of things. Business matters mixed with the war depression, which was eating away at the soul of my adopted country, had pushed me to uncommon depths of melancholy. It was definitely time to go home. It was time to be treated like the sixth Earl of Northwick once more. Yes, past time.

Upon deciding to leave the United States, I had no idea that going home would actually lead me on an adventure equal to many others that have come along in my life. A simple boat ride across the Atlantic would send me off chasing an old love, dealing with world wars, fighting an old foe who was not smart enough to let the past die in peace, and traveling back in time to give an old friend some joy.

It has never failed that whenever I think things in my life are going well, something comes along to bollox it up. Yup, it happens every single time. This time it would be those damned Bennetts. They took one of the most precious of things from me, but I prevailed. They tried their best to drive me to the grave, but I survived. They forced me to make life-changing decisions, and in the end they lost. They never understood that I am a survivor. It's part of my core being, and my little friend around my neck is the same way.

I'm obviously getting ahead of myself here. This is a story that takes many pages to tell. It has both roguish and noble figures involved. It covers many lands and stretches from the Industrial Revolution to the Technological Revolution. It is simply the story of a girl making her way through the world.

It all starts in the blood-soaked lands of America at the end of the Civil War. This was the ground that I stood on in the fall of 1865. Little did I know that the coming years, much as the preceding ones, would become an adventure that tested me to my core.

CHAPTER 2

I stood in the middle of the windows of my private study on a quiet morning in October 1865 and watched the unfolding sidewalk scene many floors below. Weather had moved in from the Atlantic in the form of a nor'easter and was pelting down a driving snow on the unprepared population. The drama had started hours before sunrise, building, changing, and fixing its eye on the city so it could deliver misery as if it were a living thing.

I'd been watching the storm since before it made landfall. I couldn't sleep so I came to my study to pace. There was a pile of correspondence on my French writing desk, and I occupied my time with it and the weather. I first noticed the storm out at sea, in between letters. My vision is much better in the dark than that of your standard human. It's one of the reasons I wear my trademark dark glasses. I like the edge my night vision gives me.

I have never really minded the many moods of the planet's weather. I think it should be allowed to do whatever it wants to, just as everything else in nature does. I just don't like being out in the big blows. That is especially true of the rain. I don't like rain. I don't know why, but I haven't liked rain since I was a little girl. It's not the getting wet, per se. It just seems like the world is mad at something and taking it out on me. I especially don't like the heavy squalls at sea. They're hard on the fleet and the men. Heavy seas tend to swallow both ships and profits.

Thinking about the ships out in this storm made me pensive. I sat and tried to read all the correspondences that had been sent from the numerous offices of the corporation as a way to soothe my mood. The first explained that which I already knew too well. Though the Civil War had officially ended in April, the fighting hadn't really ended until June, when General Stand Watie surrendered to Union soldiers at Fort Towson in the Choctaw Nation. It was summarized that the end of open hostilities would go a long way to helping two of the major expansions being undertaken on the continent.

The Transcontinental Railroad Act, which set out to build three lines across the American continent, and the Homestead Act, which gave western land for free to anyone willing to farm the parcels. Both acts had passed through Congress and were set to radically expand the size of the United States. Since these undertakings had not been conducted in the best of places, progress had been slow. With the secession of hostilities, the pace had improved. That was welcome news. I had a vested interest in the new railroad system. It was set to push trade all the way to the shores of the great Pacific. The real world possibilities of this were almost unfathomable.

The next correspondence informed me that King Leopold I of Belgium had died. He had been replaced by his son, aptly named Leopold II. Apparently, he was busy expanding his interests in the heart of the Congo. It wasn't a shock. Many European monarchs were taking stabs at Africa, including those in my homeland. It had been fashionable ever since Napoleon made the northern part of Africa French speaking.

A third letter said that a man named William Booth, back in London, had founded a mission called the Salvation Army. Though I have no particular love of religious people, he seemed interesting in that he wanted to help the masses. The letter also said that a man named Lewis Carroll wrote a book titled *Alice's Adventures in Wonderland*. Fletcher had been nice enough to enclose a copy, which sat on the corner of the desk. I was told it was quite a fanciful tale. I would need to find time for that. For right now it sat as I pondered the squall outside.

The early storm came down on the city relentlessly. It pounded snow down on the streets. It blinded the views with an opaque whiteness that was solid, like new parchment. The accompanying winds closed out all of the scurrying sounds the city produced.

What the driving winds did not drown out was the sound of young Brian Wyndell entering the residence. I could hear him stomp his heavy boots on the front step, shake the snow from his coat inside the door, announce his standard greeting to the head housekeeper, trudge the numerous flights of stairs, cross the outer study, and let himself into the inner study that lay hidden behind the stacks. It was pathetic really. I mean, the Wyndell line had lost all of their stealth in a single generation. What would go next: their secretive nature or their business abilities? I shuttered to think about the steps that would need to be implemented if such things came to pass. For now, it was simply annoying.

Brian plopped himself down in one of the two overstuffed leather chairs situated in front of the windows as the bookcase reoriented itself. He shuffled a bit in the chair and then looked about like the curious young man that he was.

"Good morning, Lady Gibbs. How is your day?"

"Brian Wyndell, does it bother you that I could hear you clearly overtop of the storm raging outside?"

"Heard me? Doing what?"

"Coming into the building, stomping your fat feet on the step, pretty much everything there was to hear. I find it odd that after numerous generations of stealthy men, you come along and wipe it all away."

"I'm not that loud."

I didn't need to turn around to see the pouting expression on his face. I could tell it was there by the change in his breathing. So, I stayed looking at the snow.

"Brain, stop pouting."

"I'm not. How do you do that?"

"When you've been alive as long as me, you'll be able to do it too. Now, onto different matters."

"Yes, ma'am."

"Do you like your occupation?"

"Hmmm, yes."

"You sound unsure."

"You never ask questions that are so suspect,"

"On the contrary, I do it all the time. I've just never done it to you before. Now, answer the question."

"Yes, very much so."

"Why?"

"Well, I don't know anyone who has a job such as mine. It is seldom dull."

"Seldom dull … hmmm, I'll accept that as acceptable."

"Why?"

"Because, we are going on a trip."

"A trip? Where to?"

I could hear the excitement in his voice. His forebears would have known better. It made me start to rethink the whole thing.

"I feel like going home. The Civil War has me longing for blood-free lands, so we're off for London."

"Sounds great, how long will we be gone?"

"Until I decide to go somewhere else." I could hear the rhythm of his breathing change again. He was getting apprehensive. That didn't bode well, especially for his longevity.

"You mean, a couple of years or so?"

"I mean, until I decide to go somewhere else."

"I'm not really sure that now is a good time to be traveling,"

"Why, because you fancy a girl across town and assume if you leave that she'll move on to someone more stable?"

"How did you know that?"

"Hmm, a pixy redheaded girl named Suzy McBenter. Supposedly, she's well mannered for a common girl. And you're right, she'll move on as soon as you're on the ship."

"So, I should stay?"

"Brian, do you remember the discussion we had when you wanted to take over for your father?" He didn't say anything. "Mr. Wyndell, it was a yes or no question."

"Yes, ma'am, I do."

"Good. Now, as you remember, you were informed that you could terminate your employment whenever you chose. And, at such time, you would be promptly removed from the planet in an extremely violent fashion."

I could hear him swallowing in an attempt to calm his building anxiety—an anxiety that was threatening to put a sweat stain on his otherwise bleach white collar, which he was tugging at with one finger in an attempt to let more air into his body. It was nice to see that he was finally coming to terms with the fact that he was not in control of his life. Apparently, it hadn't hit him until now.

"So, you've had enough of your current position, is it?"

"......no?"

"Charles Brian Wyndell, do not answer a question with a question! You're a man; I suggest you act like one."

"No, ma'am, I do not wish to terminate my employment."

"That's better. Stop being a prat. Now, head down to the office and secure us passage on the next vessel we have headed for England that has something akin to luxury cabins."

"Right away. How soon?"

"The next vessel sailing for England that meets our needs will be fine with me—just no sooner than a week."

"Yes, ma'am."

"When you're finished with that task, go ask your father if he might stop to see me at his convenience. I would like to converse with him before we depart."

"Yes, ma'am."

"Good. Now be on your way."

Young Mr. Wyndell stood quickly and headed out the way he had entered. I pondered as I listened to him trudge back out of the residence overtop of the weather just how many people had been exactly where he was now. There had been many, and they had all ended up the same way. It was sad for him, but such is life.

The snow squall blew itself out and turned into two days of sun before Master Charles graced me with his company. He was my friend. I enjoyed his company very much. I did hate what I was about to do to him.

It was early afternoon, and the sun was just beginning to make small rivulets of what would become long-imposing shadows from the buildings of my street, when Charles appeared. I was in the outer study, lounging in a luxurious rocking chair located next to the stone hearth, thinking about breaking the spine of Alice's adventure, when Charles opened the door and entered. Even in the afternoon quiet of the house, I hadn't heard him approach. He was quiet like the church mouse, that one. It was a trait of all the men in his family, save his son.

"Good afternoon, Charles. You look well. Tell me you're well?"

"I'm quite fine, Sara. Thank you for asking. How are you today?"

"My mood is sunny, much like the weather. I was just getting ready to start reading the book that your brother Fletcher sent me, but with you for company, it will have to wait."

Charles chuckled and smiled. He had that rolled-up face kind of smile that made his eyes squint. He obviously found it funny.

"Brian seemed concerned when he told me you wished to speak."

"Hmm, yes, right to business."

"We can converse a while beforehand, if you like. It's not usually your way."

"No, it's not. But then, this whole conversation is going to be my way."

"That sounds foreboding."

"We have been friends a long time now, you and I. I would say it has been more good than bad, wouldn't you?"

"Yes, Sara, I would. What's on your mind?"

"Your son, Brian."

"Yes?"

"I *REALLY* want to kill him."

Charles scratched his chin in that ominous way that he did when he was considering answering questions that could only be answered once. He looked deep into the back of the hearth, as if it knew something he didn't, and he pondered. I could tell he was thinking back over decades of deeds done in my service, wondering how he might have gotten here. The silence went on for some time before he focused and looked up with a smile on his face. It was a smile that came from a much younger man.

"It would seem that the two of you have obviously come to some impasse. He was a grown man at the onset. I would say he knew what he was getting into when he accepted your employ."

I starred at Charles in an incredulous sort of way. This I hadn't expected at all.

"That's it? He knew what he was doing? What about, 'No, don't kill my son?' 'You're destroying my family lineage?' Are you sure you're feeling up to snuff?"

Charles chuckled once more and rolled up his face. He removed his spectacles and rubbed them clean on a fine linen handkerchief.

"Sara, my lovely girl, you really are a paradox. You look so young, and you think so old. You truly can be a challenge at times."

I just looked at him incredulously.

"I suppose all the points you made are true, to some degree. I'm not really excited with the prospect of you killing Brian. I'm also not happy that my name will end with me. But to be fair, these things can happen to any man, on any day, and they don't require you to facilitate them. He could easily die in an altercation at the local tavern or at night on some slippery cobblestone street. Like I said, he knew what he was doing, as did the rest of us. If you spend your life tempting fate, sooner or later you end up paying. Apparently, this is that time."

"I am honestly not sure what to do with that response, Charles."

"How many times have you had the need to remove a problem permanently?"

"Several."

"And did you dwell on it, or just get to it?"

"Only once have I dwelled on such a decision. It, too, had similar circumstances."

"Yes, my great uncle and the members of your inner circle. They all died, yet both you and the Wyndell family went on together well enough."

I stared at Charles, dumbfounded. We had never discussed the killing of the inner circle or his uncle.

"Sara, I'm fully aware of my family's history, both the good and the bad of it. For that matter, so is Brian. I raised him, but I can't live his life for him. It strikes me as odd that you are even asking me about my opinion."

"I don't know, Charles. Maybe, it's the whole state of the war these last years, or maybe the residual power from the amulet keeping me from feeding. Frankly, I was hoping you would proxy up some grand argument and talk me out of it."

Charles pulled off his bins and rubbed them clean a second time. The amulet started to glow a soft yellow.

"Now," he said with a whimsical smile, "there's something you don't hear every day."

"Charles, please."

"Sorry, Sara, I couldn't help myself. Seriously, do what you need to do, because that is what you are going to do. But if you really want an out, leave him here with me. I will look after his mouth and movements as long as I can. Once I'm gone, so is your guilt. Then go do what you want. How's that?"

"Can you keep a handle on him?"

"I should think so. He really isn't that stealthy. We truly are different people."

"I do like the sound of that. Yes, it sounds good to me. You keep him in check and maybe get grandkids."

"See, problem solved. Now, it's lovely out. Let's take a walk around the city and discuss the state of the day."

"That sounds grand, old friend. Let me get my throw."

We stood. Charles smoothed the wrinkles out of his clothes as I retrieved proper attire. Both looking smart, we headed for the door. We broke out of the door and my opaque glasses absorbed the greater extend of the sun's rays, leaving New York City a dull gray, like after the sunset. Charles adjusted his hat and tilted his head in my direction as we walked.

"I know you have these old-world rules of etiquette regarding the ways a lady should be seen in public, being an Earl and all, but you might consider spending a little time with my daughter, Megan. She really is the most like me, of the three of them."

"I don't know. I'll take it under advisement though, old friend."

Charles smiled, and we continued on across the fashionable Upper East Side. The sun continued its march west as we discussed the remains of the day.

CHAPTER 3

The *Northern Express* slid through the North Atlantic chop with little effort and minimal rolling of the decks. The steady state of the ship had proven how far our ship building technology had come since the day I founded the Bristol Mooring. My favorite ship, *The Summer Storm,* a vessel built personally for me by the staff at the Mooring, had a significant roll to it. That is, compared to the beautiful vessel I was currently on.

At times I missed having my own ship to see me about. She had been slipped from her dry dock just after the first vampire gala, where she transported John Francis and me to Venice on holiday. Sadly, my old friend, *The Summer Storm,* foundered in a storm off the coast of Virginia in 1836. It was truly a sad day. We were close friends, that ship and me. We had partaken in many adventures together. After she went down, I couldn't bring myself to have another commissioned, so I decided to just move about with the cargo. That decision had been working quite well to date. It was still nice to have a tall ship at my bidding, one that flew the colors of Grey House high on her mast. *The Northern Express* now flew the flag of Grey House; it just wasn't natural for her to do so. Nor was it natural to have the Brimme House flag stretched out in the breeze just below it.

The quicker pace of the day meant it would only be days until we made landfall in the British Isles. Normally, I would head straight for Bristol and then make my way east to London. On this voyage I was heading straight for the Thames. That was where the ship we were on was headed—the *we* I am referring to in this context being me and young Megan Mary Wyndell.

It was oddly exciting to be in the company of a young woman. I spent so much time in the company of men that I had forgotten how young women acted. I had already noticed from the differences in our mannerisms that I had become much more tomboy than in earlier times. I would need to work on that as I went along. I was really just happy to be rid of her brother Brian.

I had to once again commend their father for his sound judgment. Megan was much more the Wyndell child I was looking for. A five foot, six inch beauty, with large brown eyes, long, curly dark hair, and a moderate complexion, she was in possession of all the attributes to attract men. It was the other things that attracted me. She had a depth behind her eyes that said she was smarter than she let on. She was quiet, well spoken, and thought on things before she opened her mouth. When you spoke to her, she listened and was discreet with information. In many ways she reminded me of her great aunt Amber. Amber also had it all together.

The problem I had was that everything that drew me to her was raw genetics. All of her good traits were merely by-products of her being a Wyndell. At this point in time, she knew nothing about me being a vampire. I had only days to give Megan an education that usually took the men in her family decades to process. It would certainly be world-changing for her, I knew that. I just hoped that she made the transition from shock to fancy to belief fairly quickly. If not, it was going to be trouble.

Fortunately for me, in 1865 the populous hadn't moved that far into the Industrial Age. All of the old ways were still there, just under the skin of society. It would only take a little shovel work for her to expose it all again. As expected, she took to it with ease. The journey was more than sufficient to get her around the base information. She had accepted belief quite quickly; she reminded me of that first Wyndell man I had known.

Megan and I made our way north from the docks, and soon enough, some five years quickly passed by at the Grey Estate. Once we had settled in, Megan began studying the numerous volumes in the library. Fletcher and I moved about London doing the fashionable things of the day, and also doing some business with the business types. I sent out some feelers in an attempt to locate Antonio. The conversation with Megan regarding my trysts had stirred my libido. My dark lord, when he wasn't being a sociopathic killer, was an excellent instrument with which to work out my sexual tension. He was my maker. He was also the one who had been responsible for making me a woman. He was very good at doing that thing that men do. Sadly, he was still being an arse. The news of the day had him off on a killing spree in Istanbul. Well, at least he had picked a good spot. Port towns are always good hunting grounds.

I passed my excess time walking the meadows of my youth. The meadows of the estate always had a way of making me happy. I would walk the well-worn paths and pick wild flowers. My friend in the amulet would soak up the sun and store its awesome power away. On occasion, Megan would walk with us. She usually filled the otherwise quiet time with questions. At points it could get annoying, but she was trying to fit a rather hefty education into a reasonable amount of time. I will say that, after half of a decade, she had managed to become a scholar on the topic. She was also a genuinely nice person, which helped my sense of calm.

I was left alone a lot as a human girl. I had some female friends, but they were all the daughters of father's business partners. After becoming a vampire and moving off to Bristol, I had found a small circle of female friends. They, too, were the daughters of my banking and business contacts. They helped me to blend into society and find my place in the world.

Even as a countess, I had some female friends whom I met with socially. But that was the extent of things. All of my confidential matters were handled with men. I had never really considered having a confidant who was a woman. It had to do with the times in which I existed. For most of my existence, my male confidant was also utilized as my escort. Proper young ladies, and those trying to be proper in middle age as well, were not seen in public without a man to escort and protect them. It was just the way times were and the way that women were viewed. I needed the anonymity that a male escort gave me. All of the Wyndell men, for their part, made good escorts. They were kind and gentlemanly.

However, with the advent of the Industrial Age, those times in the great United Kingdom were changing. Women were now going to work, often in places where they could produce mill goods. That was giving them greater status. The days of women being viewed as second-class citizens, or perhaps more aptly as men's property, were slowly going away. They had by no means left, but they were going.

Moving about London with Megan in tow, taking in the symphony, and having high tea, all made me stop and notice how things had gradually moved on since I was born. When I was alive, I would not have even considered going to the symphony with another girl my age and no nanny or male escort. Now it seemed quite natural.

Megan's cousins running my corporation, Grey's Cargo, dispelled any of the loose talk that seemed to follow two lone girls about town. It was also helpful that the only people who thought of me as young were Megan and Fletcher. All of the people who I knew in London from times past were still well alive. I might want to be more precise—recent past, maybe? There are plenty of people from my times past in London who are not alive. That being said, London society saw me as a woman of later years. The people who knew me knew the age they thought I should be, and the remainder of society just inferred from them. The glamour that made people see me as they thought I should be was so second nature that I didn't even think upon it anymore. It just exuded out from me and people used it as they needed. The amulet supplied all my power needs, so extra blood was not required. Things were just all good.

My ever-increasing years had become a topic for Fletcher and me. He had given me my last personality transformation, as it were, and I wanted him to do it again. Sadly, Fletcher was now well into his later years, and like his brother Christopher, would not be with me much longer. I could tell when I was with Fletcher that his end was about to find him, but I said nothing. It wasn't my place to depress him.

Fortunately, he had produced two fine sons, Gregory and Wayne. One was already studying the occult and working in the family business that was Grey's Cargo. That one was Gregory. Wayne had come down from Cambridge and was at the helm of the family business. He had taken over from Tiffany Brown, his cousin, the daughter of Amber Wyndell-St. Anne. I had fond memories of Amber; she was my friend. Looking at the kids, it seemed to me that the whole system would just chug along by itself. That thought made me happy.

Interestingly, to me at least, Fletcher had anticipated my request for another makeover. The template for the new me had already been invented by young Master Gregory. I had a husband who had been killed in the great American Civil War, and he was a war hero no less. My daughter was in an American boarding school and would return to England at some point. All it apparently lacked was a name, a couple of signatures, and placement with the registry.

The Wyndell family had become pre-planners. I did really like that less work than expected needed to be done. I wasn't so sure about doing things in advance. That bit went against my secretive vampire nature. Centuries of the constant need for anonymity had shown me where leaving loose ends could be a bad thing. They always came back to haunt you at some point.

Where I was sure it was unsound, the amulet was not. My friend just seemed amused, or more likely ambivalent toward it all. Where I needed to worry about being killed, she simply worried about being locked away again. She was a primal force that tended to kill large numbers before such things could happen to her. She was definitely better at the killing than I was. That explained why the war with the Brenfield Society had ensued in the first place. That didn't end well for them. Good thing for humankind that my little friend had started to mellow since she had been with me. We liked each other and got on well. Knowing that I wasn't about to let people put her in the dock helped to relax her moods.

Due to this ambivalence from my friend in the crystal, I decided to accept the pre-planning. She had been around for millennia; she must know a thing or two. So, I needed a name and a date. I figured that I could just go on vacation sometime and have some sort of accident; then my as of yet unnamed daughter could appear and inherit it all. The new name wasn't really a challenge. It would all work itself out.

As I slowly pondered my new name, I watched the things in the world unfold. The times, they definitely were a changing. In a sense, I was interested in it, because I had lived long enough to be able to see change happen. At times, it captivated me. Other times, it just made me feel old.

In 1870, one of the changes I enjoyed was the Women's Property Act, which had been enacted by Parliament. The act allowed women who were married to keep the money they made, instead of having to give it to their husbands. It also extended the rights of widows. I liked the idea greatly. The queen, for some unspeakable reason, did not. She seemed to reason that the act was mad and saw women's rights as a folly. Change was definitely slow to come to the world. The queen, of all the people on the planet, had every reason to support the act. She just viewed things from an older lens than I did, I guess. Personally, I was a big fan of the act. The government was making it easier for me to survive. That was good with me.

The government also made it compulsory to have a primary education through the passage of the Foster-Ripon English Elementary Education Act. I approved of this as well. I had benefitted handsomely from the ability to read and write—an ability that was almost nonexistent for women in the 1650s. A better-educated society turned out better trade. Better trade made me wealthy, well wealthier.

Elsewhere, Spain's Isabella II was persuaded to abdicate while in Paris. She had reigned for some twenty-seven years. That must have been some good persuasion. If I were a queen, I certainly wouldn't abdicate to anyone.

France, in a very French move, declared war on Prussia. The French decided that a preemptive strike would be needed against Prussia. That would turn out to be a disaster. The Prussians used the new railroad system and telegraph services to great effect, while the French were unable to get things all together. It was chaos. I never really feel bad when the French lose.

In Japan, the population had grown to the point where the emperor was forced to issue an edict requiring people to have last names. What would people do with two names? Those must have been crazy times in Japan.

At home, Lloyd's of London finally got around to incorporating. It had been going for some 182 years at this point. Apparently they decided they had waited long enough. The institution remained a society of private individuals but with a more secure outer appearance.

London opened its first subway in 1870. The Tower Tube ran under the River Thames. The first section of underground in the city actually used a rope to pull a carriage through the tunnel. Sadly, it never really caught on with anyone and only managed to operate a couple of months. The tunnel for the carriage was turned into a walking path.

Back in America, the construction of the transcontinental Northern Pacific Railroad had finally begun. The line that proclaimed to open the West had managed to come up with many backers, of which I was one. And, while we are on me, New York's Metropolitan Museum of Art was also chartered. They would spend a couple years buying inventory and establishing a space. It was also an endeavor I was happy to subsidize.

Finally, the British White Star Line began its trans-Atlantic service between Liverpool and New York. The steam ships of the day lacked the speed of clipper ships, so they only accounted for a small percentage of the traffic on the high seas. That statistic would change greatly in a short period of time.

There was much more shipping news from those times, more than enough to fill the pages of its own journal, but the piece of shipping news dearest to my own heart was the movement of my corporation's offices. It was a thing that filled me with both sadness and pride.

The small office of Master John Grey that was Grey's shipping and cargo had stood in the middle of the south harbor proper of the River Thames for longer than I had been on this earth. It had been as much my childhood home as the grounds of the estate. Over the centuries it had expanded its footprint many times, until it held the offices of the Grey's Cargo Corporation.

I still owned the townhouse just north of it on Banker's Row. It was where we lived during the shipping season. The southern section of the harbor was very much more my home than many other places on earth. I had grown up walking the docks of the Thames while father went about his business. It always made my blood warm when my feet touched down on the pitch-soaked timbers of the dock slips. That little piece of ground had produced more money for me than I could count. It had taken the Wyndell family from absolute obscurity to the cusp of being princes. It was a magical place. Sadly, in an age of advancement, it was also being left behind.

It is a truth that, as the years pass, things change. One needs to be able to adapt to the changes of the times, or they too will be left behind. Such was also the way of business. Over the previous two centuries, things on the Thames had been slowly shifting. I had noticed the small steps but was little concerned with their impact. At times, the Wyndells would propose changes to our location. I would think about the changes and then decide against them.

I had attempted to move the corporation's offices twice: once to Crete and once to New York City. Neither one of those moves had taken hold and both only produced chaos. The business center never really left London either time. London was where the corporation was meant to be, so I relented each time. My father used to say, "If something was working fine, don't try to break it." Father was always right about business.

The passage of time on the Thames seemed less concerned about permanence than I. Things around the area changed little by little as the years passed. One by one, the docks of the Thames moved north toward Mile End and the outlets of Canary Row. In their place, office buildings emerged. The expansion of London was slowly driving out the old harbor.

The constant push of people, trade, business, and life across the Thames had also produced more and more bridges. The river had always had a few bridges to be navigated. That was one of the reasons that ships would set anchor in deep water and wait for morning light before proceeding into the river. Over the centuries, one or two bridges turned into many. The plentiful bridges and other navigational obstacles were giving the ships more and more trouble.

I had slowly accepted the extra misery, step by step, the way I do with all such events in life. It was young Gregory Wyndell that decided enough was enough. Seemingly from the day we had been introduced to each other, he had pushed for the relocation of the offices. At first I dismissed him and moved on, but that boy was relentless. It was a Wyndell trait.

Gregory kept pushing his platform, not aggressively but professionally. He had a map of the area produced, showing all of the problem spots. He went out and secured new land on the trendy end of Canary Row. Then he went about building a spectacular new office building with ship slips and offloading areas. There were also storage buildings for warehousing goods. All of which had been built with his own funds. He restructured the shipping routes to increase merchant timing and goods capacity, as well as our profits. And he stayed at me with his ideas. Finally, five years on and building all but complete, I conceded. He was right. We both knew that he was right.

With my concession came two nonnegotiable requests. He would take the original signs from the current buildings and relocate them to the new one. He could have new stylish ones hung above them if he liked, but Father's original signs would be our signs. Second, I wanted the furniture in my office moved as is. The desk that Father had used to build a company was good enough for his daughter, and that was that.

Gregory took the requests in stride. He had a good education on the history of the company and understood my nostalgia for the past. So, in 1870, we picked up and moved closer to the sea. I returned to walk along the banks of the Thames numerous times, before the docks were inevitably demolished and modern office buildings claimed their ground.

The new offices were very nice. All the ship captains were well-pleased with the easier run to the docks. Gregory had his shiny new beacon for attracting yet more business, and I had nostalgia. Well, at least everyone had something.

CHAPTER 4

The sun rose on the morning of June 21, 1879, with a cloudless blue sky for a canvas. The happiness that the sun brought me on my birthday was almost without limit. I have always been a child of the sun. In a very real way, it holds sway over my mood. Father used to tell me that he could tell when the dull gray of winter arrived by my melancholy and when the sun of summer arrived by when my melancholy went away. He was always observant.

This day, as with so many other birthdays that had preceded it, I was up long before the sun found the edges of my London home. I had always found great satisfaction in moving about the lands of the estate at night. Practicing my hunting skills on the animals of the wood helped to keep me sharp. Their senses are far superior to those of humans, so they are the ideal training tool.

I had been out chasing stag through the wood for hours when I realized the sun was about to break in the east. The mere thought of a birthday morning sunrise had me excited. I left the animals to their own pursuits and headed toward the residence. I stopped short along the way and headed off into the maze Father had constructed in the back lawn. And, with feet that had traveled that path countless times; I found my way to the stone bench at the center. The dawn was just coming on as I unlaced my low-heeled leather boots and sat them off to one side. I folded my legs up under myself on the bench, just as I did when I was a little girl.

I have never really been able to explain my desire to be barefoot. When I was a little girl, I ran barefoot everywhere—everywhere but the docks. Even for young ladies, it was standard to wear boots while on the docks of the Thames. At the estate, however, it was barefoot everywhere. I was barefoot in the meadows and barefoot on the stone floors of the manner. When Father would host large parties, I would wear floor-length gowns so the upstanding members of society couldn't tell I was actually barefoot. It was just natural for me. It left Father perplexed at times.

When I became a vampire, barefoot turned out to be an unacceptable way to fight, especially for a girl who only weighed a little over nine stone. I instinctively transitioned to leather boots. I had been accustomed to boots when on the docks, so they seemed a good fit. They were also a good fighting tool. Most times it was a leather lace-up affair with a medium heel—something stylish but also sturdy and utilitarian. When I knew I was going to be running a lot, I opted for a lower heel. A lower heel works better under foot, especially at speed. I don't care who you are, you turn a heel running and it hurts bad. Frankly, a vampire with a swollen-up ankle is just sad. You get absolutely no respect from your peers when limping around like that.

Yes, it was either boots or barefoot for me. Megan's father had tried to convince me that silk slippers were the high style at one point. They were the fashion of the day, and they made me look like a proper lady. As I remember, I tossed them over the side of a ship.

The preceding evening, it had obviously been boots. They were a low-heeled medium brown leather affair, with fancy lace on the toe and down the side of the lacing. That was as fashionable as I got with footwear most days. Now they sat next to the stone bench, in the middle of the maze, as I waited on my old friend the sun.

I could feel the amulet jittering back and forth under my corset as I sat. I didn't wear the corset as a rule. But being naturally gifted, it helped to keep everything in place when I ran. The dresses of the day lacked a tight enough bodice to keep my breasts secure without a corset. Not having the need to breathe, I just cinched the corset down until everything seemed secure. If I still needed to breathe, it would have been a much more inconvenient affair.

Frankly, I've never historically been the biggest fan of women's fashion. Traditionally the dresses women were shoved into were either too loose and simple or just had too much cloth. I have always detested looking like a walking layer cake. I did like the fashion from the late seventeenth century. I didn't really mind the petticoats under the long skirts and dresses, and the bodices were cut nice and tight. Sadly, that style didn't last.

General Note … I have been pretty happy since about the 1950s on. The era of jeans and shirts, then tighter shirts, then sports bras has been a great pleasure for me. Running in a sports bra has to be the best thing ever for a busty vampire, but I'm getting ahead of myself.

In June 1879 my outfit was a medium blue linen dress with a delicately embroidered pattern. It was long enough, about mid-shin, with full-length sleeves that also had an embroidered set of cuffs. It had a fairly open bodice, which just barely covered the corset. Most of the under garments naturally worn daily under such dresses I had left behind for the night. I found that fewer layers of clothing helped me to regulate my body temperature when I was exerting myself. Going commando, as it were, was a useful practice.

The amulet sat in her usual spot, stuffed down between the waps, and twitched back and forth. She also knew the sun was about to rise and she wanted out. Looking about reflexively, I reached in and secured a grip on her long golden chain. A quick, smooth tug and out came my little friend. Dropping the jewel to lay against the front of my dress, I closed my eyes and waited patiently. The opaque black glasses that normally protected my night vision from the harsh rays of daylight had been left on my nightstand, so I kept my eyes shut tight.

Nature is a funny thing. I have oft times pondered the difference between day and night. When I was a newborn vampire, I was quite emphatically taught that vampires were strictly nocturnal creatures. Vampires *only* came out at night. This lesson was taught so well that even humans knew it to be fact. The only problem is that it was all rubbish.

Back in 1773, Antonio gave me two presents for my birthday. One of them was the amulet. She was a grand gift. The other was a journal. It was an extremely old codex from an extremely old member of our kind. He lived out in the wilds of what's now Russia. The journal had apparently never been read, since it was so old that it was mostly stick figures and gibberish. I had worked on the codex for days before it started to let go of its secrets, the main one being that the individual in the tale spent his time moving about by day.

Lesson in hand, I decided that if he could do it, so could I. I enlisted the help of my confidant Christopher Wyndell and decided to try it out. A few small trials at first and then I was stepping back out into the sunlit world of the living.

It turns out that the light of day is a perfectly plausible place for a vampire to reside. Like any other nocturnal creature, I'm better designed for the night and tend to fair better in that environment. That being said, it doesn't mean that I can't move about during the day. Nature works her will based on very solid rules. It turns out that I'm no different than the owl or the wolf. I hunt well at night and I also hunt well during the day.

This bit of counterintuitive information has very practical benefits. Back in the beginning, people used to wonder about the strange girl with the odd condition that made it so she never came out during the day. With my opaque glasses, I was back out in the sight of the public during the day and I was as normal as everybody else in the world. It was such perfect camouflage that my inner circle at the time quickly decided that I shouldn't tell anyone about my little revelation. This I did not, because it brought me back to the sun. The sun was my friend. He gave me warmth and colored my skin. He made the meadows bloom and produced the fragrant breezes that lifted my mood. Considering my deep bonds to the human world, I embraced the move back into the sunlight. Everyone around, save for the inner circle, thought me as human as the next girl. I was bonny.

This day, I sat cross-legged on the bench and waited. I only had to be patient for a little while before my old friend the sun was shining his radiance down on my face. I embraced the energy with the same excitement I exuded when I was young. The orb's radiation pushed on my eyelids with a steady force. I kept them shut and meditated in the morning glow. It was fine, since I really didn't need my sight in these particular surroundings. Penetrating the maze could not be accomplished without me hearing or smelling someone coming from the beginning. And then there was also the amulet. Few things in the universe escaped her unblinking gaze.

Normally I'm quite accomplished with the meditation thing, as it's a natural side effect of being a vampire. I just shut down everything that's going on in my head and wait for peace to descend upon me. It was usually a quick affair. This day I focused and focused and cleared my mind, but I could not find that blank point. As much as I tried to find blankness, an image of Antonio kept creeping into my head. He just kept sliding back into my subconscious thoughts. He was not going to ruin my birthday. He had courted me, killed me, transformed me, loved me, broke my heart, and finally dismissed me. He was *not* going to ruin my birthday.

I tried and tried, but the thoughts of my dark Spanish lover wouldn't leave me completely. They stuck to me like boils. Still, they weren't entirely unpleasant. We had seen some very good times, the two of us. We had loved together, made love together (by that, I mean incredibly good sex), and killed together. We were even business partners of a sort. He had killed me so that my business would be around as long as his business was. We could handle shipping of his cargo and commodity. It really seemed unfair a couple centuries back; now it wasn't looking so bad.

Maybe my lack of meditation was trying to tell me something. I had been thinking about sex a lot since Megan had broached the Jeremy subject back on the ship. I could definitely go for a good pounding. Maybe it wasn't Antonio I needed as much as sex. It seemed plausible to just be sex that I needed, considering all the things I had done to purge myself of Antonio when we parted ways.

I have had numerous lovers in the years since my birth. By far, Antonio—my first lover—was the best at it. Don't get me wrong, he was no Casanova. Seriously, once you become a demon, your inhibitions change. Seeing how I was a demon when he finally broke me, it was just as well. I don't scar as easily as I once did, and I have a much higher pain threshold than when I was human. Oh yeah, I also have much greater stamina. These things naturally led me back to someone like Antonio for sex, since he also had these traits. Our encounters tended to be a little higher impact than the kind humans have. Trust me when I say, "When you're all done, you're all done!"

Oddly, for a human, Jeremy Worthington was also quite accomplished at my level of bedroom games. When he was in his twenties, he had such a high stamina level that I could actually get all the way to all done. That was why even being a member of the Brenfield Society, he was allowed to live.

My meditation had descended into just thinking about sex. Oh well, I was allowed to have a birthday present, even if it was imaginary. I had completely given into the thoughts in my head when the amulet began to twitch.

"I sense her too, old friend."

Megan, making her way through the twists and turns of the maze, had broken my concentration and alerted the amulet. She wasn't actually trying to be stealthy, which made her easier than normal to identify. She also navigated the maze better than most of her predecessors, which was a skill reserved for Wyndell women. Amber was also quite accomplished at finding her way, while the men just fumbled around.

Megan made her way to the center in a particularly straightforward manner and walked to where I sat. She appeared neither surprised nor put out; she was merely the picture of steady Wyndell confidence. That was quite a nice thing, and yet odd, somehow. Her feminine vibe was strangely comforting to both me and the amulet.

"I brought you your glasses, ma'am," Megan said in a subdued tone. She sat the glasses on the stone bench and then walked several steps to another small bench, where she sat. I had a small bit of déjà vu as she sat down. I had placed the bench there after a similar experience with Amber. I put on my glasses, adjusted my vision to the new light of day, and smiled up at my old friend the sun.

"Megan, my dear, I have repeatedly asked you to call me, Sara."

"I know ma'am, err … Sara. It just seems wrong, somehow. You're a lady, where as I am a—"

"You are a daughter to one of the wealthiest families in England. You could buy five titles if you wanted. I can get you an audience with the barristers, if you'd like."

"Very funny. I'm not much for fancy things and royalty. I think I wouldn't survive it all as well as you."

"Well, Megan, that's two more things we have in common. I have never been one for the trappings that come with a title. Court can be a pit of vipers on the best of days."

"You have done so much and met so many people. Do you ever think that it's just all too much?"

"More often than you might think for … hence the melancholy. I try to live without looking to the past, as much as possible. It helps me sleep."

"I can understand that, I guess."

"Oh, it's not the killing. Well, mostly not the killing. It's just when you live long enough to see the good and bad of your decisions, you start putting more effort into making each one. Humans seldom get enough years to get to that point."

"Be happy and live for the now. It seems like a good idea."

"It is. Now, that being said, I have two thoughts swirling around in my noggin. Are you ready for them?"

"Yes ma'am, er, Sara."

"Ha, ha! You'll get to it, Megan, sooner or later. Now what have you learned about Antonio Boca?"

"A quiz? He is a vampire, transformed in the late thirteenth century, according to the gossip. He was the vampire that transformed you. According to you, he is tall, dark, and handsome. He is Spanish by birth, with residences in several locations about Europe. Rumor is he owns several major companies in Spain. Grey Cargo does a steady or total business with all of them. According to the chronicles of that group from Malta, he can be incredibly violent. They say that he's killed more people than the pox. Why do you ask?"

"Do you happen to know where he might be currently?"

"Not accurately, but I think somewhere to the east."

"That would make sense. He does like the lands to the east. Find out his whereabouts, please."

"Ma'am?"

"Just find out where is, quietly. Do not raise any suspicions."

"Yes, ma'am. Why do you want to find him?"

"Let's just say that I have an itch that needs scratching. And he's the one for that particular job."

Megan blushed and looked at the ground. She really wasn't comfortable with the topic of sex. Too bad for her.

"Megan, don't go wandering off. Do it the old-fashioned way. He is no one you want to meet in person."

She swallowed hard, but her heart rate didn't increase. That was a good girl.

"For the second thought, what is your relationship status?"

"Pardon?"

"Do you have suitors? That is what they are still calling them these days, isn't it?"

"It is, and upon occasion." She blushed, but it was the tone in her voice that told me what I really wanted to know.

"Hmm, we're going to need to work on that before you are too old to make a good wife. Shouldn't be hard in this town; there are eligible bachelors everywhere. You can even have a royal if you want one."

"Lady Gibbs, I … don't think that's necessary."

"I do. And, Megan, if you call me anything other than Sara or Lady Grey again while we're alone, I'm going to hit you so hard that you won't wake up until the morrow. Do I make myself very clear?"

Megan just stared at me.

"I said, do I make myself very clear?"

"Yes, very clear." The tone was not really what I wanted to hear out of her at that point.

"Megan, I appreciate that you're miffed, but heed a lesson from your great uncle Jimmy: defiance leads to a bloody death. This wasn't meant to send you on a bender, and it's not shash. I wanted nothing more than to get married and have a family. That was my thought as a young girl.

Instead, I got eternity with no husband and no family. You don't want what I have—trust me."

"I don't know."

"Very few of us ever have known. That is the way of such things, hence the melancholy. Now let's just see if there is a nice gentleman out there for you while you're tracking down a not-so-nice one for me. It all really isn't that bad, you know."

"If you say so."

"You are a gentle creature, aren't you? That is a very good thing. On a different note, did you know that today is my birthday?"

"Yes, ma'am. Sorry, Sara."

"It's all right. Let's head for the manor. I'd like to talk to Julia a while, and then I think I might go out and kill someone."

We stood and quietly started out of the big conglomeration of hedgerows that formed the maze. The sun was getting high in the sky and its daytime warmth was comforting. The grass under my feet made me think back on human times. That, too, was comforting on this day.

"Sara, why do you spend so much time talking to Julia?"

"She has known that I am a vampire since she was somewhat younger than you. She is a good keeper of secrets and has a perspective of the world that is older than yours. We get on well enough, I guess."

"Sara?"

"Yes."

"You were joking about killing people, right?"

"No."

"Oh."

And we continued quietly on to the manor. I could tell that my birthday was going to be a good day.

CHAPTER 5

It has been said that times change when you least expect them to. It's a true statement, and yet I am always shocked when I realize that my way of thinking has become antiquated. In the years that made up the start of the Industrial Revolution, the ways things worked changed many fold in the blink of an eye. I mean, I knew that there were trains and telegraphs and that iron was being utilized in construction. Man had harnessed the power of steam to work the mills, freeing him from the rivers of the world. But, as it's all happening, it just takes time to set in, I guess.

My case in point here was Megan and her search for Antonio. In years gone by, my confidants actually had to leave and go find people when I wanted them found. That process, at best, could take many months to accomplish, and that was if they started with accurate information. Sometimes the search for an individual could be a one- or two-year endeavor. My confidants would gather the information and then head out on the hunt. They would just come back whenever they came back.

In conducting her hunt for Antonio, Megan went as far as her cousin's office building on the far edge of town. She came wandering back into the study a month or so later with some notes scribbled on a ledger sheet. She calmly proclaimed that Antonio was moving through the lands east of the Dead Sea again. He was slowly making his way west toward Europe and should make Istanbul in a month or two at his current pace. I naturally assumed she was taking the Mickey out of me for some reason, until she sat the ledger sheet on the edge of the desk and asked what was next to do.

My inquiry into how she could possibly know so much, so fast, produced a one-word response: telegraph. She had sent out messages over the telegraph to trustworthy people who had knowledge of such things. The results narrowed the search pattern to a reasonable area, and then she did the same thing again. Accurate information was quickly generated. After all, Antonio owned several large companies, so people naturally knew where he was. He apparently just wasn't quite as easy to find as I was.

Megan went on to tell how she even utilized the new telephone system, which had only come to London the previous spring, to talk to some people over on the European mainland.

"You mean to tell me that you can just pick up a thing and talk to someone in another place now?"

"Of course you can."

"Well, that's slightly unsettling. Imagine what might come next."

Megan continued on with her educational lecture, explaining that we could now cross the channel and take a new rail system most of the way to Istanbul. Europe's rail system, and Turkey's as well, were a series of big chunks of rail. We could actually ride a piece of rail, and then take a coach to the next piece of rail, and so on, until we reached Istanbul. It would now be much faster to travel across the continent by rail rather than to sail, and it would be more luxurious as well. Frankly, it all seemed fantastical.

"Railroads replacing tall ships? I just don't know."

"It will all be grand, Lady Sara. The luxury train coaches are quite nice."

"You say he's coming to us? And should make Istanbul by early fall?"

"Yes, ma'am."

"Well then, let's just see if he stops in Constantinople for the winter. If he does, we can go fetch him in the spring."

"We could be off at week's end, according to the railroad time tables."

"No, that's not wise. Let him come to us. If he stops for the winter, we'll go east. If not, we'll see him in Europe."

Feeling the finality of the conversation, Megan didn't press. That was always a good thing. The uneasiness of the conversation had left me with a desire to get up to speed. I knew my fashion was slowly going out of date, but I hadn't realized that I was behind the times. This conversation had obviously proven otherwise. Well, at least I now had something with which to occupy my time.

The following months definitely showed two things to be true. Megan's assessment of Antonio was accurate. He made a quiet landfall in Istanbul and quickly blended into the background. Apparently, he planned on staying a while. He would probably need to be off in the spring but seemed otherwise content. Secondly, I was truly slipping behind the times. Somehow I had let myself linger too long. I was a horse-drawn cart in a railroad world.

The winter months I spent waiting on Antonio I also spent changing my lifestyle. I used the hours to read relentlessly. I found excitement in all the topics of the day. There was the newest philosophy, new and strange advances in science, and new styles of art. One of my favorite books of the day was *A Manual of the Practice of Surgery* by W. Fairlie Clarke. The human body has always held a deep fascination for me. I mean, it is how I survive. Many found the choice in topics macabre. I found it to be insightful.

Megan was a little put out by my choice of reading topics. She was also a little put out by my choice of suitors for her. I think she was so bashful when it came to men that she would have died an old spinster. That wasn't really high on my list of outcomes for her.

A friend to the Grey Estate, Sir Reginald Longmore, knighted servant of the Crown, had a son named Harold. Harold was a military man, strong in spirit yet gentlemanly and kind with women. He was of appropriate age for marrying Megan and still had many good years ahead to make her happy. The empire had not sent him abroad in some time, and he was now training younger men to fight. He seemed the most likely of choices.

Megan was awkward in her relationship with a man for some time, but as I suspected, Harold prevailed. She never really did get past her bashful phase. I, and everyone else, found it to be endearing. By the spring of 1880, when we departed for Istanbul, the couple was quite well on.

I had been looking forward to seeing Istanbul again. The trip would not only plant my feet on old ground and reunite me with my former love, but it would easily do something else. It would allow me to change my persona. Lady Gibbs would go on vacation and befall an accident of some kind, and then my daughter from America would need to come back and take over. My daughter, who came from America, would be a new me.

I had spent several weeks contemplating on what my new name should be. It needed to have a current sound to it. I tried a few names out on Megan, all of which she liked equally well. She would obviously be no help in the matter. So, after a fashion, I decided upon Mary Beth Alcott. Having been called by several names already, this one was no worse than those others. It would do fine for a generation.

Mary Beth had a nice Catholic sound to it. Mary Catherine did more so. The thought of that made my mind wander off toward church. I hadn't had anyone from the opposition's camp to converse with in a long time. Father David had passed on some years back. It made my heart sad. He was a good man and gave sound judgment. I was at a stage where I would have liked to talk some more, but seriously, where does one find an open-minded priest in 1880? Maybe my friend at the Vatican could be of service on that front, if he was still alive. I would need to think on that.

Come April of 1880, the channel waters had let go of their ice and ships were escaping the Thames for fair winds and trade routes. It seemed the right time to be off on a holiday of my own. All of the required paperwork had been done for my change of being. Megan had tracked down Antonio and he was still right where he was supposed to be. All was ready, so we were off.

The trip across England was as uneventful as always. We took a grand coach on the new island rail system south to the cliffs of Dover.

Upon reaching Dover, we caught passage on a Grey's vessel across the channel. The French had expanded the Port of Calais since I had been there last, but it was otherwise the same as in years past.

In the town of Calais, we boarded a French train that transported us to Paris. Megan and I spent a few days shopping in the French capital before heading south once more. It was everything that I had heard it to be. We shopped, took in a show at the Grand Theatre, and even toured Louis XIV's great palace turned museum. The Louvre had a truly exceptional collection of art.

Moving along, a fashionable car kept us content as the countryside sailed past. The train ran from Paris all the way south to the shores of the Mediterranean. The train made many stops as it made its way south, but none were of any duration as to be a bother. Soon enough, we were disembarking our train in Nice. An opulent coach collected us in Nice and transported us to the seaside kingdom of Monaco.

OK, it was a tiny principality. And, it was sandwiched between the irritable French and the domineering Italians. But, a kingdom is a kingdom, independent of the size. They had their own land, so more power to them.

We spent a day in Monaco, waiting on a train to take us east, and it was quite fine. The company had a long history of quality service in the area, and due to some quiet posturing on Megan's part, we were warmly received. The prince and his family were quite warm and we passed our time fashionably.

General note … appreciating the fact that I am a lady of the court and an extremely wealthy woman, that doesn't mean I'm toff when it comes to lodging. On many occasions I have passed the time quite happily in a quiet inn or a roadside house. As long as the room is clean and neat, I am content. It comes from growing up on the docks, I think.

East out of Monaco, we held on as a clambering, banging, and clanging behemoth, belching steam and coal smoke, dragged us through the Alps and on to a thankful stop in Florence, Italy. Getting off the torturous beast in Florence made me very, very happy. That section of the ride was different enough to even give Megan pause.

We paused two days in Florence, waiting on a train that would take us east. That time allowed us ample opportunity to explore the signature site of the European Renaissance. Well, it allowed me time to explore. Megan made it as far as touring the Duomo and then rested the remainder of our stay. I was on the prowl. I wanted to see all that I could see. Who knew when I would ever make it this way again.

Florence was the first time in an age where I allowed myself the pleasure of hunting for a meal. I obviously didn't need to, but something about Florence brought up memories of Venice. Those fond memories made me want to do a little hunting. The residents of Venice had all been so accommodating in producing adrenaline-infused meals. I really liked the sensation of adrenaline-laced blood sliding down the back of my throat. So, as night slipped down full upon our arrival, I slid into the shadows and looked around for a good place to find a meal. Moving about for a time, I settled on the outer fringe of the Piazza della Signoria. It was a beautiful square with good traffic flow. It was a place rumored to be built upon ruins dating back to the thirteenth century. Its open space was flanked by Renaissance architecture and anchored with a fine bell tower. Bronze statues took up station in all the proper places. The square was a hive of traffic and contained many political buildings. There were also numerous social scenes unfolding, which gave life to the space.

I wore a long, blue muslin dress that evening, with long sleeves that had been finished in a decorative floral stitching. The opening around the neck was decorated with the same floral design and made it look quite pretty. The length of the dress's hem hid my sturdy brown leather boots. I had covered the whole affair in a black cloak with a full hood, which I pulled over my now longer black hair. I had been growing my hair out and it was now exposing my blonde roots. It was annoying, but the hood covered it all nicely. I could tell that when I became a new me, I was going to be blonde again. The raven hair, however elegant, was simply too much work to maintain.

The chosen hunting method of the evening was simple enough. It was a simple case of misdirection. I came to the square by a dark and tightly woven route. At a spot where a bit of discretion could be had, I stopped and wrote down the street address on a small piece of parchment. Having the proper bait, I proceeded slowly through the square until I came upon a likely victim. He was alone and looked the type to be chivalrous. I proceeded to him, excused myself with the five Italian words I knew, and waved the note at him as to give him the impression that I couldn't find my way. As expected, he was chivalrous. He read the note, recognized the address, and made several sweeping hand gestures suggesting that he would escort me to that place. This was followed by him offering me his arm. Bait taken, I smiled and accepted his arm.

The man walked confidently to his death. He escorted me directly to the narrow corner of the dark street. Turning, with the obvious pleasure of making another grand gesture, he was greeted by the image of large eyes and gleaming white fangs. The second in time that it took him to process the information was his downfall. I clamped a hand so firmly over his mouth that I was sure I had broken his jaw. My second hand went to a free arm, my knee behind one of his, and the big man was down on my level.

I slammed his side into the uniform blocks of the stone building behind him as my ivory fangs sank deep into his neck. I will say that he gave it all a gallant effort, but it was of little use. He died in a dark alley off the Piazza. He was kind to me, and in return I drained him dry.

It had been some time since I had drained a body. I paused after feeding and inspected myself thoroughly. Fortunately, I found myself to be proper. That was good, as I hated to have to do cleanup. I propped the dead body against the building and faded back into the night from which I had come. I was long gone before anyone happened along.

The rich, heavy blood pulsed through my system and made me giddy—I mean, right chuffed. I love the feeling of blood pulsing through me. I love my amulet and her mystical ways of making me content, but she couldn't really reproduce what the blood did. It was the thing that really did it for me. It still is.

A lone dead body wasn't enough of a problem to keep us from leaving Florence unbothered. As planned, we boarded another train east and continued on toward the lands of the Ottoman Empire. Megan could tell that I was different somehow, but she wasn't able to pin it down. I couldn't bring myself to ruin her guessing with a simple answer, so I just let her ponder.

There were a couple more train changes and a coach or two to get us to the building mass of humanity that was Istanbul. We came into the fabled city and made our way east across the Bosporus to the Asian side. All pieces of Constantinople held equal opulence, but the section known as Harem was the place for us. Harem held the commercial docks and the large business areas. That was the place the owner of Grey's Cargo would be if in the city. Megan had secured us proper lodging in the way of a large Ottoman-styled home. It was grand and set the mood for the days that were ahead.

Megan harbored concerns we would have trouble tracking down Antonio in such a large place. I did not. Even in a city of eight hundred thousand people, I could tell when he was about. All I had to do was get that initial scent, and then I could follow it wherever it led. It would take me straight to my old moody comrade. There was nothing to it but to start.

CHAPTER 6

Istanbul turned out to be a nice change of pace for all three of us. Megan and I were escorted all about the sprawling city by a gentlemanly English-speaking chap who worked for one of Grey's larger clients. We all had a wonderful time viewing the sites. A city as old as Istanbul had many sites of note to see. We viewed the mosques, ate in the cafés, and even partook in the curious custom of smoking the hookah. It seemed to me a very male way to lounge away the day at the local casbah. Megan just seemed excited. As women, we were allowed to participate because we were foreigners.

Istanbul, or Constantinople as it was known in earlier times when the Romans owned it, was truly an ancient place. The area that the city sat upon was first settled by King Byzas from Megara in the 600 BC range. It was locally inhabited long before that though, as it was the major crossing between Europe and Asia. Some say that that settlement period extended all the way back to the seventh millennium BC, but who really knew?

All of these ancient roots pleased the amulet. She embraced the city's ancient energy in a very real way. I could sense her almost humming with energy all the time we were there. The two of us had traveled to many places much older than the headquarters of Byzantium, and she had never had such a visceral reaction to a place. There was a power in the city that she embraced. I was happy that she was enjoying herself; however, the rivulets of energy that swirled about her jeweled case left me unsettled. I wasn't going to ruin her fun. She had proven upon occasion that she could be miserable if crossed.

It turned out that as the journey unfolded, the thing I thought would be the most problematic part was the least eventful part, thanks to my friend in the amulet. I knew I could locate Antonio with little fanfare. I knew somewhat how he traveled and what areas in which he felt comfortable. I also could sense when he was nearby, so I knew I would find him at some point. But I didn't need to worry, because the amulet did that for me.

We were all but finishing up our tour of the local sites when the amulet placed an image of the far bank in my mind. The image was of the old European side of the city. Apparently, Antonio was milling about in the Daya Hatun section of town. My friend had helped me do things upon occasion, but she usually wasn't this precise. Maybe there really was something about the city that she tapped into. She took a lot of the legwork out of our trip. It would be nothing to find him now. Knowing that he was still moving about exclusively by night, all I had to do was go there during the day and wait him out.

General note …Vampires are generally able to know when other vampires are about. It's an extrasensory type of thing. I can just tell when another vampire is close by. Most rumors say that it's a natural adaptation to keep the vampires of the world from congregating in one place. Too many predators in any one area is always hard on the prey. Knowing others are about helps to disperse our number. I'm not a neuroscientist; I don't know why it works. I just know that it does. It's one of those things in life.

I left Megan in the capable hands of the nice Muslim fellow, hoping he didn't secretly whisk her off and sell her to someone, and headed back across the Bosporus, toward the old Thracian settlements of Lygos. The tight streets and changing landscape of the Daya Hatun district were comforting to a vampire. It was a perfect hunting ground. Sadly, I hadn't come to hunt. Well, I wasn't hunting a meal anyway.

I sat quietly at a café along the Kaputcular Sokak and waited for the sun to drop below the rooftops. It took some time, and several cups of mint tea, before it was dark enough for the nighttime creature to stir.

As the darkness came on, I removed my glasses and allowed my vision to adjust to a natural setting. Seeing the world in its natural hues was always nice. The glasses' opaque lenses washed everything out into a dull gray, like twilight in the city.

I was finishing up a glass of mint tea and was admiring the handsome glassware as Antonio stumbled out of the domicile he was utilizing. I wondered if he had actually procured it or just killed its original occupants. Either one was fine, I supposed.

Antonio made his way a short distance along the street, continuously stopping to look about. He looked every inch the person I remembered him to be. The image before me was a tall and powerful man with long, dark hair pulled back, exposing a strong expression. Just seeing him on the street made my heart start beating faster. I hadn't seen my dark prince in some time, and I apparently still missed him on some level.

His instincts honed to razor sharpness, he was keenly aware something was amiss. The cagey old killer continued along his path to a small bench and sat to take in the lay of the land. The bench was in a small open area with green space, next to a cross street leading to Saka Mehmet Sokak.

"That's as good a place as any, my little friend."

The amulet's energy pulsed in my brain with recognition. I stood, dropped enough money on the table to cover my lingering, and casually ambled over to the bench. I sat next to my maker and smiled. He turned his head in acknowledgement but said nothing.

"Hello, lover, we're out of bed late. All the good prey is heading inside for the evening."

"Why can't I move?"

"Because me and my shiny friend like you right where you are."

"Grey, this is not the best way to get back into my good graces."

"You know what your problem is? You lack the ability to not be in control. Sad, but it explains so much about our relationship, doesn't it?"

"You're really starting to aggravate me, Grey. What do you want?"

"If you promise to be a good boy, I'll tell you."

"Fine, I won't kill you."

I laughed at his slight. He didn't.

"Let's be perfectly clear about something, lover; you couldn't kill me if you tried. I'm faster, meaner, and just a plain better killer. You taught me that. History says that you kill many. It says that I kill effectively. You know it and I know it, so do stop posturing."

"You're not so big, I think. Without your magical bobble, you're not so much for me."

"Antonio, I didn't come all this way to get in a big row with you. After a hundred years, you're still being a right git. By the way, you never even thanked me for coming halfway around the world and breaking you out of prison."

Antonio glared at me for a second with menace I had not seen out of him before, and then he calmed. Maybe he had changed back to the person I knew … somewhat. The amulet relaxed her grip a tad so he could adjust his posture.

"All right, Grey, thank you for coming to my assistance. Now, what did you come here for?"

"You. Not to put too fine a point on it."

"Pardon?"

"I have had an itch for some time. You were always very good at scratching itches. So …, you."

"Last I had heard you had no trouble finding sticks with which to scratch your itches."

"Oh, I'm wounded by your sarcasm."

"You came all the way to the Ottoman Empire to find a casual lover?"

"There has never been anything casual about our loving. And is it so hard to believe?"

"From you? Yes."

"We are really not going to get past you being an arse, are we?"

"I am who and what I am."

"You, sir, are an arse."

"So be it."

"I agree. I'll tell you what; when you're done being like this, you come find me. Until that century rolls around, I'm gonna sod off. I guess I'll have to get stuffed in some other fashion."

"Colloquial."

"I grew up on the docks, remember? That was where you found me. You remember, the pretty human girl?"

"Grey."

"Good-bye, lover." I stood and wandered off toward the carsi kapi, without looking back. It seemed a century wasn't enough time for some people to change. Being moody was just counterproductive. I realized as I walked away that just talking to him had left me knackered. We hadn't even really fought. He was just exasperating.

I could feel Antonio moving off to the south. It appeared that he didn't like our little exchange either. That was too bad for him. Oh well, it was a nice night for a walk. The sights and sounds of the city mingled together in the streets and mixed with the pungent salt air from the Bosporus. The straight that separated Asia from Europe was as much an integral part of the city as the Daya Hatun. It all was soothing and enticing. I decided to walk back to the other side of the city. The night air was warm, and that was contenting enough. I was also full of mint tea.

My unplanned path had slowly moved me to the tip of the Golden Horn when a new sensation came to me. Well, it wasn't new, just unexpected. It seemed there was another vampire in the sprawling city. This new predator was somewhere over in the area of the Golden Horn. I wondered if it might be someone I knew, so north the path continued.

All the traffic moving north toward the Vefa merged and headed to either the port, where the ferries crossed back to the Asian side, or to the Galata Bridge, which crossed onto the Golden Horn. The solid stone edifice that tied the two sections of the city together was long and disappeared into the blackening night. A pair of men, who were obviously part of the night watch, passed by as I was making my way onto the sturdy bridge. They gave me a hard look, but otherwise didn't stop to bother me. That was just as well. Most men who conducted the night watch were as much criminal as they were protector. I didn't really want bodies in the river quite so soon.

The walk across the Galata Bridge turned out to be more exercise than the casual stroll I was intending. Maybe, that was what the night watch men were looking at? Nevertheless, the other side of the crossing finally appeared and I planted my feet on the fabled Golden Horn. If nothing else, the night was going to produce some new experiences. I had already been to the city of Istanbul in past years, but that stop had strictly been to the Asian side. I had to see a man named Akmed. Our earlier tour had led us over to this side of the city, but tours aren't like exploration. I find it a much nicer affair to walk about in a place, to get the smells and hear the languages, to connect with its streets and mood. It was the real way that people explored. The most interesting things in any city weren't churches and museums; they were corner shops and casbahs.

This night my exploration took me to the far end of Simsir Sokak, a short distance inland. As with all of Istanbul, at the end of the street was a small tea shop. Men sat outside in the mild night air and smoked the nargilah as they conversed about the affairs of the day. I made my way by the scene and into the establishment's dimly lit interior, my cloak's hood pulled up tight to disguise my features. Everyone there knew I was a woman, which was the way of the Turks. It was the white woman part I was trying to hide. I knew that they knew that as well, since good Ottoman women didn't travel to such places. I just didn't want to advertise. Fortunately, there was a vacant table to one side of the door leading out the back to the kitchen area, which I quickly occupied. The men sitting about the room all gave me the hard onceover and then returned to their own affairs.

In the far corner of the room, at a similarly sized table, a gentleman seemed to be intrigued by my presence. He didn't simply return to his smoke, but lingered on me. He was the one. The vampire radar confirmed what my gut told me. The amulet threw in her two pence on the subject, as well. It was yesses all around. He was like me. He must have also been a traveler, since I got no vibe that he was put out by me being in the city. That, in and of itself, was very good.

A thickly mustached man appeared through the back door and sat a container on my table, along with a nicely decorated tea glass and some cubes of sugar beet. Great, I was going to have more tea! The mustached man said something in thickly accented Turk, which I did not understand. I simply pointed at the tea, smiled, and said thank you. The young female "thank you" that escaped from the hood of my cloak made the mustached man smile broadly, as he turned to head back through the door. I really needed to become a better linguist. I could have responded in Greek, but that would have offended him. Apparently, I needed to learn some Turk.

I prepared a glass of the thick black tea and stirred it to cool. I was happy it wasn't mint. The mint tea leaves a taste in your mouth. As I handled the caydanlik, that shiny double-stack tea pot the Turks use, my new friend stood and made his way across the room.

The first observations of my new friend were rewarding. He was tall and fit, possessed well-cropped blond hair, and a look of capability. He had a sturdiness that obviously went back to when he was human, a military man perhaps. He seemed sure of himself. He paused by my table in a gentlemanly fashion and waved his hand with a small flourish.

"Good evening, madam, my name is Sebastian Coslovich. I was wondering if you might enjoy some conversation, if that is not too forward a request."

"Good evening, Mister Coslovich. Please, join me and help me with my tea. I confess I have already consumed quite enough tea for one day."

Sebastian sat and instructed the mustached man's assistant to relocate his smoking pipe from the other table. His native tongue was obviously neither English nor Turk, though he spoke adequately in both. The young assistant brought the contents of his table and changed the coals on the pipe as the tea cooled.

"So, are you a traveler, Mr. Coslovich?"

"Please, call me Sebastian. I travel to Istanbul now and again. I like its people and long history."

"Please, call me Sara, Sara Grey. I, too, like the history of this place. Your English is quite good, by the by."

"I have heard that name many times," Sebastian said in such a low tone that it was inaudible to all save me.

"I am pleased to meet you as well," I responded in like manner. That was that, the vampire handshake. We were kindred spirits, Sebastian and I.

Sebastian sipped his tea and then explained that I was better disposed to learn the ways of the nargilah. One or the other was the customary thing in the Ottoman Empire, and if you didn't smoke much, that was okay with them. If you didn't drink the tea, they took it as an offense. I thanked him for the information, as it would definitely be useful, and let the conversation turn casual.

It turned out that Sebastian Coslovich had been a member of the Serbian Army when he was a young man. Having been shot in some battle many years past, he was found on the battlefield by another of our kind. Seeing it as a better alternative to death, he embraced the transition. He had been traveling the dark path, as he put it, for some seventy-five years and was enjoying it all quite well. He was now your basic situational opportunist, the way that most of our kind are. It was a lifestyle that suited his skillset well.

Sebastian explained that he had heard my name from many others with whom he had crossed paths. They all spoke very well of me, and a few who had been to the gala's raved of my hospitality. Apparently, my exploits were well-recited tales amongst my kind. It wasn't really my fault that I was different from them.

I gave Sebastian my own story. He listened with great interest as I explained the many misadventures I had been involved in over the centuries. He seemed quite interested in the way I confided in humans. It was something very few of our kind did. It was just natural for me. I explained that you needed to really have a sense for people. There were people in the world that saw things differently than the majority.

Our stories went back and forth throughout the evening, until the shop started to empty for the night. It was late, well into the wee hours of the morning. The sun's return to the Bosporus was mere hours away. I wasn't sure if we had time enough to get back to the Asian side, but I asked Sebastian if he would like to escort me anyway. He asked if I would be missed by the humans. If not, he would be happy to escort me to his local residence. It was much closer and we could easily get there before sunrise. He was young and feared the sun. It was fine. I wasn't going to explain away his irrational fears.

I stated that his residence would be grand, and we were off. Worst case scenario, I ended up pulling his heart out, like I had Constantine's. I was hoping that would not come to pass. To my great pleasure, it did not.

Sebastian had fed earlier in the evening, so he was at the top of his game. Once we made our way to his residence, all the posturing was off. It was time to get to the matter at hand. I will say, as lovers went, he was quite good. He was sturdy of frame and well skilled at the trade. When we finished, he seemed quite satisfied with himself. I was exhausted and extremely pleased.

I admit that the quickness of it all made me feel a bit of a slag. But he seemed very well-mannered about it all, so that helped. We both got what we were looking for. Besides that, he was just nice. I wasn't sure if it was his age or his human upbringing. Either way, I didn't care much. I enjoyed talking to him as much as I did having sex with him. And I enjoyed the sex a lot!

As quickly as it had started, it seemed to be over. The full disk of the sun was all but down in the west when we stirred for the night. The next night was also spent with Sebastian. We toured the city and viewed many fine architectural achievements as we talked about all manner of things. Come sunrise, we retired to his residence and used the day for satisfying our libidos. He wasn't Antonio, but otherwise, it was exactly what I had wanted when I came to Istanbul. I was happy that I had made the trip.

On night three, I explained about Antonio and his mood. I explained to Sebastian how he might locate me in both England and America and asked that he do so. He embraced my kindness and said that he would travel to my country with a great heart but not too soon. With that, I was out the door and down the hall. I went back across the Bosporus and explained to Megan that I had made a new friend, and he was the good kind.

CHAPTER 7

The autumn of 1891 was a pleasant enough time in the world as far as the weather. It was just starting to return me to my otherwise exuberant self. It had taken some time for me to shake off the trip to Istanbul. I really had wanted to smooth things out between Antonio and me, but it appeared the time still wasn't right.

I had spent some time wondering if our romance had all been in my head, a silly manifestation of my human mind. Could it have ever really existed at all? Was wanting something you couldn't seem to acquire all for naught in the end? Was the purpose of eternity just to create misery?

All of this circled around my brain like some relentless polar current. It had actually all happened the way that I remembered it. Antonio was just being a ponce. It was all too human a thing, for being as old as he claimed to be. Maybe he wasn't as sage in his wisdom as he seemed when I was young. Oh, well.

I used some time to dwell on Sebastian. He was nice for a vampire and seemed well adjusted. But, in the end, I decided that he would not be more than a mere distraction. He was, after all, a vampire. And, as Antonio had taught me so well, vampires are not to be trusted. No, if there was to be a new stallion in the stable, he would need to be human. Real men had better control over their emotional senses than the demon kind.

As all the thoughts receded into my subconscious and the ideas of the day came to light, I started to notice that the world had continued to become a smaller place. The French had been ambling around the Sudan, killing the natives for a while. That always went well for them.

Empires did have to expand, I guess. Britain had become permanently tethered to Europe by the new telephone system, and a London-to-Paris telephone connection had been established.

In my adapted homeland of America, the Dalton Gang had committed the first great train robbery. One of the remaining Hatfield's had finally married a McCoy and stifled that twenty-year long infamous nuisance. The state of Nebraska had introduced the eight-hour work day. That I found to be a novel concept. And Carnegie Hall opened in New York City, with none other than Tchaikovsky as a guest conductor.

On a personal front, I had become well-adjusted to being Miss Mary Beth Alcott. I had utilized most of my Turkish blood lust, and a little nudge from my jeweled friend, to produce a fine head of shoulder length blond hair. It did take some time for me to readjust to being a blonde. Though it was my true color, and very much matched my mood, the raven hair fit my demonic nature. The sunshine blonde was completely its opposite.

I had gone around the city and remade some old human friends, so they would know me anew. I had reinserted my nose into my business, as would naturally be expected. Not enough to be disruptive mind you, just enough to let the Wyndells know I was still around. The remainder of my time was easily taken up with high tea and country manor living.

My once-young confidant Megan was now Lady Megan Longmore. She was a happy wife and mother of three. Their family had moved into the city and acquired a fine place for raising children. Megan and the children still spent some time every week at the estate. It gave the children room to be precocious, and Megan liked it.

The early part of the year had gone on in such fashion, and it wasn't till the later days of summer that things were afoot once more. Things for a vampire are never quiet for long. Sadly, the troubles that tracked me down this time were all too human.

I had been spending a great deal of time out with the humans. I tended to do this, so I wasn't really full in tune with my internal radar. It had been so long since I had been confronted with a significant dilemma, I had just let my guard down. The Brenfield Society had long ago ceased to be a bother, and the crown liked me well enough. I had slowly given in to being human with the humans. I swear that one day it's going to get me killed.

It was interesting that on this occasion the amulet recognized the sense of danger long before I did. Her unrelenting gaze had seen the trouble and attempted to tell me, but I wrote it off to her encountering another human she didn't like. That happened often, so it wasn't anything that wasn't to be expected in my day. Untrusting, she is.

This particular bit of drama that was putting her on high alert came in the form of a well-dressed smooth talker named Christian Smith. He was nice and educated and seemed knowledgeable in the old ways. I should have known better!

It all happened innocently enough. I was at tea, down Piccadilly way, with Megan. We were at one fashionable hotel or another, having a quite good occasion, when he appeared. He was handsome and somewhat dashing. I had noticed him out of the corner of my eye as he sat with some younger women around my age and conversed. Fit young men were not uncommon at tea, just a pleasant addition. He conversed with his group for some time and then excused himself to leave. As he passed cross the room, we happened to make eye contact. I took the onceover as flirtatious. The amulet took the look as inspection. I was unassumingly pleased. She was put out at best. And that was it. The start of bloodshed and problems had come to me once more. It was all downhill from that point.

It remained quiet for days after that encounter. I was at the estate and had no need of the city. I had taken him in and dismissed him that quickly. The amulet continued to twitch away. I could tell she was unhappy, but I really didn't see what all the fuss was about. The push of her will upon my subconscious mind could easily be equated to a migraine if left alone, so I only let her go on a little while before confronting the situation.

I made my way through the halls of the manor and into the study. I continued on to the sunlit patio beyond and took up station in my favorite outdoor chair. Overlooking the lawns that led off to the maze, I pulled my friend's jeweled case out from under my dress and let it fall against my chest.

"Come hither, my friend."

The amulet slowly lifted off my breast and came to a hovering position out at chain length in front of me. The smooth surfaces of the fused crystals shimmered in the sunlight and the magick symbols carved into the surfaces seemed to dance in midair.

"Come now, show me a picture. Show me what is causing you such consternation."

The air began to ripple all around the open space of the patio. The waviness slowly consolidated and focused itself into an object. It continued refining itself until a translucent image of Mr. Smith stood on the patio.

"That Smith fellow, he bothers you this much? How can that be?"

The single pulse in my brain signaled that the answer was no. The air began its rippling once again, and soon enough Mr. Smith was surrounded by five other hard-looking men. I paused to inspect the scene, but the amulet wasn't finished. Rivulets of energy swept across the stone pavers of the patio until a bloody pool appeared. I audibly drew breath when I realized that the body in the pool was my own. The body writhed several times before the dashing Mr. Smith planted a wooden pike handle through its chest. The tornado-like whirlwind of dust that consumed my body was quite unsettling.

" … "

The amulet thumped out a "yes" in my head that almost hurt.

"Bloody hell."

Yes. Thump.

"But … assuming that this hasn't happened yet, how do you know this? Are you telling me that you can see the future?"

"At times, when I choose to, I may look into the void and see what is to come."

The voice came out of the air as if it just appeared. It was a clear, sound, and young voice that was matter-of-fact and direct, a voice that was too young to be feminine. The voice could only belong to a child.

"You speak?!"

"Of course I speak. I control the power of the void. You think I don't speak? The same way that you are basically human, I am basically human."

"Why is it you have never spoken before?"

"I didn't feel it was necessary. Truthfully, after several millennia of being alone with my thoughts, it was nice to see your thoughts. The idea of speaking to you didn't really come to mind until now."

"Not that we don't need to discuss this all at length, but for the moment, let's jump back to the topic at hand. Mr. Smith means to put an end to me?"

"Yes. Several days from now, he will befriend you at tea. Later, while being escorted down a darkened street, his comrades will descend upon you and kill you."

"So, they succeed?"

"That is precisely why I am sharing this with you."

"So, that wasn't the future?"

"That … was one possible future. It is what may happen to you. Choices always have at least two outcomes associated with them. This was one of those possible outcomes. I showed it to you because I would wish that you did not decide upon it happening. Besides, I won't let things escalate to that level."

"I do like that very much."

"And I you. You have a gentle nature, even though it's wrapped in a demonic presence. You have no desire to use me, and that makes me very happy."

"Isn't that what we are doing now, using you?"

The surfaces of the amulet danced and pulsed with light. Apparently, my statement was amusing.

"We two are friends. We have a mutual need for survival. This is what friends do. Humans, and a great many demons, too, oft times desire what they cannot get for themselves. They tend to use my power to accomplish these things. Like you, I understand what I am and why I am here. And like you, I accept it, but I don't enjoy it."

"Well, that's good to know, I guess."

55

The surfaces of the jewel bounced and shimmered in the sunlight even more than before. My friend was definitely happy to be talking to me.

"So, what happens now?"

"Now you do what it is that you do. Seeing how you know bad things are afoot, you meet them head on and remove your enemy before he removes you."

"You really do have no problem with killing?"

"All the great plagues of the earth are but a small cup of water compared to the numbers I have killed. I don't mind killing in the least, as long as it serves a purpose. Sadly, the majority of my killing was for empire building. Empire building seldom serves a purpose."

"But survival is acceptable?"

"Survival is survival."

"Then six dead men they are."

The illumination from the amulet mellowed and the scene playing out on the patio shimmered into nothingness. The strange magick symbols floating in the air reaffixed themselves to their crystal surfaces. All was quiet. No breeze stirred. No bird sang in the meadow. No sound made its way out of the manor behind us. Total peace had descended upon the patio.

"Do you have a name?"

"Efuru, that is my name. In my own language it means 'daughter of heaven.'"

"That is a very nice name. I am pleased to be your friend, Efuru."

"Thank you."

We sat quietly, the remainder of the day. Efuru soaked up the sun. I pondered all that had just come to pass—that and how I was going to kill Mr. Smith and his little band of blighters.

CHAPTER 8

I utilized the next several days by getting myself back up to speed, as it were. Not that I had slowed, but I had just gotten out of the practice of killing. Since I had decided not to kill Brian back in 1865, I had pretty much removed myself from the killing game. I would get blood when it was needed, but otherwise the amulet handled things just fine. It seemed that I had been in a stage of avoiding conflict. It just seemed easier to walk around it. That time had now passed.

I noticed over the course of days that there was a downfall to having a female confidant. Unlike all of the preceding Wyndell men in my world, Megan couldn't fight to save herself. Violence just wasn't part of who she was. Normally, I appreciated that quality. At this point, it was definitely a hindrance. I couldn't even begin to provoke her to violence. It was slightly disheartening; she was a Wyndell after all.

The solution to my issue came, once more, in the form of the amulet. Though her images were puff and willow, they were very fast. Shadow boxing something that you can't hit or catch makes you up your game. After a couple days of chasing Efuru around the dungeon, I was as fast as I had ever been. Effie, as I had taken to calling her, seemed to enjoy the game very much.

In the dim of dungeon light, the bins were unnecessary. Most times, they sat on a small table by the settee. Sometimes I would keep them on. I wanted to be able to fight in daylight as well. I would definitely need to keep them on my face to do that.

I had owned several pairs of the dark black glasses over the decades. They didn't seem to wear out as much as they went out of fashion. Being up with fashion is what young girls do. My original pair, along with a half dozen additional pairs, was in a locked storage drawer in the study. The changing times had produced glasses with a curved loop over the ear. They were quite sturdy once properly in place on my face. I could move quite freely without worry, unlike previous pairs.

The thing that I had come to miss about the sparring was the change out of fashion. In days past, I would change out of my cumbersome woman's fashions into trousers and a shirt. I enjoyed the freedom of movement that men's clothing afforded. I did also spar in dresses and boots, because that was how I killed. Most days, though, trousers were the rule.

One of the things history had done to please me over the centuries was the evolution of trousers. There had always been some women wearing them, even back when I was human. They lived down the docks or on the streets of London. They had no station in society. The Industrial Revolution and its mass migration to the cities had started producing a generation of women working in factories. The transition of dress from standards of society to something a little bit more utilitarian was a natural side effect of that situation. There was a whole new lower class of women who now wore trousers as a matter of course. It was still basically unacceptable for a lady to be seen in such attire, but the times they were a changing.

I had hit the streets in trousers on several occasions. Add a dark-colored shirt and a hat with a brim, and I was just another working woman on her way home from the factory. It was great camouflage. Sadly, I couldn't employ this tactic with my current situation. For the hunting of Mr. Smith and his comrades, it would need to be high fashion. He was the type of prey that you trapped with a dapper bit of bait. I admit, fighting a half dozen men would be much easier in trousers, but I had done the same in bulky dresses before. I would just need to choose as moderate a wrapping as possible.

The women's fashion of the day was of dresses that produced a slim appearance. They had tight sleeves with puffy shoulders, which helped make them maneuverable. The floor length hem meant you had to hike them up to run, but that was always the case in my world. As a matter of course, they all seemed to have a closed-up bodice, most times with some type of lace or seamed collar. Frankly, hiding away my chest in a tightly enclosed bodice was just fine with me. Getting away from the loose bodice fashion was grand. Getting away from the bustle was also a plus. I have always found bustles to be a big pain. Let's face it, all the satins and heavy velvets of the day made it all look like well-kept upholstery. Though the fabrics were still heavy in 1891, the style was a major improvement.

For the day in question, I chose a full-length, heavy, cotton dress of checkerboard design. It had a full collar and a tight bodice. That allowed me to get away from wearing the corset. It also had long sleeves, which flexed well at the elbow. Though tight at the waist, it wasn't overly tight in its skirt, so I could move about and kick quite well. And I looked quite good. A pair of black lace gloves, a small hat with some lace about the brim, and short-heeled boots to finish off the ensemble. All in all, it was the very statement of fashion.

I inspected myself in the large bathroom mirror for no particular reason. Even though there was no image returned by the mirror, I could tell that I looked pretty. It was a knack I had developed over the years. It also made me feel a little more demonic. The lack of an image reinforced the idea that I was not human. I was a vampire. I was not a pretty, frail, teenage girl. I was a 250-year-old killer. It was just one of those things I did to get in the right mood.

That day I was fully in the mood. I dressed and made my way downstairs to my favorite overstuffed chair in the study. One of the girls from the kitchen was shortly behind me with a steaming cup of tea. Megan was shortly behind her. She said something about me looking nice. I returned the compliment and we had tea. She asked why the wrapping. I explained that I was headed to the city. She asked when we were leaving. I explained I was going alone and smiled, my large enamel fangs glinting in the morning sun. She drew a breath. We continued our tea.

Megan was many things, but the two things I liked the most were smart and secretive. Her quiet human disapproval of my lacking humanity was exactly what I needed to set my mood on the killing at hand. Finishing my tea, I made my way to the stables and found my carriage waiting patiently. How my driver knew in advance that I wanted to go somewhere was always a mystery to me. I would think I wanted to go somewhere, and the carriage would be ready. Secretly, I liked it quite well. As a vampire, it always left me feeling suspect.

Today, young Vlade Templeton sat in his seat, waiting patiently for me to appear. I liked Vlade well for a human. He came from a family of immigrants who had made their way out of Eastern Europe. The family had done their best to adopt and thrive. Young Vlade was a worker. He was quiet and unassuming. He was not so far removed from his roots. He still believed in the old ways. I could always tell that he wasn't 100 percent sure about me, which in and of itself made me happy. Britain had lost hold of the old ways long ago with its relentless march toward the future. Progress and mechanics had replaced folklore and superstition. Society forgetting made me perfectly happy. I liked unhindered anonymity when I could find it, but I also liked Vlade's subconscious curiosity.

My young driver took me quietly along to the office out the other side of Mile End. The day was pleasant and the city bustling with activity. The docks and office of my corporation were fully stocked, and the stevedores were busy as bees. It had been a while since I had spoken to Gregory. As expected, he was waist deep in some shipping issue. I liked that about him, he was hands on. I had been hands on for many years. It was the best way to maintain leadership.

We conversed for some time. The status of the corporation was covered in full. The state of the family was also covered in depth. Gregory touched on the well-being of each of his five children. They were all well. Wayne, his brother, was also doing fine in his pursuit to increase the family fortune. Megan's brother, Brian, had succumbed to some type of disease. He had produced no heirs. I wasn't shocked.

I left Gregory to his busy affairs after asking when he would be stepping down and moved along. Gregory was no longer a middle-aged man, and his kids were old enough. He should be allowed a few years of peace. He just laughed and said that he would consider it later.

I reboarded my carriage and we headed off toward Piccadilly Circus. The area was the usual stomping grounds of one Mr. Smith. The amulet lay in the cleft of my breast, as quiet as could be. My pulse was all but nonexistent. I had a little flow, to maintain color, but that was it. If he already knew I was a vampire, then there was no need for pretense.

The opulent hotel on Regent Street had a wonderful salon. I made my way in and secured a table with good viewing of the crowd. I ordered some tea to complement the niceness of the day. Then I waited.

Unlike humans, most vampires are very good at waiting. I can wait as long as I need to wait if I want my own ends to come true. Waiting patiently is the sign of a good predator. Most humans aren't good predators. It sounds odd, since they do manage to kill just about everything on the planet, but it's true. The real predators among them are few. The vast majority of the human population is a herd of sheep. They fidget and go off half-cocked. They don't wait or observe situations before acting. They lack the patience of the hunt. Vampires do not lack patience.

Fortunately for me, on this particular occasion, I had to wait but a short interval. I hadn't even finished my first round of tea when Mr. Smith strolled casually through the doors of the salon. He made a stealthy turn around the room, stopping to converse with several couples before making his approach.

I do have to say that he was smooth enough on the approach. Most of men's flash moves are lost on me. I like gentlemen. He definitely had flash, but it was subdued by a quiet sense of supreme confidence. As any woman will tell you, confidence is the ticket to getting your chance. He got his chance.

"Good day, madam, my name is Christian Smith. I would like to say that you look radiant today sitting here in this magnificent salon."

"Why, thank you, sir. A woman always appreciates a compliment from a gentleman. Would you like to sit and join me for tea?"

"Oh, that is quite nice of you. Thank you, but I wouldn't want your husband to be unsettled upon his return."

"I am a single woman, thank you. And I happen to be unescorted today, so the seat is free."

"Well, in that case, it seems only right that I should accept your gracious offer and help you pass the time."

Mr. Smith sat as I introduced myself. He seemed momentarily pleased when I gave my name as Gibbs. I think he was actually planning on hearing me say Grey.

We conversed for some time. All of the usual topics of the day came and went. He was versed in business and politics, so the conversation was solid and well-paced. We talked all the way through tea. As the service staff came to collect the china, Mr. Smith asked if I might like to take the air in Saint James Park. I said that would be lovely. We collected ourselves to go out into society, and the real show began.

My escort and I strolled down Regent Street, almost to the Admiralty. At a small alleyway just before the massive stone building complex, he made some coy statement about taking a shortcut and pointed toward the closed-up ten-footer. I nodded in a demure fashion and followed him into the alley. About fifty feet or so from the road entrance, the alley turned a blind ninety-degree corner to the right. Mr. Smith ever so casually let me go around the corner first. In a ladylike fashion, I acknowledged and turned the corner.

Three sturdy men stood in the alley on the other side of the corner, all wearing the long coats and black-brimmed hats of the Brenfield Society, just not the canes their type were known for. Not unexpectedly, the missing two men came up from behind to reinforce Mr. Smith. They had picked a good spot for their attack. The alley was no more than eight feet wide and was shear-walled a solid two stories high.

Deciding not to let them have the advantage, I attacked first. Pivoting about on one foot, I kicked Mr. Smith so hard I could hear his ribs break before he went crashing into the men behind him. They had no more than started their tumble to the ground when I turned on the men playing blockers. The middle one took a shot to the throat. The one on the left, a stunning blow to the chest followed up by a bone-crushing blow to the hip. My left palm came to rest against the temple of the man on the right about half a second before his head impacted the brick wall behind it. The sound of his brains squeezing out from in between the smashed bits of skull was a bit discomforting.

Four men down and two to go. Two were fully dead and two were of no bother. I spun back around on my heels to find the last two a little better off than I had expected. They had recovered and were closing the space between Mr. Smith and me. One of the men dove and hit me at the knees. The two of us flipped head over tea kettle and came to rest against the one wall. The other man was directly behind him with the damned pike handle that Effie had shown me.

The man with the pike slammed it home, but as was usual for humans, he was a good five steps slower than I. When he slammed the pike handle into the back of his companion, I was no longer underneath him. The snapping of bone as the wooden beam shattered the man's spine was gratifying. I reached out and grabbed pike man by his exposed wrist. A quick yank and he spun around uncontrollably, like a toy top.

I normally don't strike people with a closed fist. My light body doesn't produce enough kinetic energy to be an effective boxer. The martial arts–style blows are much more effective on large men. The equalizer on most days is that vampires are naturally stronger than humans. This day it took three strikes to produce the desired effect. The first two strikes loosened up the man's nasal bone, and the third one shoved it straight through his skull. Then eighteen stone of sturdy man hit the cobblestone like a sack of cabbage.

The new count was all men down, with four dead and two barely alive. Total combat time elapsed, less than one good minute. I stopped and straightened my attire. I didn't need to look like I had just killed a pack of people.

I stepped over to the last of the hired help, who was trying to crawl away on his busted hip. He squirmed about in a pathetic fashion. It was a sad end for an otherwise capable man. Feeling momentarily benevolent, I decided that he didn't require further suffering. I place a heel on his throat and pushed until it produced the familiar sound of breaking bone. There was a pronounced twitch under foot and the squirming stopped. I ran my hand down the front of my dress, the same way one does when wiping crumbs from an apron. Then, I turned my attention back to the dashing Mr. Smith.

"Mr. Smith, you seem to have and alternate agenda. What happened to taking the air in the park?"

He tried to respond as he clutched his flailing chest. He was not as much a fighter as the men he had hired. It was sad, really.

"If it makes you feel any better, I am not going to feed on you. Frankly, I find weak men to be unsatisfying. You will simply die in a pool of your own blood."

With the strength of a 250-year-old vampire, I secured a grip over the pathetic man's mouth and sliced open his throat with a sharp edged piece of cobble that was lying about. He kicked and twitched as adrenaline pushed the blood from his body at twice the normal rate.

Pausing for a moment in the utter silence, I checked each man to make sure they were all dead. Deciding my work was done, I picked up Mr. Smith's hat and filled it with all of the men's valuables. When found it would seem that they must have been robbed by some street gang.

Strolling casually back to the entrance of the alley, I found my carriage waiting patiently. I climbed in the back and smiled at Vlade.

"Will the gentleman be joining you, ma'am?"

"No, Vlade, the gentleman will not be joining us. What do you say we take the long way back today?"

"Very good, ma'am."

As we crossed Westminster Bridge, I tossed Mr. Smith's hat into the Thames. A small splash was heard in the distance as we made our way toward the far side of the river. I was pleased with the outcome of my afternoon's exercise. I was also disconcerted by it. They knew me, and I did not know them. That needed to be addressed when I got home.

CHAPTER 9

The days passed along as days always tend to do. Except, unlike days of old, the days following Mr. Smith's untimely demise came with lingering consequences. In days gone by, all one needed to do was to dispose of the body in some reasonable way. I had always found the Thames to be a perfectly reasonable place. In lieu of floating them downstream to the sea, disguising them as mugging victims was the second best approach. No one ever really spent much time on dead bodies in a port town.

Sadly for me, the city of London was slowly transitioning from being a big port town to being a modern urban center. As cities go, it was now loud and dirty, but it was also educating itself. The law of the day was doing its best to maintain the new ideal. That was good for the city and bad for me.

Two days on from my little tussle with Christian, a nice man from Scotland Yard came to visit me at the estate. He kindly informed me that a man I had made acquaintance with had been murdered some days past. Apparently, this man had managed to put himself into some spot of trouble while in the city. The fellow, along with five of his friends, were murdered and robbed. Since he had been seen in my company some time before the events may have transpired, the detective wanted to see what my recollections were for that day.

The nice detective told me that considering the size and number of the men, there must have been some sort of gang robbery or mob killing. I told him that the whole affair sounded quite ghastly, and I was sad for the man and his friends.

The nice detective and I conversed for some time. Since he obviously wasn't looking at me like Mr. Smith had been, I was on my most ladylike behavior. The one interesting bit of news that did come out of my meeting with The Yard was regarding Mr. Smith's past. I told the detective while we were talking that there were many dashing men about the city and it seemed odd that someone would single him out. The detective agreed. They thought it was odd that he would have trouble in the city. It seemed that young Christian Smith was the direct descendent of Grand Duke William Bennett, and apparently resided at the family estate in Stratford.

The detective and his peers assumed he had come to London on some business and run up against the city's darker elements. I knew that the policemen were correct, but for different reasons. I passed on my deepest sympathies and explained that I had not known of his station in the chain of nobility.

The two of us continued to talk for some time about my title and my family's long standing in the area. The detective had grown up on the London street and knew well of Grey's Cargo's history in the city. The man really did seem to be nice, and making friends with the law could be advantageous. In a pleasant and girlish way the questions were answered, and the good detective was placated. I asked him to return at some convenient point if he would like a tour of the estate. He departed, seemingly pleased by the Earl of Northwick's answers. I explained to him that I might be out of the city for a time, as I needed to return to Bristol and inspect the manor. He wished me safe travels. I thought it nice that he wished me well.

I sat out in the summer sun on the study terrace and drummed my fingers on the table. I had actually never been visited by the law before. I had killed countless people and had never before been questioned about them. The omen that this was something new to come with the times hung over my head like a black storm cloud. I was obviously going to need to change up my tactics if I was going to keep killing people. And, seriously, if I couldn't kill people when I wanted to, what was the point? Being a predator of the human species meant that I killed humans. It appeared to be getting just a little more complicated with every generation. That was the price of change, I guess.

Now, the seemingly minor fact that Christian Smith was the nephew of dead old Grand Duke William Bennett was a complication of a different matter. This was the thing that had actually produced the finger drumming. Could Smith possibly be a member of the Brenfield Society? Did they even still exist? Had they resurfaced to settle an agenda item, or was it a personal thing? Whatever the case, I needed none of it. Things had finally calmed down. I was as anonymous as anyone else on the planet, and then the ghosts of my past rose up again. Did I really need to kill every one of them and all of their families, too, before they left me in peace?

General note ... Looking back on the world with a clear view, the men from the House of Shadows, and all its differing incarnations, were all great men of industry. Their exploitation of nature and their polluted factories killed many more humans than I ever have. If you counted all the vampires of Great Britain, the society still had us outdone many fold with its lethal nature. This is not a justification, simply a statement of fact. Preying on people is preying on people, no matter how you go about it.

The idea of going to Bristol had been a reflex idea in the midst of conversation. The more I considered it now, the more I came to like it. I had been residing at the estate for some time. It would do me good to get back to the country and spend some time at the manor. Brimme House had always held a special place in my heart. It was also a good place for some killing if need be.

I had spent my vampire youth in the secure seat of the earl. Though it was the manor house for an earl, Brimme House was much more a castle than it was an estate house. Built in a time when lands needed to be secured, the fortress of Brimme House had full command of the countryside. The house itself was a massive three-story stone structure that sat inside a thick defensive wall. The river ran around two of its sides and produced a natural defensive mote. Secure gate towers and a parapet let one completely walk the surround connecting the main gate to the corner watchtowers and produced a very defensible dwelling.

In more current times, with the lawns manicured and the weapons stowed in show armories, Brimme House had transitioned into being a prominent object projecting extreme status. Extreme in the sense that most of the nobility, save the crown, could not muster better lodgings. It really was a shame that I didn't spend more time there. Yes, a trip to the country was in order.

I promptly informed Megan that we would be taking a trip west to visit the country. Quite unexpectedly, she informed me that she would not be accompanying me to Brimme House. I somewhat understood. She was a wife and a mother and had responsibilities outside of me. Normally I would have gone off on a tirade, but her obligations had been of my making. I couldn't chastise her for doing what I prompted her to do.

It quickly looked like I was traveling solo for the first time ever. I had never been left to my own devices before. I was sure I could manage it; it just felt wrong to be alone.

In days of old, no young lady traveled without a sturdy male escort to protect her. Nobility simply didn't travel unescorted. As the times had moved forward, and moral codes had softened, I had come to traveling with a female companion. Now, I was sans an escort. It seemed immediately strange to me, yet at the same time, girlishly liberating.

Megan did come through and make all the traveling arrangements for me. I would be taking the train west across England, from London to Bristol. At the train station in Bristol, a carriage would take me on to Northwick. Once the arrangements had been finalized, she sat with me and explained about scheduling the return. I was educated on whom to contact and what modes of transport were most suitable. It is sad to admit, but up until that time, I had never been forced to make my own travel plans. I had always had a nice Wyndell man to do that for me. Even in the days of the tall ships, one of the Wyndell boys would track down *The Summer Storm* and have her at my bidding. The longer Megan's tutorial went on, the more alone I began to feel.

I was old by every standard and still had never been left completely alone in the world. There had been father, Antonio, Charles, followed by numerous generations of the Wyndell family, a couple of goodly priests, and Megan. Now, I was out in the wilds. I wondered if this was another sign of things to come.

Don't get me wrong, I wasn't completely alone. I mean, it wasn't like I was sleeping under a bridge alone. No earl is really completely left by herself. There are always residual people, bankers and such, circling around the outside. They just weren't remotely close enough to be useful to me. There was also my constant companion living in the crystal case around my neck. Effie was with me at all times and a better defense than ten sturdy men. We were good friends and could do with just each other's company for long periods. It was just that I had always had a live human confidant to talk to and discuss things with. I had come to both like and take comfort in their presence.

A fortnight from the detective's visit I stepped onto the train in Paddington Station and prepared to head west. I liked Paddington Station. The station had housed the western line since somewhere around the 1830s. A large piece of it had been updated in 1854, and its platforms were the point for destinations to the west. Well, at least the point for traveling to destinations west in style. The new style of traveling the countryside by rail was quite comfortable and solidly faster than the older alternatives.

Megan watched from the platform as my train pulled from the station. She wore the look of an expectant mother. I wondered if she actually saw me, at times, as one of her children; another young charge for her to take care of. She stood on the platform and watched as I was released into the world. Young Earl Lady Allison May Gibbs, the 250-year-old vampire, was finally out on her own.

The ride west across Britain was liberating for me. I really was out on my own. I was traveling the world of my own accord. The longer the train clanked and banged its way along the tracks, the more certain I became that it was a good thing. I was capable of living my own life, by myself. I decided that if this excursion to Brimme House proved successful, I would continue on alone. As much as I liked the humans, it would be good to live on my own a while.

It seemed like no time at all and the locomotive pulled into the Bristol station. A kind man from the railroad appeared and explained that my luggage would be offloaded at spot number two on the luggage landing and that my driver could acquire it there. I thanked him and exited my train car into the hustle and bustle of the Bristol station. Not five or six feet from the end of the landing stood a man with a thick mustache and a large, black top hat, holding a small sign with my name on it. I proceeded to the man with the sign and introduced myself. The older gentleman said he was from Brimme House and was there to escort me to my waiting carriage. Effie pulsed in my subconscious, telling me that he was who he said he was. I told the man what the train steward had informed me of regarding my luggage. The man informed me that a boy had already been sent to fetch the trunks and deliver them to the carriage.

As I was escorted to my waiting carriage by my mustached driver, I passed other well-to-do individuals receiving similar treatment. It interested me that where I was newly in awe of the whole experience and the kindness of all the people I had interacted with, the other well-off people looked almost put out by the experience. They were obviously all people of means, so why wouldn't they be happy to have people helping them? It momentarily made me wonder if I had been killing people in the wrong social circles. There was really no reason to look down on society. I had every reason to do so, as the humans of the world were just food to me, but I had never done such things in all my years on the earth. It struck me as wrong. The scene made me wonder if that was also something in my dislike of the Brenfield Society. They were all such people: ones who thought that the better people are better people. People who think that way annoy me. They always have. Maybe that really was it?

I had no more started to be put off by the thoughts in my head when a young man came scurrying out of the throngs of humanity with my two large trunks pulled behind him on a rickety wooden cart. I tossed him entirely too big a tip for the service and he disappeared back into the crowd, beaming from ear to ear. My driver simply smiled at the gesture and loaded the trunks onto the back of the carriage. I watched the young lad scamper away. It was all good. It all even made Effie happy for the smallest of moments.

My mustached driver hopped up onto his seat with a spring in his step that I wouldn't have assumed he possessed for his obvious years. Never judge people, I guess? A quick yank on the reins and we were on our way to the country. The landscape of the area had changed since I had seen it last. Bristol had expanded its limits and the surrounding area had grown along with it. I had been noticing that the revenues of Brimme House had been expanding, but I hadn't really given it much mind. As the carriage made its way to my ancestral home, the increased humanity on the lands it passed made me reconsider the balance sheet.

I became taken up in the changing countryside and how it affected me being a landowner, and the ride ended up a short-lived affair. All too soon I was entering the gatehouse and arriving at the front drive of the manor. The site of Brimme House's sturdy walls and the family flag at full mast did my heart a world of good. As much as the Grey Estate was where I lived, Brimme House was who I was. It always did me good to return.

I was escorted through the main doors and into the sitting room. My driver introduced me to the members of the staff on duty. Everyone seemed kind and they all asked numerous questions. It made me feel welcome.

They quickly enough departed and returned to the never-ending toils of running the house. I made my way to the grand ballroom and out onto its large patio. On my way through the ballroom, I stopped to look upon the portrait of myself I had hung alongside the other members of my family line. I hadn't seen my own image in many years, but I could tell that it still hadn't changed significantly. That, too, made me happy.

I sat at one of the large, iron patio tables and looked out over the lawns. As orchestrated, a young girl appeared with a tea set and placed it on the table's sturdy glass top. She explained that a currier had delivered a message for me earlier that morning and it was on the tray. Then, she disappeared back into the house. The tea was nice and steamy. The message was short and problematic.

Lady Gibbs,

We at the Enfield Trust hope this message finds you well. The actions of Mr. Smith were unfortunate but were not activities that had to do with the Trust or its older collaboration, the Brenfield Society. Please accept my open invitation for tea at any time that is of your liking.

Respectfully,
Eugene Stone, principal
The Enfield Trust

A short note from the Marques Eugene Stone inviting me to tea. Yet it was also a statement that the Brenfield Society was still alive and well. It, like me, had transitioned to a new look and a new name. It seemed that they were also still paying attention to the quiet troubles of the world.

Just maybe I would need to have tea with this new watcher of the darkness. He was a man of station and should be cordial during tea … maybe? I picked up my own tea and stirred it, watching small ribbons of steam bend in the air. Being home made me happy and reading the note made me sad. I could just tell that things were going to get all bollixed up again soon.

CHAPTER 10

The following day at Brimme House reminded me why I am who I am. I molded into its grounds and forested woods with ease, the paths of my youth containing the same joy and optimism as they had in centuries past. It was refreshing and made me feel good about life. My newfound sense of pleasure was also having an unplanned side effect on my little friend. My jeweled companion was quieter and mellower than she had been in some time. It was good all around.

The requisite inspection of the estate found everything to be in proper order. The following inspection of the ship yards and Bristol business interests found them with progress unreported by the London group. The Bristol Mooring had expanded and was a frenetic beehive of activity. The same slips and docksides that had produced *The Summer Storm* now produced commercial ships of all shapes and sizes. The heavy timber of the tall ships was gone, replaced by steel and steam. It took me days of inspection to even believe that it was the same place from my youth.

Hanging in the yard manager's office was a faded black and white painting of the christening of *The Gaelic Wind*. She was a massive, wooden ocean-going galleon of days past. The manager liked it because it was nostalgic and showed the age of the Bristol Mooring. The men in the yard found it fancy. I remembered the day that the mighty *Gaelic Wind* slid down the dock skids and splashed into the North Sea. It really did seem like a different world, compared with the hulking ironworks of the modern-day mooring.

Timber had given way to steel and sail cloth had been replaced by steam engines, but the money remained. This new Mooring saw out ships that produced great wealth. The profits of the shipbuilding business were truly well intact. That, in and of itself, made me like the changes to the Mooring.

Liking the changes I saw around me was one thing, but understanding that time continues to change is quite another. I spent several days casually wandering the paths of the grounds, pondering the relentless march of time. I had been overseeing the same things for centuries. Why? I had promised Father that I would continue the company. But for how long? Eternity? I had made deals with Antonio so that my company would handle the needs of his companies. That had been handled long ago. I had promised Charles that I would look after his family as if they were my own. But, once again, for how long? Did I really need to continue on with relentless progress just to maintain a centuries-old status quo?

My father, God rest his soul, would not even recognize the multinational corporation that had replaced his little two-room shipping company. Antonio's needs were handled so easily that they now got lost in the dizzying amount of business conducted by Grey's Cargo. The Wyndell family was no longer one but now a fully branched tree of families. And they were no longer subservient working-class people, either. They had amassed so much wealth that they wouldn't even recognize the street-level existence that Charles had started out with. Everything had become bigger, better, more, and yet somehow the same.

I will admit that all of that change had also changed me. The quiet and almost shy little human girl that lived with her comfortably employed father was a distant dream compared to my current noble, super-wealthy existence. I had changed so much. I wasn't even the same bloody person. Well, that's not completely true. On every internal level that mattered, I was exactly the same person. OK, I was now demonic, but that really wasn't any harder to control than being wealthy. It was all the exterior trappings and things that had accelerated and expanded around me as the centuries had marched on.

As I came back to the house from my walk, without a confidant to converse with, another change was reinforced. The sheer act of being left alone in the world for a time had forced me to view it all differently. There were times when Effie wanted to remind me that I actually was not alone, but she let me go on with my thoughts.

As near as I could tell, I had done all I said I was going to do. I had actually done it a hundred folds over. Did I need to continue? The thought of being free from it all left weeks of beating another question to death: If not this, then what?

This life I lived is all I had ever known. The docks and salt air were what I was raised on. They were my entire life. Being a vampire and killing humans had been with me almost as long. I had been what I was so long that I couldn't fathom being anything other than what I was. Yet, that wasn't completely true either. When I was young, I ran my company with my own hands and I killed the humans that I needed to stay alive. As time marched on, I had come to being a casual observer in the events of my corporation and I had moved on to killing for cause, as the power of the amulet gave me what I required for life. Over time, I had evolved. I was now a hybrid of what I once was.

I decided that I needed to do a little work on this topic. I needed to spend some time observing what ultra-rich women did here at the turn of the new century. I had a good idea what a noble woman did, but wealthy women were a somewhat new area for me. Just being an earl would take up some of my time. Continuing to be a vampire would take up some more time. I would need to observe rich women to decide what I was going to do with the rest of it. Of course, that was if I decided to change anything at all. My well-serviced human sense of comfort did not like change.

I decided the topic was valid enough that it was worth exploring from the fringes, but I would hold off on doing anything rash for a couple decades. You don't want to rush to judgment. That usually goes badly all around.

Another topic of thought that had been reeling in my head as I walked the meadows of Brimme House was this Enfield Trust matter. The House of Shadows had changed into the Brenfield Society. That group had now mutated into the Enfield Trust. As in days of old, this new Trust was also led by a high-ranking member of the British nobility.

I had managed to stun the House of Shadows. I had put a sword through the chest of the Brenfield Society. I wasn't keen on doing combat with the Enfield Trust, but from the correspondence, it didn't sound like that was what they were after either. The House of Shadows was an observant group and did its business with less than hostile intent. The note from the marquis sounded like the Enfield Trust was coming back around to this way of thinking. Less confrontational definitely sounded better to me than fighting. If I could make a truce with the Catholic Church, maybe I could do the same with the Enfield Trust.

As I walked the meadow on the far side of the river and picked wild flowers, I formulated an idea.

"Effie, we are going to have tea with this marquis I think."

"Why?"

"Let's see what he has to say. Let's try a new plan, old friend—diplomacy over violence."

"This seems to be part of this soul searching that you have been engaged in."

"Yes, it is."

"Well, then, let's you have tea and see what the human has to say for himself."

"I agree. It's tea with the marquis."

And with an earl-like efficiency, it took not more than days for the staff to set up a convenient time with the marquis' people. It was accidental fortune that he happened to be wandering about Wales at the time. It definitely reduced the travel.

One day, perhaps a week farther along, the Marquis Eugene Stone sat comfortably across a moderate-sized iron table on my terrace. Upon meeting him, I saw that he was everything that anyone would expect of a member of high nobility. He was probably six feet, three inches tall and sixteen stone, with the polished features of both a military man and an educated scholar. Brown hair and brown eyes were set on a sun-stretched face. The age lines his face possessed only added to his unspoken sense of accomplishment. The thing I admired most about him was his sense of calm. His calm was greatly reassuring to Effie.

"I'm pleased to see that you were in a position to accept my invitation for tea, Marquis. I confess I found your note both relieving and perplexing."

"I have to admit that considering our otherwise mutual history, I was surprised to receive your request. There was no way I could possibly turn it down, Lady Gibbs."

"Seeing how we do have an otherwise mutual history, as you put it, I suggest we dispense with some of the English pleasantries. I would like it quite well if you called me Sara. Besides, the last member of the nobility I entertained was Prince George, and we spent most of our time hunting."

"There were notes in the chronicles that you were quite good friends with both King George III and IV."

"It was more the queen. The men just fancied me. It was all that 'young country noble girl comes to court' thing. The queen was very nice to me and a wise monarch."

"Well, that being said, Sara, would you please call me Eugene. As an academic, I am much more comfortable on a first-name basis. I use my title daily, but for business purposes. And my military days full of structure are all far behind me."

"It is nice to make your acquaintance, Eugene."

"And I am honored to have this audience with you, Sara. As a sign of this I have brought you a present of sorts."

The marquis reached down and retrieved a small leather satchel by his feet. After some fumbling inside, he retrieved two extremely old-looking books and laid them on the table midway between us. As the books touched down on the iron table's glass top, Effie quickly began to spool up the dark energy.

"Effie, sweetie, calm down please."

With that, she began to let the building energy subside. The marquis said nothing but was obviously transfixed by the electric blue glow emanating from under my dress.

"You'll need to forgive us that little display, Eugene. My friend is … edgy."

"I had read as much, but I didn't realize the workings of the amulet were so libertine."

"She can be double quick, even by my standards. Now, I am sorry, please continue."

"I would like to make an offering. A show of good faith, as it were."

I raised an eyebrow but said nothing so he might continue.

"There were reported to be five books surrounding the history of the amulet. Three are currently in the Vatican archives and two are in the Trust's private collection. These two books are the two that you haven't read. They are at your disposal until such time as you feel you have learned all that you seek. When you are concluded, I would request they be returned."

I stared at the books and at Eugene, in an alternating fashion. My instincts were saying "trap," but my frontal lobe was definitely saying "truce." Effie was full-on thinking trap, but she hated people, especially people like the Enfield Trust.

"Forgive me once again, Marquis Stone. But why would you do such a thing if it wasn't bait for something else?"

"Caution really is a hallmark of your kind, isn't it? I suppose that's probably a good thing. Well, Sara, it's not some cleverly disguised ambuscade. It is, for lack of a better phrase, a truce. We at the Trust are a different lot than those of the society that preceded us."

"That is very nice to hear, Eugene. What kind of truce did you have in mind?"

"The same kind we have with Europe." He began to laugh. I did the same as I got the intentions of the stress the British flag had on our neighbors across the channel.

"Let's just say that the Enfield Trust is returning to its roots in academia. We would like to lay down our warring ways, with you in particular. We won't hunt you, and you don't hunt us. A truce."

"I like this idea. Conflict is always problematic. How long do you see this truce lasting?"

"As long as it lasts—that's the nature of such things. But the books are a sign of good intentions."

"They are greatly appreciated, and a truce is most welcome."

Eugene exhaled audibly, as if he had been holding his breath. If he had been somehow unsure as to its outcome, he didn't show it. He was a man that was cool under pressure. Effie interpreted the exhale the same way and relaxed completely.

"As a further example of this newly formed understanding, I would also like to pass on a bit of information."

"Please."

"Our sources tell us that young Mr. Christian Smith and his thugs that you dispatched in London are just the tip of a spear—a spear that is not of our making."

"You made mention to as much in your note. Please elaborate."

"Mr. Smith is a member of a large family. That family contained one of our preceding directors, Grand Duke William Bennett. You remember him? I think you had the queen stick his head on a pike?"

I smiled a bit too fondly as the memory resurfaced.

"Yes, well, his extended family is some one hundred strong. They are well-to-do, well-educated in the occult, and they ALL HATE YOU."

My smile faded. "So, Mr. Smith wasn't an isolated affair?"

"No, Lady Grey, he was not. And, sadly for you, they all know all about you."

"That will require a new footing, I guess."

"What you do to the descendants of William Bennett is up to you. We tend to think that you will prevail, as it's your way. We would just be happy if you didn't take it out on us."

"Eugene, you have my word. I will do no harm to any member of the Enfield Trust, unless they are entwined with the Bennett family."

"That seems more than acceptable."

"I have to say, I'm happy I invited you to tea."

"I, too, am greatly pleased. However, if you would indulge me, I would like to change the topic slightly."

"Please."

"As an academic, I do have some curiosities about your vampirism. It seems unlikely that I will ever get the opportunity to converse with another member of your kind."

I laughed loudly. It was a position I had apparently been in too many times. Why was I always educating the competition?

"Eugene, feel free to ask any question you like. Some of them will get answers and some of them will not. And please feel free to come for tea again. You seem nice, and that is as good a harbinger of good will as anything else in the world."

The marquis began his questions, and I did my best to answer them. The conversation continued on for most of the afternoon. As Eugene finally made his way down the drive and out through the portcullis, I sensed that I had made a new friend. He really did seem honest. I would keep him for as long as he lasted. I would kill all the members of the Bennett family and anyone else associated with them. It seemed I was right when I sensed that the quiet was over again.

CHAPTER 11

The sun rose, breaking warm, bright yellow rays through the leaded glass of the study windows, like in some early Hollywood movie. I sat at the large wooden desk that took command of the space's open middle area and bathed myself in the solar radiance. As I did so, my mind swam with possibility.

On a day just like this one, but long ago past, I sat at a similar desk in a similar study at the Grey Estate and wrapped my intellect around an ancient stick figure story told by one of my kind. The study of that olden vampire's life had changed my own life greatly. The amulet I wore, which came with the story, changed it even more.

Later on in that century, I used that same curiosity to decipher the tale of my shiny jewel. A tale so old that it, too, was all but stick figures set in far off lands. The tale of woe, though hard to glean, brought me much closer to the individual entity that came to be my best friend.

Now, coming up on the end of that century, I find myself sitting at a large desk in front of two more very old tomes—these current editions being the last two of a five-book set. They composed the basic initial history of the amulet. The story that the five books had been slowly laying out was both horrific and spellbinding. It was the reason that countless ruthless humans, over the course of millennia, had sought to hunt it down. The incalculable power it was capable of unleashing could produce and depose kings with equal whimsy.

All five books had been written, if written is the correct phrase, in the same pre-hieroglyphic text. It was a series of stories in pictures. The two books housed at the Vatican had been stories of first, the need for great power to dispel enemies, and second, the price Efuru had paid for men to have that power. The third journal of the five, which I found in the Лyx Fortress while freeing Antonio, was the story of how my young friend reacted to being transformed into ethereal energy. I can sum up that story by saying it did not go well. Diligent study of that work on the voyage back to Rome produced a story as compelling as the first two in the Vatican.

The shaman of her day had attempted to train her to wield the vast power of the void, but as with all such situations in life, no one is ever really ready. When the young girl, schooled in the darkness of the world and knowing scant little of the good it could also possess, was combined with unlimited universal power—well the ending was explosive.

Oh, the amulet accomplished exactly what it was meant to. All the enemies of the land were laid waste before it. No one else would rise up and challenge the rulers of her land for fear of her reprisal. The problem came when there were no more enemies to decimate. The young charge that they had given unlimited power had somehow become lost in the never-ending blackness of the void. Having an outlet for her anger was good. Not having an outlet for it was definitely bad.

Young Efuru slowly and methodically ate away at the rulers of the land to go forth and conquer. She needed more people to subjugate. Her drive was to break the will of men. The power granted her was so great that the rulers of her time crumbled under her lust for conquest. The humans fought against her incredible might until, like is expected of a child, she threw a small tantrum. Her little mood swing decimated all the rulers of her kingdom.

Seeing the ultimatum imposed, the rulers that rose in replacement were somewhat less inclined to let the amulet just do as it chose. That reaction pleased the young girl in the jeweled cage even less. Feeling slighted, she razed the capital of the kingdom. Not one stone was left unturned as the power of the void spilled out upon the men that had made it. In the end, all that remained of the once-great city was rubble. There was just an endless sea of rubble, with a sun yellow jewel hovering in the air above it.

Successions of humans attempted to placate the powers of the amulet in any fashion that seemed acceptable to her. Young Efuru in return acted just as one might expect. It seemed that the learned men of old had ripped the top off Pandora's Box and then kicked it for good measure. They had created something so uncontrollable that they were worse off than before they made it. They ended up looking back upon their decisions in horror. The amulet, on the other hand, just kept getting stronger and stronger as its young guardian slipped further into the void. The power of the amulet now radiated out over all the lands of the African continent, and those affected by it looked on in awe. Well, as nearly as I could tell, it was awe and fear.

That's what I had grasped as I traveled west from the Black Sea. My friend did nothing to tell me I was wrong as I formulated my story from the pictures in the book. While I gleaned out the tale, the amulet simply watched on in mild amusement.

That was the story from the volume that I had returned to the Vatican. It was still hard to equate the story in those books with the jewel hanging around my neck. My shiny friend was still pushy and quite powerful, but she seemed neither chaotic nor childish. She was, for all purposes, just exactly the opposite. She was smart, rational, calm under fire, and when necessary, quite violent. But mostly to the opposite, she was not really the manipulative sort. She was a giver. She gave to me constantly. She was not the same amulet as in this tale I had been reading, but the tale was also thousands of years old. Maybe she had mellowed.

It appeared that the term mellowed was exactly right. The two volumes that Eugene had presented gave me the remainder of the picture. It has been said that people learn with time. That is certainly true with vampires. Obviously, it is also true of my little friend in the jeweled cage.

I sat at my study desk and pondered over the fourth book for a good day before it started to make some kind of sense to me. The story picked up where I remember the castle book leaving off. My young friend was laying waste to all that seemed opposed to her. The problem with children and authority was that she saw everyone as opposing her.

It has been said countless times that humans are inventive creatures. Nowhere is that statement truer than in the human's response to the swirling destructive power of the amulet. Someone apparently stopped long enough to think and decided to fight magick with magick. It really was the only way out of the situation. There seemed to be some of this and some of that at the beginning, but once the shaman of the day realized that they couldn't actually destroy the amulet, since the shaman of old were apparently cleverer, they decided to put it somewhere that it couldn't do more harm. They were thinking of what might be considered a really old school time-out, which was exactly what she needed.

Sorcery fashioned a container, a second Pandora's Box of sorts, and sealed it with all of the magick that they could muster. It was not the power of the void, but it turned out to be enough to keep the focused power of the amulet at bay. They decided that they wanted to put the evil back into Pandora's Box.

The real problem they faced wasn't in fashioning the box; it was in the act of getting the jewel inside. Efuru was no fool. She could see straight into the minds of men. The first one to attempt the task died quickly. The second one died not quite so. The third and fourth proved no better at their tries. A half dozen died before they all realized that they were no match for the amulet. So, in a small leap of insight, the shaman went back to the magick for help. The shaman of the time used the dark magick on himself, which gave the amulet nothing to see and fear. The man finally managed to get the amulet into the vessel designed to hold her at bay.

Now, when the vessel was closed and the amulet realized what had transpired, let's just say that she had a fit. Young Effie wailed and lashed against her new prison with such untimely force that the shaman of the day didn't think it would hold her in. However, it did hold her in, and with time she began to calm. It would seem that some small sense of sanity had now been restored to the land.

The lands of the once-decimated kingdom slowly recovered. The men rebuilt the cities and power returned to new leaders. Knowing not to let apathy direct their actions in the future, the new rulers built a massive stone temple and placed the caged-up jewel inside it. Every wall of the temple was covered in stories of the evil that would befall anyone trying to open the vessel. Once completed, all of the passages were sealed. To me it seemed that in a very real way they had finally brought Pandora to life.

The problem with men is that they have short lives. It seems humans never really live long enough to get past the apathy that comes from time. Such was the case when it came to my jeweled companion. As a couple of centuries passed by, the tales of the amulet became folklore. The very real fear of the ancestors slowly turned to superstition. The knowledge of the power remained, but the history of uncontrolled destruction had been forgotten.

The harshness of reality faded and some centuries passed before men came looking for the amulet once more. The amount of time was really hard to tell from the pictures, but it felt like centuries. The monks entrusted to the temple fought off numerous invading kings from distant lands. They managed in fending off the invaders for a time. Eventually, a suitably sized army with a ruthless king succeeded in defeating the monks and obtaining the vessel. The ruthless king broke the magick seals and pulled the amulet free of its cage. He hoisted it up around his neck and stood before all, ready to conquer all in his path.

Sadly for this guy, a couple of centuries in solitary confinement were exactly what Efuru had needed to get it all under control and calm down completely. She had solidified and extracted herself from the void, fully understanding now how to wield the power infused in her being. In short, she understood the fine art of manipulating people. *That was a good lesson learned,* I thought as I studied the book. Manipulation was the only thing that had ever happened to her, so she should be allowed to do it to others.

Efuru spent the final book of the five manipulating anyone foolish enough to want to wield her power. As the millennia passed and kingdoms changed, she traveled a long road of men. She stayed with the Egyptians for a time. She helped the Hittites pound out new ground. She rode with Alexander across Persia and was there when Genghis Kahn subdued the Chinese. The Germanic tribes fell before her unrelenting glow as Rome created an empire. She was the force of change.

I was happy that the fifth book actually contained writing. It started as pictures but transitioned to language as successive scholars added to the tale. Now, I'm not a linguist, so there was a lot of dictionary work to be done, but it was all there.

Somewhere during the fall of Rome, Effie disappeared from history. That was where the book ended. The later parts of her story were all myth. They were stories of mysterious happenings that had groups like the Catholic Church and the Brenfield Society wanting to lock her away again. What none of them ever understood was that she just wanted to be left alone. She had done more in ten thousand years than anyone could do in another ten thousand. Now, she just wanted to be for a time. That was the reason that we got along so well. I was the only one she had come across who found her and wanted nothing from her. Ours was first a friendship. Later, I gave to her and she gave to me. We still get along fine this way.

After three straight days of sitting at my desk, reading and studying the cryptic works, the staff had started whispering behind the closed doors. The amulet quietly hung on a hook in the window, looking out on the patio, and paid it all no mind. I closed my eyes as I closed the last book and thought back upon a much younger me, sitting and studying the journal of Karynkouthu without pause. That old vampire had taught a young vampire so many lessons. Time had done the same for the amulet and the girl locked inside it.

I stood, retrieved my friend from her window perch, and wandered out into the fading rays of the sun. A dull orange hung over the meadows and gave everything a calm and peaceful appearance. I looked at it all as my mind slowly wound down to neutral. I had learned a great deal about my little friend. She, like me, was the victim of her situation in life. She was existing the only way she knew how. The fact that others didn't like it was simply their problem. It did explain why she had come to really hate mankind. They had done her nothing but wrong. I guess I couldn't argue with her about that.

"So, my little friend, you control the powers of the void. Tell me, is there really a God?"

"If there is such an entity, I have not met it."

I laughed for a while. The jewel glowed a mild orange-yellow color, like the fading sun. We were fine, the two of us together. We were just fine.

CHAPTER 12

The next decade and a half moved along nicely for both Effie and me. We spent several more of those years at Brimme House. I casually watched the passage of time with new interest. So much had come to the land of men since last I stopped to take notice. The state of railroads had matured greatly. They seemed to connect everyone and everywhere. The possibilities they now produced were simply amazing. The horse drawn carriage was slowly being replaced by a motorized version. The automobile was a wonder of human invention. I had a European model delivered to Brimme House.

Even as impressive as the automobile was, my main interest of the day was that of the airplane. Those Wright brothers had done an amazing thing. And, as these things tend to do, everyone else took their invention and improved and then capitalized on it. Quick as the sunrise, the prospect of flying somewhere was the new dream of man … and vampire. I couldn't even imagine all the possibilities that came from it.

The constant filling of agricultural lands around Northwick was also of interest to me. The country was increasing in population. The endless spaces of my youth had slowly been settled and developed. I stopped to notice that empty space has slowly become an increasingly rare item. To me this was a double-edged sword. More people about means more food for me, but with Effie around my neck I didn't need to feed on the masses as I once had. Less open space meant less ground on which to be alone. That certainly wasn't good for me. I really was becoming a solitary creature, like the majority of my kind. I was different than most, thanks to my constant human interaction, but I was still in need of solitary space. I found that I enjoyed the peace that came from separating from humanity's steady pace. Oh well, nothing is constant, save for change.

At some point in the years I spent at Brimme House, Megan did manage to visit. She came over from London with her family and spent the better part of midsummer in the country. I do remember that she was very impressed by how I had gotten on. Her praise was nice to hear. I was glad she thought me capable. I had actually been capable for centuries, but this seemed a nice affirmation of my social skills.

It wasn't long after Megan returned home that Effie and I headed west. I hopped an ocean-going vessel and headed back to America. Planting boots on the New Amsterdam streets was another confirmation that life was good to me. I had always enjoyed my time spent in New York City, so coming back to her was like coming home. London, Northwick, and New York City, that's where I lived. Sadly, my island residence in Crete had suffered from the passage of time. A great shaking of the earth had razed it all but to the ground. I sent a release to the landlord that he may dispose of it in whatever fashion seemed best. That brought me to living on just the two shores of the Atlantic. I did like the age of Eastern Europe, but I was just as happy to trade it for the possibility of America.

So, by the fall of 1908 I found myself quietly walking the streets of the great city once more. I was perfectly content. By all accounts, 1908 was a good time to be alive. I had been in the city for Yule and ended up at a party where a large ball was dropped down a pole in Times Square. It was to signify the start of a new year. In retrospect, it was the start of a new tradition.

Let's see … shortly after New Year's, the great Rhodes Opera House in Boyertown burned to the ground. The loss of culture always made me sad. In New York City, an ordinance made it illegal for women to smoke in public. Not that I approve of tobacco, but regulating what people can do has always annoyed me immensely.

A bunch of crazy men left New York in what was called the New York to Paris auto race. They went across America to Siberia. Once in

Siberia, they continued on to Europe and then to Paris. It took some eighty-eight days of racing to produce a winner.

The territory of Oklahoma became a state. I had to buy a new flag when its star was added. A great fire in Chelsea, Massachusetts, ended in some seventeen thousand homeless people. They invented a new holiday called Mother's Day—I appreciated the sentiment. The fourteenth of May brought the first passenger flight in an airplane. It would only be another six years before the first commercial airline was established in 1914. Passengers in airplanes made me almost giddy with excitement. Not to be outdone by all of the airplane business, the British ocean liner *RMS Lusitania* crossed the Atlantic Ocean that year in a record time of less than five days. It seemed the days of the sea had not gone completely.

Elsewhere in the world, the Olympic Games started again back in London. They were the fourth hosting of the resurrected Greek tradition. A world congress for women's rights opened in Amsterdam. The advocating of equality was something that I followed closely. The bank of Italy founded a new headquarters in Clay. It caused me a momentary flutter, as I had a significant amount of wealth sitting around in Italy at the time.

Down on the African continent, the Congo became free and changed its name to the Belgian Congo. I'm still not sure that they were really any better off. Russia annexed part of Poland. Bulgaria declared its independence from the Ottoman Empire. And back in my American home, my good man Henry Ford introduced the Model T, starting what would become the total transformation of America.

While all this change was going on, I was quietly going about my existence. My little friend Effie was doing the same for herself. We both liked the pace and culture of New York City. I had slowly taken up hunting humans again. I decided that keeping my skills sharp was a good idea. I did greatly enjoy the adrenaline-charged blood that humans produced. The sensation of adrenaline coursing through my arteries was something that Effie couldn't reproduce for me. She had all of the energy but none of the punch that the fear brought.

I was on maybe one body a month at that point. It was a nice, quiet body count. At such a slow pace, the city didn't even notice me. Random immigrants disappearing were common enough, even without my help. The odd body washing up in the harbor was also not surprising to anyone. It felt good to my senses to run a little wild in the streets and skulk around the dark alleys in search of the unsuspecting. I have always enjoyed acting like a predator. Mainly, I suppose, because I am a predator.

Socially, I was out in the throes of the rich at every opportunity that seemed exciting. I had settled back into my youthful outer appearance when landing back in America. Fending off potential suitors was somewhat of a pain, but otherwise my youth and beauty presented me with numerous opportunities. I had collected a couple of young and secretive sexual partners. I liked the young men of the city; they had the stamina to keep up with my sex drive. They were also quite content to be of service without attachment. That and quiet discretion were what I was looking for in those days.

The only real thing I was missing in life was someone to talk to. I mean, I had Effie. She had slowly turned into a natural conversationalist since I had managed to get her talking. She was nice, but I did like the human touch. Neither one of us had the human perspective on things. In days gone by, I had a human confidant to converse with. They kept my decisions planted in the realities of men. Those days had passed. Now I lacked a sounding board. That had begun to nag at me a tad.

One day in mid-autumn, I found myself staring off at the roof tops and a church spire in the distance when it hit me: a priest. I did like priests. Was there a good priest in the city of New York? I didn't know, but I knew of a place that would. And I had even had a friend there once. Maybe someone from the House of Peter could help me with my issue.

I considered this idea for some days. Effie was not keen on the idea of contacting the Roman Catholic Church for any reason. I wasn't quite so unsure about it all. They had offended my companion greatly, but they had done me no ill will. They had been given the open opportunity to do so, and instead, they chose détente. That showed common sense. If handled correctly, it should be possible to contact the right sort of priest.

As was the start of most good business in those days, I chose correspondence. I penned a nice correspondence, to-whom-it-may-concern, to the Vatican post. It was a small note of a simple nature about a relative who corresponded with one of the Vatican historians, one Cardinal Father Michael Falco. I figured that my name, and his name, would lead me to whomever succeeded him. My problem was in having to assume that this new person would be of the same mind as he had been. It was a chance, but how else was one to find a good priest in a foreign land? I certainly didn't want to do it the way I did it the first time. That was reckless, but I was younger then.

I signed my correspondence "Lady Mary Beth Alcott, New York." My current name would be anonymous to the mail people. The intended reader should be able to attach it back to Sara Anne Grey easily enough. I paid a private currier company to deliver the letter to Rome, and then I sat and waited.

The twentieth century was not like the nineteenth century. What I thought would be months of silence lasted but weeks. The pace of the world was truly an ever-increasing thing. One day an unassuming young man appeared at the door and requested a signature for receipt of a letter from the Vatican. The housekeeper did so and then brought the news piece to me. I sat and stared at the letter for a time. I had asked for it, but what was it that I was about to get? I started to become anxious as I stared at it. Was it good news or bad? Finally, Effie seemed to have had enough of my posturing.

"Sara, please open the letter. This is becoming annoying. I could tell you what it says, but I won't."

I could see her dull blue glow through the cloth of my dress. She was right…. in for a penny, in for a pound. The message in the letter was short and direct, which was comforting.

Lady Alcott,

I would be happy to help you with your request, as your family has been generous to us over the years. I recommend that you contact Father Oscar Ryan, Church of the Heavenly Rest, Fifth Avenue, New York City. You will find him of similar disposition to Father Burman.

Sincerely,
Cardinal Father Salvatore Costa
Vatican City

A cardinal who was direct and to the point—he obviously knew who I was and of my connection to the late Cardinal Falco. He gave me exactly what information I was looking for. It was either continued détente or the perfect trap. I was willing to view it as peaceful. Strangely enough, so was my suspicious and sometimes hostile little friend.

So, I picked a nice warm day and made my way over to Fifth Avenue. I selected a seat on a bench across the street from the church and sat to compose myself. I had chosen a modest blue outfit and buried Effie deep down in the fold of my breast. She was always happy there and I didn't need her acting up.

Looking at it from across the avenue, the church was a large, hulking structure. The building was powerfully gothic. It was large, made of limestone and had many windows, possessing a look that was actually quite elegant. Founded by the Carnegie Family, it had apparently been designed by a distinguished firm. It was a New York City landmark. Most interesting to me was that it was also an Episcopal church. My new friend at the Vatican had known enough about me to give me back to the Anglicans. That was a true sign of good faith. I had quite well-expected to end up in the Roman Catholic regime, yet they sent me to the Anglicans. I had always liked the Anglicans. I understood them. I liked the Catholics well enough, but I had just spent more time with the Anglicans over the centuries.

I sat on the bench and thought a while. I figured that, if nothing else, I would get to enjoy the stained glass. That was if it all didn't go tits up first. Guess I would just have to go inside and find out.

CHAPTER 13

I sat on the sturdy wooden bench opposite the church for some time. The little space containing the bench backed up against Central Park and saw many people come and go. I hadn't actually spent much time around this part of Fifth Avenue and quite enjoyed the pedestrian traffic. I had enjoyed Central Park on numerous occasions. It was lovely after nightfall.

I had observed the congregation come to the building for evensong. The church's attendees were large in number and seemed to comprise multiple layers of New York City society. This priest drew a good crowd. That spoke well of him.

I sat on the bench patiently and waited until the first of the faithful started to exit. I had learned from the vicar that this was the best time to make an entrance. People would be busying themselves with leaving and paying scant attention to another body in the crowd. I did enter and found a seat in an already empty section of pews directly in front of the heavy wooden entry doors. People fashioned themselves for the outdoors or gathered up stray children, all while paying no mind to me.

The interior of the space was definitely decorated in the Anglican theme. In a word, it was sparse. Apparently, they had spent all of their money on the building and forgot to save any for flash. I knew that wasn't true in reality. Anglican churches, as a rule, were not known to be overly ornate inside. There were some exceptions, but they had a standard theme of minimalism.

They did, however, dump money into glass. Oh, how I love good stained glass. In the 21st century it has truly become a lost medium.

But then again, most everyone can read these days. Back in 1908, things were starting to change, but the times still saw a goodly part of the population as illiterate. The glass still served a practical purpose in those days. It wasn't just large decoration.

It took almost half an hour to empty the nave and transept. There were but a few people still milling about when I got my first vision of Father Oscar Ryan. He was not what I had expected; although I must admit that I didn't really know what to expect. My last two priest friends were of good build and solid disposition, so I figured I would get a more scholarly man this round. Seeing how times had changed to a more intellectual age, it just seemed to make sense. That was apparently not the case here.

I couldn't speak directly to his disposition, just from looking at him, but I was wagering it was solid. He was a well-built man, over six feet tall, and in possession of a thick, sturdy frame. He had a square jaw and close-cropped hair. He looked—well, in a word—yummy! I could feel my temperature rising just looking at him. That certainly didn't happen very often. It must be because I was in church again.

As I watched him move about, he seemed to do so with purpose. I was betting on ex-military of some sort. He just had that bearing to him: an unspoken confidence obvious at a distance. I took him to be on the young side of middle-aged, maybe thirty years old. That was definitely old enough for both the seminary and the military.

By the time I had shaken off the temporary infatuation, the massive place was empty, save for the two of us. I sat patiently for another quarter of an hour or so before he finally noticed that there was still someone sitting and waiting.

Father Ryan made his way in a quiet but direct manner to where I sat in the back. Yup, he was definitely a military man. I casually waited for him to speak. It always seems to go better if they speak first.

"Good evening, ma'am. Are you finding what you need tonight?"

Hmm, direct and not overly religious, he was definitely a keeper.

"That depends. Perchance, are you Father Ryan?"

"Yes, my child, I am Father Ryan."

"Father Oscar Ryan?"

"Yes, that's me. I don't believe we've met before. Your accent sounds English. Am I acquainted with your family? Do they attend the services here?"

The thick Irish tongue started to spill out as he talked. I had thought the name Ryan to be Irish, but in the New World it was hard to tell anymore. His accent, however, made him first generation at best.

"No, no, dear Father Ryan, this is our first meeting. Though my family was all basically of the Anglican faith. My name is Lady Mary Beth Alcott. And while we are both technically Anglican, I believe we two have a mutual friend in the Vatican."

The priest cracked his neck from side to side. I could see all the sinew in his muscles stiffen for combat, though he never actually moved a muscle. His eyes did narrow in an inspecting way. That was to be expected of him. Effie didn't as much as twitch. I gave the young priest the time he needed to calm himself.

"Ma'am, I do recognize the name. It isn't often I receive letters from the Vatican's House of Historians. I had assumed it was some clever bit of business, until now."

"Were they correct in their assumptions? Or do I have the wrong priest?"

"No, I think you have the right priest. I tend to pride myself on being open-minded. And I have studied many of the more esoteric parts of history."

"Esoteric? Oh, I like you already! Please, Father, have a seat and let us converse for a time."

The priest sat in a meaningful and deliberate fashion, leaving an arm's length between us. Once seated, he slowly shifted himself around to look at me. It was a more conversational posture. It seemed to feel natural for him, which was good.

"May I start our dialogue by asking you a question?"

"Certainly, Father."

"The correspondence from Rome. It led me to believe that you were a ..."

"A . . .?"

"Well, a . . . vampire?"

"Quite correct, Father Ryan. That is exactly right. I like the way you said it in such an academically interesting way."

"Academic, because vampires don't really exist. If you are what you claim to be, that would be fantastical. It might also require proof of your claim."

"What, Father, no faith?"

The young priest flushed white at the jab. It probably was a bit early in our relationship for prodding.

"I am sorry about that last bit. I was just having a bit of fun at your expense. Please, hold out your hand, I promise that no harm will come to you."

Father Ryan extended his hand without reservation. He probably still thought me a jokester. Smiling, I reached out and wrapped my dead-cold hand around his and shook. He immediately picked up on the temperature change and looked at me in a harder fashion. I smiled broader and both thick enamel fangs gleamed in the church's evening stained glow. Red blood flushed through my eyes, giving them an unnaturally menacing appearance. He swallowed as hard as any man ever had, but he made no motion of retreat. He really was the one I was looking for.

"You're a vampire."

"I like your change in tone, Father. Sometimes, acceptance can be a hard thing to come by. Trust me—I was a good half century getting to terms with it. I do like the industrialized world we live in now. No one believes in me anymore. That makes me happy, but it leaves me with no one to talk to. I do miss having someone to talk to."

I released his grip and folded my hands back into my lap as ladies do. He rubbed his palm and then mellowed deeper into his relaxed posture. Effie continued to remain calm.

We talked for some time. The longer we talked, the more the priest came around to the reality of it all. I could tell instantly that I liked him. He just seemed so nonjudgmental. It was nice to have a small amount of equality in the world. I say equality because that's what friendships turn out to be in the end. I accept and like him for who he is, and he does the same. By doing so, we both receive some measure of surety that we are right in who we are and gain comfort from the compassion. Wow, that almost sounded like I was philosophizing. I need to stop that—now.

We talked and talked and talked and talked. The moon was full up and night had encapsulated the city by the time I departed his house. Father Ryan had slowly become Father Oscar, and Lady Mary Beth was now Sara. I explained that it was necessary for me to change names as time moved along. The anonymity made good sense to him. I have always liked my long-term friends to call me Sara. After all, that's my name. It's the one my father gave me and the one I plan on keeping.

It turns out that my new friend was actually a military man. He had done time as a young man in the king's regiments, before leaving to find God in the New World. Apparently, he had seen all he wanted to see of the bad end of life. Now he wanted a little good. His move to America wasn't shocking to me; so many before him had done the same. They came here for adventure, faith, wealth, or to be food for ones such as me.

He had taken to faith well. It gave him sureness in mankind that the military did not. It also gave him time to pursue other avenues of thought. In his case, that was folklore. That too wasn't shocking, as he was Irish after all. If any country has folklore, the Irish have folklore.

I gave my new friend a week to process what had happened and see if any loose talk filtered out. I wanted him to be my friend, but I also wanted to make sure that he wasn't just a pretty bit of camouflage. Good for all, he was steadfast.

About eight days on from our first encounter, I ambled into the church again. Evensong was finished and I took up my customary seat in the back by the doors. I knew I was safe enough in the Lord's house, but I still wasn't willing to take too many chances. Father Oscar was about finished conversing with his flock when he spotted me in the back. He merely smiled and continued on about his task, just the same as if I were anyone else in the world. When he was finished, and the church was quiet, he wandered in my direction.

"Good evening, Father Oscar. You conduct a lovely service."

"Thank you, Sara. I didn't notice you in the crowd. Can you, by the way, attend services, I mean?"

"For the most part, yes. I'm fine until it involves touching something ceremonially religious: bibles, crosses, and the like."

I removed my white lace gloves and showed Father Oscar the scar from the small cross Antonio had put in my palm—a baby present from my much older maker. The priest inspected the scar, still smooth and fresh despite being in place for hundreds of years. He seemed to intuitively understand the duality of the situation.

"Did it hurt ? I mean, when it happened?"

"At the time, it was more shock from the act than it was pain from the event. We have an increased resistance to pain, so most things in life don't really bother us much. I've had considerably worse experiences over the years."

"And given as well, I would imagine."

"True."

He was uncompromisingly direct. My other two priests had been somewhat more subtle in their approach. This new tact was refreshing. He was like the Wyndells of much older days.

"If you can't embrace symbols of the church, how is it you wear a cross around your neck?"

"You don't miss a thing, do you? The cross was a present from my father on my twelfth birthday. I wore it every day when I was a human girl. When I became a vampire, I carried it with me in a small cloth pouch. I had it deconsecrated by a shaman long ago. I wear it because it reminds me of my family and where I came from."

The priest puzzled over the statement for several moments. He seemed to understand the situation.

"The images of religion are present to remind people of why they have faith and to reinforce that faith when it weakens. If that cross does the same for you, in the fact that it keeps you in touch with your past and the goodness that a family gives a person, I would say that it still does what it was intended to do."

"Thank you for that. I miss my father, even though it has been so many years. He was a good man. He possessed a calm and good nature."

"When did he die?"

"He was laid to rest long, long ago, in the family cemetery at our estate in London. I go back and speak with him often."

Oscar's gaze narrowed in that inspection-oriented way once more. He scanned my features for several seconds, obviously confused.

"No offense, it isn't really a question that one asks a lady, but … how old are you? I mean, you look like a child."

I laughed. I couldn't help myself.

"Aren't you sweet? I was born in the month of June, 1633. I died on a very pleasant evening in July, 1651. Yes, it was a very, very, very long time ago. I was a young lady once, but now I just look that way."

"So, you were eighteen when you died?"

"Correct, Father, which explains why I look as if I'm eighteen now. Trust me, being perpetually young and pretty can be a double-edged sword."

"I'll have to take your word for that."

We both laughed this time. He really did mean well. I like people who are able to see others for who they are and not just what they are. I spend way too much time interacting with the *what you are* crowd.

General note . . . Humans, especially businessmen, are all carnivores. They are very much "what" driven. It is either what you can do for them or what they can get out of you. When you are pretty and rich, you very much become a "what" to most people. Men generally don't chase me, they chase what I have. I know that it's a bad way to look at the world, but it's oh so true.

The priest and I talked religion for a time. He was pleased that I had such a good grasp on the topic. I had to remind him that in the 1600s religion was pervasive in a person's life. It wasn't an optional experience, like it currently seemed. He seemed to understand.

"You said earlier that I conducted a lovely service but that you didn't attend."

"You leave the doors and windows open. I sat on a bench across the avenue and listened to the evensong."

"And you enjoyed the experience?"

"Very much so. I thought your choir had a lovely depth of sound and a good, moderate tone. It was quite soothing."

"I wouldn't have expected that."

"Back in earlier days, I used to sit by the windows of Westminster Abbey and listen to the songs as they came wafting out on the warm summer breeze. It was always nice to just sit and be unbothered by the troubles of the day. My first priestly friend led the congregation there. I remember the nun wanting none of my presence, but Father Josh had a much more sensible nature."

"They could just tell you were a vampire?"

"Well, it was a different time, in a different land. Things were much less industrial and much more spiritual. The things you consider to be superstition were all very real once. In a way, she was right. It was her ground, after all."

"On that note, how is that you are just able to walk in?"

"What? You think there is some type of mystical force keeping me out?"

"Well, yes, I guess."

"When we are done, go outside and look at your church. Every church I have ever seen has the words, by or over the door, proclaiming that "all are welcome." They are there to invite the masses to enter. But because you make an open invitation, you also allow people like me to enter. If the words weren't there, I would need to ask for permission first."

"I never considered the ramifications of that statement before."

"Not to worry. Most all demons are terrified of religion. I came in for the glass. I love the stained glass, and the singing is nice, too."

"Well, just in case we work on the exterior anytime soon, you are officially welcome here in my church."

"Why, thank you, Father Ryan. I will do my utmost to be on my best behavior."

We laughed again. I liked his company. The conversation continued on a while longer. Sadly, once again, the moon overtook us. I departed and left the young priest to his duties. I did make him promise to show me the glass on my return. He said he would be glad to.

CHAPTER 14

New York City was being quite nice to me, and the years passed by with little fanfare. I spent much time with my new priest. He made me content. He had knowledge but lacked the conviction of reality, as my priests of the past had possessed. I decided not to push his level of faith the way I had done with Father David. Even for me, that was probably wrong.

America was also less stressful for me. Europe had started to bicker with itself, as it tends to do. One could feel the tension continuing to rise all around the continent. I wasn't sure where it was headed, but having seen the show before, I knew that it usually ended in bloodshed.

I have oft times wondered why people can't seem to get along with each other. All the little countries of Europe continuously flexed their tiny muscles, as if they were someone of great power. America had gone through the same throes of misunderstanding. The stink of death that the great Civil War produced had actually driven me back to England. These days, they had all settled down and started to put it back together. They were just taking the baby steps that would lead them to being a Super Power.

In 1912, it was peaceful. I had taken up going out into the city for afternoon tea—that and to socialize for a fashion. Not having a confidant had made me embrace humanity a little more directly than I had in centuries past.

I had started haunting the fashionable salon at the St. Regis Hotel. John Jacob Astor's magnificent creation reminded me of some of my other haunts back in Europe. I have to admit that since my days on the docks, I've turned into a five-star bint. If I can afford it, why not do it? Now, I'm still quite comfortable on the dirty cobbled city streets, but I prefer the high end when it comes my way. These days, New York City had a lot of flash to offer those with the cash. The full marble lobby and Waterford crystal chandeliers at the St. Regis got that done most days.

The NYC as it would come to be called, was just starting to do that thing where its people fall in love with all things French. The fancy Parisian cuisine at their restaurants really did remind me of France. And while it was all well and fine, I was happy simply sitting and taking in the strong black tea in the salon. It was a great place to stop before an afternoon spent at the shops on Fifth Avenue. The world famous shopping mecca was a shadow of its current spectacle, but it was still upscale.

I would stop, take the tea, socialize, and then go on to shopping or a visit with my priest. Some days a walk in Central Park would be a nice distraction. When the park was quiet, it reminded me of the lawns back at my estate north of London. When it was loud and overrun, it reminded me of New York.

I had maintained a lazy lifestyle for several years. I should have known it wouldn't last. I have said many times that my main fault is short-sightedness. In business, I can see the long-term quite easily. For some reason, that same skill eludes me in my personal life. I just can't ever seem to shake off being predictable. So far it's been correctable, but I swear that one day it's gonna get me killed … or worse.

In the summer of 1912, it came back on me once again. I had been having this sensation for several months that everything was not as it seemed. I had written it off as my demonic senses overreacting. Effie was sometimes uneasy, but she didn't seem put out by anything particular. I just pushed it all into the back of my mind as if it were nothing and continued along about my existence.

One day I was walking out of the St. Regis, on my way to some shopping, I noticed a man standing across the street. He looked the same as anyone else in New York. The city was so full of people that noticing one out of the throngs was odd. Still, something deep down in me said trouble. I didn't know how or why, I just knew it was trouble.

I casually paused, as ladies tend to do, and motioned to the concierge. Jonathan, a sturdy Jamaican fellow, and I had become well acquainted in the years I had been coming in for tea. He was the good sort. I calmly drew his attention to the man across the street and explained that I would un-modestly compensate him for any available information he could come by. My concierge friend had a weblike information network stretched out over the city that had proven useful to me at times. He requested I come back for dinner; he would see what he could do. I asked him not to dawdle. He simply nodded his head professionally and opened the door of my auto for me. I smiled appreciatively. My black 1910, type 15 Bugatti pulled away from the entrance and I was gone. So was the mystery man.

I made my way through traffic with little effort. My flashy car always drew looks from people on the streets. It was a little upscale, even for the streets of Manhattan, but the fact that a woman was driving it seemed to draw the majority of the gawkers. I loved to drive it. It was such a feeling of freedom to bomb down the city streets with my long locks whirling in the wind. The sensation was akin to being astride a solid steed at full gallop—only faster. Or maybe it was like standing on the weather deck of *The Summer Storm* as she plowed headlong through an Atlantic gale. I love that feeling of being free with nature. The sensation that you are living life is something I still look for constantly. It's easy to become complacent to life after a couple centuries. I simply refuse to give in to it all. I am here to live life, even if I am not technically still alive. (I could tell you a story about the first time I went skydiving, but that is a whole different affair.)

My afternoon wandering about the shops on High Street passed slowly. I couldn't enjoy any of it because I couldn't shake the feeling that bad things were afoot. Well, they would certainly be bad for someone. I hoped it was just overreaction, but I knew that it really wasn't. As I wandered about Fifth Avenue, I considered the conversation that I had with the marquis. The last time that humans had bothered me, they were relatives of the late Grand Duke Bennett. That ponce had a big family. What was it Eugene had said? *They have money and they hate me.*

Oh, why do people keep bothering me when I have obviously not bothered them? I guess they just all needed killing.

As I walked and pondered, Effie made not one gesture that anything was amiss. I think she was letting me get around to the killing idea. Well, I had already made it there. It was probably time to go see what my man on the street had dug up for me.

I took the long way back around to the St. Regis, and let the Bugatti run loose for a while. Driving the auto at speed seemed the only time that my mind was calm, even with the wind rushing by. Having to concentrate on seeing all of the things that could be found in a city street and being mindful of all the people walking about pushed most everything to the back of my mind.

Pulling up to the front of the opulent hotel, I found Jonathan right where I had left him. The steady look of professionalism on his face gave no indication as to the success of his endeavors. I slid to a stop and pulled back on the brake, letting the street machine rumble. Jonathan promptly opened the door.

"Good day again, Lady Alcott."

"Why thank you, Jonathan."

"In for dinner? The French cuisine is especially good tonight. I believe that you will find your table very much to your liking."

"That sounds delicious. I do like good French cuisine. I believe there is a cloth in the glove compartment, would you be a dear and wipe down the windscreen when you have a moment?"

"Absolutely, Lady Alcott."

"Thank you, Jonathan. You are always such a dear."

The sturdy Jamaican doorman turned informant held the door as I made my way into the lobby of the hotel, and then he shuffled off to move my auto. Even if the information he was going to provide me was a full dissertation with supporting documents, the envelope of money wrapped up in the cloth would be overpayment. That was the plan. Nothing secures loyalty like the liberal application of money. That fact has been true as long as I have been on this earth. The ones that are going to betray you were going to do it from the jump. For the rest, the security of position produced by payment breeds a loyalty that is irreplaceable. Back in the 1600s, security came in the form of a roof over your head and food for your children, a place that was free from typhoid and the pox. These days it came in the form of cash. The perils of life hadn't really become any different; just the medium of exchange had changed. In the beginning I had kept the families of the estate safe and fed. In return, they all happily worked for a vampire. Now, I pay extravagantly well, and people are more than happy to discreetly service my needs. It's a system as old as time.

My usual table in the far corner of the dining room, adjacent to the views of the city, was free and the maître d' quickly sat me. The day was lovely and the room was, as a result, quiet. A young waiter came along and filled my water glass. I ordered a bold red wine and he nodded his approval. The young man scurried off and returned with a bottle of red and a thick yellow envelope.

"Compliments of the valet, ma'am," the waiter stated as he poured the wine.

I returned a small smile and the young man scurried off once again to retrieve the menu of the day. The waiter was of no worry. He was in the employ of the valet. Jonathan ran a professional business, which was why I utilized him. His information was also always accurate.

I sat the envelope aside and waded into the wine. It was refreshing. I have always liked a spirited red, as long as it's not too dry. It's red and sweet and attacks the pallet, just like blood does. And the small lightheadedness that I get from the alcohol is entertaining, even now.

I do remember the meal being quite enjoyable. I don't really remember what it was, just that it tasted good with the wine. I didn't need, or really desire, the meal. Eating was and still is good camouflage. It makes you look just like everyone else in the world. I didn't desire it because I needed to invest enough conscious thought toward the basal part of my brain so that my body would push the food through my defunct digestive system. It is pretty much the same as when I want my heart to beat and circulate the blood. There was nothing to be gained from it, other than camouflage. The sliver of power that the amulet peeled off and gave to me infused my body completely and kept me running at full stride. Effie was nice that way.

I did still enjoy a good blood drunk now and again, when it might come along appropriately. It gave me the full-on high that vampires crave, and it gave Effie a day or two off. I tended to hunt my food whenever possible. That way I kept all of my skills at top notch. Upon occasion, my very discreet butler, Randolph, would procure fresh blood from a slaughterhouse for me. It was almost the same. Animal adrenaline, though chemically the same, just doesn't have the punch of human adrenaline. It is like an 80-percent fix. It will definitely take the edge off; it just won't put you over the top.

My young trustworthy butler, Randolph, was a present from the staff at Brimme House. He had apparently wanted to come to America, so I had him sit in my library and educate himself on the ways of my kind. Naturally, until he actually met me he assumed it was some type of academic fad. They all do anymore.

Needless to say, he took the jump to his new situation without resistance. He really was a smart and secretive young man, and very polite. He spent most of his time at King's College, receiving a proper education. King's College, properly known as Columbia University in 1912, was a solid institution. It was old enough to make me believe in its academic fervor.

The investment in Randolph was of no consequence to my bank account; it was more of an investment in the future. He was smart and capable. He would probably go on to become a fine businessman. Even if he just returned home to Brimme House, it would be money well spent. Helping the people that help me is a cornerstone of my existence.

I finished my meal and made my way back out to the valet. Jonathan nodded his appreciation as he placed me in my sporty motor carriage. I did the same and was off into the fading sun. The ride home was much faster than in days gone by when I used to traverse the streets of New Amsterdam in a horse-drawn carriage. The old way did possess an elegance that this new style did not, but I did like this new way much better.

As expected, the main door to the house opened as I approached. My doorman was ever efficient. I smiled and thanked him as I strode through and headed straight toward my secret little study on the top floor.

I paused in my bedchamber and disposed of my wrap and a fashionable hat that had spent the majority of the day on the seat of the Bugatti. I discarded my small leather boots into one corner and padded barefoot into the study. I pulled on the book in the stacks that released the catch so the stack could slide soundlessly out of the way and allow me access to my private study—my quiet space, as Charles Wyndell used to call it.

As the book case slid silently back into its original position, I looked at the two elegant chairs stationed in the middle of the room. Charles and I sat there often and ruminated on the events of the day. These days it was Randolph and I who took up station in the chairs.

I sat and opened the envelope. There were papers explaining the styles, traits, and backgrounds of a dozen or so men. The one on top was named Griffin Waynewright, the man from the street. *Griffin? Who in the bloody hell names their child Griffin,* I pondered as I read about the ex-infantryman turned adventurer. He seemed to be the sturdy, determined type.

I scanned the workup for several minutes until my eyes finally landed on the piece of information I knew was coming. Mr. Waynewright was great nephew to one dead Grand Duke Bennett. I knew it! I could just sense it. The damned old blighter was a problem for me, even in death. It seemed that I really was going to have to kill the whole damned family.

The summary of Griffin's compatriots read basically the same as his. He had recruited a dozen seasoned men to help him with his task. There was a baker's dozen against little old me and Effie. Even if it was just me, it wasn't fair for them. Effie and her amulet of destruction made it quite ridiculous.

"Effie, sweet girl, you probably should keep an ethereal eye out for these men. Just so they don't sneak up on us."

Before Effie could respond with her trademark nonchalant affirmation, another voice interjected.

"Keep an eye on what men, Lady Sara?"

"Ah, Randolph, just a little talking out loud is all." My butler looked down on all the papers scattered about both the table and floor and raised a solitary eyebrow.

"Whatever you say, ma'am."

"Ha, ha! Yes. It is most of the time, isn't it?"

"Ma'am?"

"Please, sit, Randolph." I motioned to the adjacent seat and he took up station. Randolph looked at me for several moments. I knew the look he possessed quite well; it was what I liked to call "confused longing." They all get it at some point.

"Yes?"

"Well, ma'am, I was just thinking how I fancy you much better with your natural blonde hair, more so than that raven black coloring. I spent many days in my youth looking at your portrait. The blonde hair suits you better, ma'am."

"Oh, Randolph, dear boy, stop with the ma'am. Sara is more than acceptable for general conversation. Please."

"Yes, Sara."

"I'm happy that you approve of my blonde locks. I had trouble being talked into having my hair colored the first time. I did, however, enjoy the experience of change. I don't really ever change; it's part of being undead. I am static. I have been with darker hair upon a couple of occasions, but I, too, enjoy my natural blonde hair much better. It's who I am."

"Well, I think it does you justice."

"Thank you, Randolph."

We sat and continued to discuss the state of both my style and the events of the day for some time. I enjoyed his company greatly, or maybe it was just the thick Welsh accent. Whichever, it was pleasant and soothing. I would stay distracted for the remainder of the day and deal with Mr. Waynewright on the morrow.

CHAPTER 15

As always, the new day dawned. I like that about time: it's consistent in its movements. I hadn't always enjoyed it. When I was younger, I wasn't the best at waiting. Back in the days of tall ships and hearty steeds, time moved at the same rate, it was just that everything took five times longer to happen. When I was a human girl, I was impatient. You probably wouldn't know it from the tale I've been telling, but it's true. My impatience, of what I'm not exactly sure, was what led me to wander the docks and to go talk to the working ladies over street. That same impatience has lingered along with me since I died. I would imagine that since I have tried very hard to keep hold of my defunct human emotions, it has just stayed by proxy.

These days I actually don't mind it so much. My stronger demonic instincts keep me calm. They allow me to wait and plan and stalk quite well. My human impatience now helps to spur me into action. It is the nudge that says I've waited long enough and it is time to act.

That's why I like my human emotions—they keep me in check. I am not simply a killer. I don't just overreact to situations. The human and demon have fused over the years to make me a much more deliberate creature able to think things out. I can't change being a demon, but I can hold onto my lingering humanity as best as possible. It's where I started and who I am.

With regards to Mr. Waynewright and his compatriots, being deliberate was the plan of the day. They had obviously been studying my ways and my movements about the city. It seemed clear to me from our limited encounter that Mr. Waynewright was a stealthier adversary than his relative had been. A direct frontal approach did not seem to be the plan this time. That was fine with me. It saved on potential collateral damage from both sides. So, the questions of the day had become: If he knew my nature and my movements, where would he plan his attack? And, consequently, when?

It took me a day of quietly considering my own movements over the last months to divine a time and place he would choose. I thought about every place I had gone, every way I had traveled to each place, what time of day I had traveled, how long I spent at each place, and how long I had waited in between. I considered every person I had seen along the way and everyone I had conversed with at each stop.

Every waiter and valet, every shop girl and casual acquaintance was thought over.

I have said several times that the true weapon of a vampire is the mind. The repurposing of different bits of one's brain upon becoming a vampire gives us much better mental acuity than any human. My situational recall, memory, interpretation, and reasoning skills are leaps and bounds ahead of your average human. It allows the predator in me to plan quite effectively.

I can walk down an alley in some foreign city and a year later I can show up and run down it with blinding speed. I can meet a person somewhere and years later, even with changes of age, I will know them again as soon as I see them. Little details of people and things and layouts of areas just stick in my brain. It is a superior survival skill. In my current position, I would say that they were definitely survival skills. Men were hunting me, and I was not in the mood to be hunted. I was not someone's trophy.

After a fashion, I decided my life really needed some change. As near as I could tell, I was a boring person. Ha-Ha-Ha. I know I wasn't really leading a boring life, just a repetitive one. That was what posh people did. They did what they did repeatedly. Seeing how I no longer ran my company, a topic that slowly ate away at me, I tended to make my repetitive tasks more social. The ones that stood out as predictable were shopping on High Street, going to see the priest, taking in the symphony, and walking in Central Park.

I had developed a habit of taking a long walk through the park once I had finished my session with Father Ryan. The large, open green of the park reminded mc of the woods from the estate, the same way riding the cliffs of Crete or running through the Boston woods had. It gave me time to consider the father's words and kept me from longing for home.

The park also appeared the optimum place for my opposition to act. It lacked the masses of people that the remainder of the city possessed, so it was a prime location to act without being caught. I usually took my walks at night. This gave my opposition the natural advantage of working under the cover of shadows. It also gave them an easy escape from the scene. Finally, it was a place that required no cleanup on their part. Since I was pretty sure that if they killed me, my body would rapidly transition back to the dust from whence it had been previously spared becoming, they would have nothing of which to dispose. Yes, sir, that would be a proper attacking point. And if I managed to stay on my usual routine, it would transpire a mere three nights on.

Three days' time seemed ample for the limited preplanning I required. I had noticed as I looked forward that it also would be a night with a new moon—complete darkness, as it were. That was good and bad for both camps. Complete darkness was bad for them. Sharp light appearing in the complete darkness was bad for me. I knew that Effie could override my ocular response in an instant, but it was just another problem to consider. Working under the cover of darkness also played into the opposition's well-honed military sensibilities. Yes, it seemed like bloodshed in the park. Hopefully, it would be in three days' time.

I woke and dressed on the day, choosing something conservative enough for the priest but minimal enough to be comfortable for fighting. As in past events, all unnecessary thickening undergarments were excluded, as to increase mobility. Being stronger and faster was my great advantage. Being heavier built and of greater number was theirs. Overall combat ability was probably level pegging. We all seemed like accomplished killers; we just had been schooled differently.

As always, sturdy leather boots were the choice of the day. They laced up tight and possessed a solid wooden heal. The toe cap of the boots was heavy leather. They would leave an awful dent in anyone they hit. A fashionable hat and some matching gloves and I was ready for the day.

The standard milling that the day brought on passed by quickly enough. I was somewhat relieved by that. Time had moved slower in years gone by. I liked that I could now put things in the back of my mind and let time pass. A little shopping and soon I was enjoying a pleasant philosophical conversation with my priest.

I asked him what he thought about killing, since it was something that I was naturally inclined toward. He seemed to accept the nature of the universe. If one needed to kill, then kill. He seemed to be comfortable with the idea that as long as it was needed—in war, for survival, or some such thing—then it was in our nature to do so. Murdering someone for no good reason didn't appear to sit well with him, but survival was survival.

Then we discussed his views on survival. He laughed a lot while this part went on. It seemed we were both natural survivors. I had been doing it much longer, but he was also accomplished. In an interesting way, he also led me to understand that we were both emotional survivors. He had survived the throws of combat while in the army and the emotional wreckage that went along with military service. We both had managed to live our lives without losing ourselves in it all. He really was smarter and wiser than the sum of his years.

We finished our talk and I thanked him for his time. He gave me his appreciative smile and returned to his tasks. I collected myself and headed for the door.

The sun was removed from our side of the earth when I exited out into the city air. Darkness had consumed all but what the faint lamps of autos and such provided. I made my way down the church's imposing steps and crossed the avenue to enter the park. It was not many steps more into the woods of the park and the darkness was total. I had placed my glasses in my hand bag when entering the church. In the nearly complete blackness of the park, I possessed the eye sight of a jungle cat. I also had the hearing to match.

I made my way along the same route that I naturally traveled, all the time listening and looking for the opposition. I was sure that they were out there; I just wasn't sure where.

About halfway into the park, the path that I normally traveled took a series of abrupt left and right turns. The night seemed quiet, so I made my way into them at a casual stride. I had navigated the first turn and was about halfway around the second when a loud retort shattered the silence. I was stunned by the large caliber bullet slamming into my chest a split second before my ears were stung by the noise. The energy of the impact knocked me backward several steps. The pain that the bullet produced as it ripped through my body was searing.

One of my knees buckled and I started to falter. As my body showed the first signs of buckling, large flood lights snapped on to illuminate the kill zone. The onslaught of the piercing light overwhelmed my senses. I was blind and in massive pain. What was happening to me?

A second gun blast sounded out somewhere beyond the curtain of light. The bullet screamed at me and creased the side of my neck. As it slid past like a red hot knife, it impacted Effie's golden chain. The energy of the lead bullet snapped the chain in two and ripped it from my neck. Out of the corner of my eye I could just visualize Effie's jeweled cage cartwheeling through the swirling night air. It was strange, but in the midst of everything that was transpiring, I could hear—plain as anything—the amulet touch down on the grassy lawn in Central Park.

My body hit the path with a resounding thud. Numerous shadowy images appeared in the streams of light. I swung my head from side to side, trying to get a grasp on my situation. The figures seemed to hold numerous weapons, varying in age from maces to modern hand guns.

I tried to leap to my feet and fight but the slug in my chest sent shockwaves of pain through my body. Then, unlike the chivalrous days of old, all the shadows attacked at once. I tried to move, to stand, to ready myself for the coming blows. I needed to survive this round, so I had time to get my wits about me and retaliate.

I had never been shot before. I had been punched, branded, stabbed, hacked at with an axe, and run through with a sword, but I'd never been shot. I couldn't believe the difference in the intensity of the pain.

I tried to push the pain out of my head as the shadows closed the space to where I lay sprawled on the walking path.

I wondered if this was the way it was all going to end. Was this where I would die? Should I feel bad that I was going to die? Well, I wasn't dead yet, damn it!

I managed to get to one knee as a large bloke with something resembling a pike slammed the pointy end into my shoulder. Fortunately for me, both the pike and the bullet had managed to miss my heart. That was most excellent, and the only good thing I had going for me.

The man's momentum pulled the pike from his hands as it fully inserted itself in my shoulder. I spun around toward the blow and impacted the ground again. I pulled the pike from my shoulder and tossed it as the big man regrouped, yanking a large revolver from beneath his coat. All the remaining figures advanced to the big man as he retrieved his weapon. I braced for the end—an end that—did not come.

As I lay on the path, streaming blood, watching my apparent end unfold, it seemed as if time itself began to slow. The figures of the men moved as if they were submerged in a vat of heavy syrup. They slowed till they were but wax statues of men in action. Wax statues with artificial light stationed all about them. Not a sound entered from beyond the canopy of light around us. It had instantly become as quiet and stationary as a still painting.

From the corner of my now-blackening vision I noticed little blades of grass begin to stir, as if a breeze had slowly come up. I could feel no breeze, though I could vaguely see objects swirling about outside the curtain of light. Things swirled around in a growing maelstrom. It was as if I had landed myself in the eye of a hurricane, with reality cycling in a torrent around the scene. And then, as if some outside hand had struck a flare, a piercing ribbon of blue-white light shot out horizontally in all directions, cutting the scene as slick as one cutting paper with scissors.

I could feel just the slightest ripple from the thunderous shockwave as it shot through the static night air. It was a second swirling torrent out at the limits of my blackening vision, almost like a tornado inside the hurricane. But I could hear no sound. The night was deathly still.

It was surreal—so much so, that I was sure it was the limits of my life coming into view.

The ribbon of energy impacted the waxy shadow men stationed all about me and they shattered, as if someone had slammed an ice sculpture with a sledgehammer. The countless bits of shadow men swirled around in the funneling torrent of wind and light until it all faded to naught, leaving only lingering wisps of blue crackling static energy behind to dance in the air a mere moment longer. Then, all was gone.

I lay in a thick, metallic-smelling pool of blood and attempted to process what had just transpired. Out at the limit of my almost completely diminished vision, the blue-white light returned. This time it was a gentle glow dancing in the complete still of the night air. I rolled fully onto my side and tilted my head back as best as I could. Slightly off behind me, the amulet that had been ripped from me by the second bullet hovered in the still air some five feet off of the lawn. Its long, broken gold chain moved around it as if held up by strings. Standing very calmly in front of the jewel, the blue-white ethereal image of Efuru stood, her round gentle face smiling down at me.

I couldn't really process the whole scene in my faltering state. I was pretty sure that Effie was welcoming me into her netherworld. I was sure that wasn't good for me. Effie seemed to sense my feeling of impending doom, because she raised a tiny hand toward my direction in a calm and reassuring way. As she lifted up her hand, I could feel the large lead projectile slip slowly back out of my body the way it had entered. This time there was no pain, just the sensation of movement.

A summary yellow glow shimmered into reality and enveloped my body. The pool of blood around me began to shrink. The liquid oozed back into my body the way it had exited. I was consumed by light and warmth. It truly was what being embraced by a higher power must feel like.

Once the puddle was gone, I slowly stood on shaky legs. Discounting Effie, there was nothing else about. There were no bodies, no weapons, no remains of technology, nor even any scuff marks on the path. The whole scene had been wiped clean. No one would know that anything odd had ever happened here.

I smiled at Effie's glowing image and her smile broadened. Then, as if it never happened, she slowly shimmered back out of existence. I walked over and placed my cupped hands under the floating amulet. The jewel slowly lowered into my hands and calmed its glow. The broken length of chain came back together at its ripped ends and fused as if it had never been damaged. I stared at my mighty little friend for a moment, somehow having forgotten that she was a weapon.

"Thank you. I don't know how I will repay you, but I certainly owe you for this."

"You're welcome. And ... it's fine."

CHAPTER 16

Time slipped by like foamy waves from a sandy shore. My body had healed itself completely by the time I had left Central Park. My mind was somewhat slower coming to terms with the whole affair.

That was my time. It was the day I normally would have died. I should have moved from this earth to the great beyond. The thing that caused me pause was that I was somehow so accepting of it. As I had lain on the warm walking path, blood seeping out of my body, my expert night vision slowly going black, men swarming in to finish me, I was somehow content.

I mean, I knew I had to move, to fight, and to keep not giving in. That was who I am. But below all of that, I was also ready. Ready to just be done with it all. If it hadn't been for my little friend coming to my aid, it would have been my time. I would have just let it happen.

The thing I was really having a problem with was that I couldn't tell if I even cared anymore. I had been going through the motions for so long that I had completely forgotten what the motions were all about.

When I was a little girl, it was all so easy. I would grow up, marry a nice man that would provide for me, and make a family. In that context I would spend my time.

When I was a young vampire, it was also simple. I would use my enormous energies to create a place for myself and then maintain it for the duration—an empire created by my loving father, brought to full maturity by my hand, and designed to outlast us both.

The problem with all of this was that I had succeeded. Well, I had succeeded at the second one. I had built a business empire and climbed inside of it, but to what end? In the end, all I had really invented was another crystal cage. It didn't look like the one Effie lived inside, but it was as sturdy as hers. I could no more escape my confinement than she could her own.

I puzzled on the question: Was this all that I was. I stayed to the task so long that it hurt my brain. Effie, for her part, didn't interfere. She had already been down this road a millennia ago and knew all of its twists and turns.

What I eventually came to realize from my deep introspection is that it's all a cage. If I had somehow found my human husband and the family he was supposed to give me, I still would have ended in a cage. I would have climbed inside that cage and closed the door until years too far gone, when I realized it all for what it was. It was a lovely, warm, comfortable cage.

Human family, a shipping company, an earl with lands and responsibilities, an amulet with magick incantations etched upon its surfaces—they were all different forms of control and confinement. They were just pretty little cages to put oneself into.

My lack of concern over impending death was a glaring sign that I had become unhappy with my cage. I seemed discontented to some huge degree. But what could I really do about it? To live was all I really had. Yes, the corporation and the title were things I didn't necessarily want to part with, and they were things that made it much easier for me to survive. That was what I was here for: survival. Survival was what was left when everything else had gotten washed away. I couldn't talk to God, not anymore. I couldn't talk to Satan, or I didn't really want to. All that I actually had for my lot was the space in between the two. I was here for as long as it all lasted, as long as I could survive. After that, who knew—I certainly didn't.

I thought and thought. I talked to my priest. I discussed it all with my jeweled companion. It took months to shake off my funk. As I did come back up for air, I looked around and realized that things had changed. The world I was somewhat sure of before looked different to me now. It had slowly and then quickly become something else. Suddenly, it was less sure, more violent, and strangely unpredictable.

This new landscape was uncomfortable. This unstable frontier I found did me good. New landscapes had presented themselves just when I needed them to.

It was now September of 1914, and the world had found itself at war. I had lived through several major conflicts, and they usually left me wanting. This, however, was a new kind of war. World War I was so large that it consumed the whole of the industrialized world. Even from its opening salvos, I could smell big change coming from its deaths. The change that would come, it would be good.

History would show, somewhat ironically, that a Serb named Gavrilo Princip, who was interested in freeing the chains of ethnic and political control, bollixed up and assassinated Archduke Ferdinand. That little misstep threw the whole region into war. The region finally drew in all of the surrounding major players and the world spiraled into conflict. Well, that would have made for good tele I guess, but it's only some of the truth.

Don't get me wrong—Princip really did kill the archduke, and his wife to boot. I'm just saying that, in and of itself, that wouldn't be enough at any point in history to produce a world war. Hell, it probably wouldn't muster up a good skirmish.

What the whole event really was-was a catalyst. The real cause of World War I was Germany, France, Russia, Britain, and the rest of the industrialized world. Decades of military maneuvering, imperialism, and backdoor alliances had resurfaced the chess board that was Europe. The festering that all of this had produced had been left unchecked. By 1914, it only required something to release the cork from the bottle. That something came in the form of a bullet in the month of July.

History would also show that WWI was a perfect case study for the problem with alliances. If you tell someone with surety that you have their back, then eventually you have to make good on your claim. Now, America and Britain had much more vested interests in it all than just saving face, but it was the thing that mobilized them into action.

This was also the thing that had mobilized me into action. I didn't have any specific attachment to my new homeland, but I did have a very specific and concrete one to the land of my birth. All associate members of the crown were obligated to assist in times of war. Being a well-heeled member of the larger nobility, I needed to get my act together fast.

I knew from wars past that even if the conflict was centered in the middle of the continent, it still required lots of shipping. There were also naval concerns and numerous merchant issues. The merchant issues were my primary concern. War goods and troops needed to be moved in for the army, and wounded troops needed to be ferried out. Considering war losses, numerous ships would be required for a conflict of this scope. Apparently, Grey's Cargo was going back into the arms transporting business. Ah, the joys of war.

I first needed to mobilize my corporation into action. So, to the New York office I proceeded. As I trudged through the door of the building and into its grand entryway, I realized that I hadn't actually been down to the offices in some years. I was happy to see that it hadn't changed from what I remembered it to be. I was also happy to see that it appeared to be busy. People scurried to and fro with obvious necessity, none of them noticing me. I stood for a moment and watched the business of it all. It wasn't this hurried when I ran it. People had some sense of decorum.

Deciding that I could have stood there all day, I made my way to the reception person and asked on the status of one Mr. Julian MacTavish, the office's manager. I liked Mr. MacTavish; he was a large, commanding Irish fellow with good business sense. The receptionist informed me without flourish that he was entirely too busy today to see anyone who was unannounced. I would need to make an appointment and return some other day. I calmly informed that woman that if she, and he, wanted to keep their employment, she had best toddle off and find him post haste. When I turned and headed off for his office, she realized I was serious.

I opened Mr. MacTavish's office door and proceeded in without knocking. My imposing office manager looked up past two well-dressed businessmen and smiled at me warmly.

"Lady Alcott, how lovely to see you today."

"Good morning, Mr. MacTavish. It's always a pleasure to be down to the offices. You seem involved."

My office manager introduced me to the other gentlemen in his meeting. They again introduced themselves quite professionally as the receptionist lady came click-clacking down the hallway. I introduced myself to the businessmen and dismissed click-clack with a wave of my hand.

The gentlemen with MacTavish seemed to have concerns about the transportation of their merchandise. In the deteriorating months, the seas had become a rough and ready place. MacTavish had been in the middle of alleviating their doubts when I burst through the door. A young voice, speaking with an underlying sense of knowledge regarding the mysteries of the seas, simply assured them that their merchandise would be delivered, and was insured, as Grey's Cargo had practiced since the days of the Dutch East India Company and Caribbean pirates. Though the face was young, the words were sound, and the men departed the office content in their affairs.

Seeing all was quiet for the moment, it was time to get down to it. I took up a seat in one of MacTavish's comfortable leather chairs and properly adjusted myself.

"Lady Alcott, you seem spirited today. To what do we owe this honor? Not that you need purpose to come look upon your company." My office manager took up station behind his large mahogany desk, a wry smile on his face.

"I, too, have concerns about the unfriendliness of the seas. War can be a good thing for business, but it can be a bad thing for ships."

"The main shipping lanes are well clear of any misery. Some ships have gone missing along more obscure routes, but they weren't the standard merchant cargo," he responded.

"How long do you see this lasting before the standard lanes become compromised?"

"That's hard to say, really. All of the common routes in the North Atlantic and in the Mediterranean will go tits up as soon as full-on war commences. I would imagine that the main Atlantic artery will stay strong until America gets involved. When American troops start heading off to Europe, I'd say those lanes will be bonjaxed as well."

"Hmm. That's exactly the same conclusions I had come to. That's good. I like that you and I are on the same page here."

"Thank you, ma'am. That, after all, is what you pay me for."

"Very true. Tell me, what are your thoughts on these submarines I keep hearing so much about?"

"The German U-boats? They are some type of vessel that can travel beneath the waves. I haven't heard of them being any kind of bother. I was under the impression that even though they were armed, they weren't really intended for sinking ships."

"That is what I have been hearing as well."

General note...Sadly, it would only take days to prove us both quite wrong. On September 22, 1914, a German submarine sank three English warships, one after another. The age of war in the form of ships shooting at ships on the open seas had officially changed.

My office manager leaned back in his chair and studied me for a long moment. He seemed like he was trying to decide what I wanted. I figured that I'd save him the trouble.

"What is your plan for our shipping interests, once the primary shipping lanes become problematic?"

He furrowed his forehead, seemingly not liking to have to explain himself. Men could be that way.

"I have conferred several times with Mr. Wyndell about this. We are going to reduce our shipping to the necessary cargo contracts. The ships that do go to sea will run in groups, escorted by either American of British naval ships, depending on their destination. We have already been asked to task several ships to war service. The businesspeople will only be mildly inconvenienced. Cargo will be delayed but put to sea as scheduling allows."

"And how would our customers be taking this news?"

"Mostly positive. A large amount of the European-bound business was already something that could generally be a war commodity, so it's unaffected. The remainder? Well, they would rather see their things show up late as opposed to not at all."

"Very good. We should think about making them some concession if they become too inconvenienced."

"Lady Alcott?"

"We should make our clients some concession if they become too inconvenienced. There is nothing safe about the sea, independent of war. But business is business."

"I will pass your thoughts on to Mr. Wyndell for his consideration."

"No need, Julian—I'll do that myself. When is your next ship sailing for England?"

"There is one in two days and one in eight days."

"Eight days should be fine. Please save me passage accommodation on it."

"Ma'am, *The Southampton Star* is a cargo vessel. She has almost no accommodation, save some spare berths the crew doesn't use."

"And I am sure that one of those will be adequate for my needs. I'm not fragile, Julian. I require transport in that direction. If we have a ship going in that direction, then that is what I require. It'll be peachy."

"Ma'am, there are more comfortable options departing later on. Let me look into one of those for you."

"The *Star* will be fine, Julian. I need to be returning to meet with the other nobility and to discuss affairs with Mr. Wyndell."

"Since you seem settled, I will make arrangements."

"How is Mr. Wyndell by the by? It has been some time since I conversed with Gregory."

"Gregory? You mean Tracey, ma'am. Gregory is his father."

"Yes. Yes, I meant Tracey. How is he doing these days?"

"Well as can be expected. Running a corporation the size of Grey's Cargo is hard on a seasoned businessman, let alone one just years out of Kings College."

"Well, hopefully he has it all in hand?"

"He really does seem to. The Wyndell family members are very good business people. They run their business very effectively."

"Their business?"

Julian instantly sensed that he had made some unfixable blunder. I smiled it off as best as I could. "Ha, ha. It's quite all right Julian; they have been heading up affairs for quite some time now."

"Yes, ma'am."

"Well, we'll just see what he has to say when I see him. Eight days till sailing, you say?"

"I will make all the arrangements for you."

"One more thing: that receptionist lady out front … is she new here?"

"No, not really. She has been with us going on a year now."

"Well, in that case, I'm sure that she would love the experience of new employment elsewhere if she has trouble with the corporate hierarchy again."

"Yes, ma'am."

I stood and smiled at Julian, who instantly got the point. He really was a good man. I needed to go put some affairs in order before I departed. Apparently, it was back home to London for this North End girl.

"Always a pleasure, Julian."

"And for me, Lady Alcott."

He stood. I departed.

CHAPTER 17

Even with the added stress of the war and all, I must say that the twentieth century was a high-paced affair for a quiet, old-school vampire like myself. In days of old, a trip from New York City to Bristol and on to London would have taken the best part of a year's time. As the sun rose on New Year's Eve of 1914, I stood in the study of my London estate and pondered just how fast I had crossed the Atlantic. I had even spent several weeks in Bristol, checking on the state of affairs in the house. Finding all to be well, I had headed home to London.

As the current Earl of Northwick, I had notified the crown of my desire to do my utmost for the cause as soon as I had planted boots in Bristol. Britain had declared war on Turkey through an alliance with Russia some two months back. Churchill was mobilizing the might of the empire and directing it across the channel toward the continent of Europe. In one of the countless twists of historic fate that only I find to be interesting, Britain and France were both allies with Russia. How often had the two empires exchanged cannon fire across the channel? How often had Russia tried to plant its double-headed eagle everywhere that it could? Three, once and present conflicting empires all mad at Turkey? It had been a long while since the Ottoman Empire was threatening to anyone. If they hadn't thrown their lot in with Germany and its naval campaign against Russia, no one would have bothered getting out of bed. The world really is a mad, mad place.

I pondered on the state of man, the duty required by the crown, and the impact of war upon my business as I looked out the window and sipped a cup of tea. The one possible problem I seemed to have with America was that no one could make a decent spot of tea. I really did enjoy a nice cup of tea. Sadly, America was a land of coffee and beer. Neither of those made me happy. I was a tea and Scotch girl. OK, nowadays it was blood, tea, and Scotch.

On this particular day, the tea, a steaming Earl Grey, was quite fine. The heat of the liquid soaked into me and somehow warmed my soul. I did have a piece of business to handle, and the tea was just my way of procrastinating, while I watched my old friend the sun make its way off of the horizon. Soon enough, though, my chauffeur appeared and informed me that the auto was ready whenever I desired. I thanked him and stated that I would be ready presently.

Living in New York City, I usually drove myself everywhere. I loved the feeling of unconstrained spirit that the Bugatti gave me. It was impulsive and showy, two things an earl was not. In my homeland I utilized a chauffeur. On the soils of the empire, a member of the nobility was required to act noble. It was an easy concession, and the drive allowed me to enjoy the countryside as the Rolls Royce Phantom casually cruised along. And not that I am one who is fixated with status, but the Phantom, with my young and fashionable driver, Antwan, at the wheel, said "Move out of the way because I'm important" much better than the Bugatti.

Antwan settled me in the back seat of the luxury carriage and commandingly headed out the drive. The Grey Estate slipped away behind us as not even to have been noticed at all. In the beginning, horses could dispatch me at a pittance of the speed that Antwan could now. It was just one more thing that made me wonder if time was moving too fast for me.

Antwan sped me along to the fashionable South End, past the Thames, and into the quiet countryside manors of wealth and privilege. I had a need to go to my company. But first I needed to go converse with the man who had been running it for me. I didn't want to barge in with change and end up looking like a ponce. That had happened before and it didn't really play well.

More to the point of the trip, I could also embrace Gregory. He had steered the corporation into the second biggest shipping company on the planet. He had done quite good service and deserved more respect. If he saw fit to transition the reins of the corporation over to Tracey, then he obviously thought his son capable of the task.

Yes, Gregory Wyndell was no fool. He was a clear and resourceful businessman. He simply made money. He was so good at making money that he had become an advisor to the crown. He and his brother, Wayne, who was at the helm of the vast Wyndell fortune, were both regular guests at Parliament. Probably because their money combined with my money was more than the empire's money. It pays to be nice to people who can buy and sell you over breakfast biscuits.

I found Gregory tending to his greenhouse. He looked very fit for a man who had gone for retirement. He met me with genuine warmth for not having personally interacted in so long a time. He had always been a nice boy, and now that he was on in years, nothing had changed. It reaffirmed my faith that good was good and bad was bad. He was good.

"Lady Mary Beth Alcott, you look as if you haven't changed a day. Time has been good to you, yes? Mary Beth, I have always liked that name quite well."

"Thank you, Gregory. I am grand. I see that time has also been kind to you. You appear fit enough for the both of us."

"Thank you so much. You are too kind. Sadly, you of all people know that both age and health are but illusions. I have weathered well enough, but the pain of time is still there, deep down."

"Are you ill? I don't sense anything out of the ordinary."

"No, no, my girl, just time catching up with a machine that has no spare parts." He smiled broadly and it immediately put us both at ease. He had a command of people that was natural in its implementation. It was comforting.

"I have to say, I am very glad that you came to see me once again. I mean, before the end of my days. I have wondered many times of late as to how you were getting on over in America."

"I enjoy New York City well enough. It isn't my home, though. I do relish coming home."

"Do you miss the business as well?"

"I miss the intrigue and busyness of it all—the actual business, not as much. Besides, Wyndell men have been running my business for so many generations that it would seem more yours than mine."

Gregory smiled and adjusted one of the potted plants on his table. It was noticeable to the trained eye of a vampire that he lacked the fluid movements of a young man. The movements of the old are always noticed by the studied predator.

"We do what we do, Mary Beth. In the end, we all get treated with riches."

"Yes, we do, don't we? While we're on the topic of business, I know nothing of your son Tracey. What kind of man is he?"

"Studious."

"I'm not sure if that's a comforting answer."

"Oh, he's capable enough. He will ensure your riches as easily as others have. The studious actually applies to you."

"Once again, I'm not sure that that's comforting."

"Let's just say that you … intrigue him in a way that I don't believe you have the rest of us. I suspect it's because he's never actually met you or that he didn't grow up with you. Right now, you're a myth, so he studies."

"I hope he's learning the right lessons. That's been the downfall of some of his ancestors."

"Yes, he's learned that, too." Gregory smiled a wry smile to himself, as if he were thinking back on some childhood event.

"You know, Sara, I have always held you in high regard despite your, um, condition. You have treated my family kindly since before I was a child, and you have been kind to me personally. You are good at knowing business and people and how to interact in different circles. It all makes me like you quite well. I hope that this family affiliation transfers on to Tracey."

I looked at Gregory quizzically. He had never been one for being roundabout.

"How so, Master Wyndell?"

"Let's just say that all of the rest of us grew up in your presence. We know you. We knew you long before we came to understand you, for lack of a better phrase. My son is a good man, but he only has books and stories. He doesn't know you. I fear that he views you differently that the rest of us have."

Now, I smiled. My old friend was being protective of his child. That was truly a nice touch. He was a Wyndell, and they tended to be more stone and merit.

"Oh, Gregory, I've known more generations of Wyndell men and women than I care to count. Some of them were prats and some were the dog's bollocks. Each one of them managed to face life on their own terms. I would generally suspect that your schoolbook boy will be no different."

"Yes, the long view—you have always been wise in the use of that. I take the short view on some topics."

"As did my father in times past. What do you say that we go meet this boy of yours and see what he has to offer me?"

"That sounds like a fair idea."

"Fine. I will fetch my carriage while you fetch your coat."

Gregory Wyndell attired himself in an obviously expensive tweed jacket and motoring cap and appeared at the door of his residence as if he were a young man headed out on the town. Pretty girl, nice car, sunlit day, impressed friends—I suppose all were true. That's what was good about him: he was always too keen to be pretentious.

The ride across London to the East End and Canary Row, like my earlier one in from the estate, was much quicker than in days gone by. It seemed we had no more than left the Wyndell residence than we were pulled up in front of Grey's Cargo. I noticed as we stopped that my corporation had gotten another facelift.

"You've put up a new storefront?"

"About a year past. It was a grand year for the corporation and Tracey wanted to do something fancy."

"Before my blood starts to boil, where is my sign?"

"It is VERY safely crated and stored in the secured warehouse, along with other business heirlooms. I do still remember the conversation we had when you allowed me to move the offices."

"You are a good man, Gregory. It means a great deal to me. Could you have it sent out to the estate for me, please?"

"Absolutely, ma'am. Consider it done."

I smiled. It was going to be a good day, or so I thought before I got out of the auto.

We walked into the large lobby and onto the wide stairs that led to the upper floor executive offices. All in the office stopped to stare at the senior Wyndell escorting a pretty blonde woman, as if he were someone's valet. I could just feel the gossip flowing behind us as we walked.

The secretary stationed at a desk, front and center of the hallway, gave me a quizzical look as the senior Wyndell nodded approval. Gregory simply stated "the owner" as we passed her by. The lady's eyes went wide. Apparently, no one knew I was so young. That amused me.

Gregory paused in front of the door of the corporate manager and looked at me.

"Do we knock?"

"Did I ever knock for you?" I reached out and pushed the door full open so I might enter with a flourish. Gregory followed, obviously trying to hide the smile on his face.

"Excuse me, ma'am. I don't believe we have an appointment. I am sure we could—" Tracey's retort stalled as I calmly raised my small gloved hand.

I took up station on his fashionable settee, which was situated to one side of the room, and Gregory sat next to me. Tracey's office was large and richly appointed. It presented the image of power. Hmmm.

"Your office is grand. It has a lot of flash. Do you have another down the hall where you actually get work done?"

Young Wyndell looked equal parts confused and put out. Gregory's inability to contain his smile wasn't helping him. But, needless to say, Tracey was fast on his feet. Only seconds of confusion and he was on his feet rounding the desk and headed for the settee.

"Since you arrive with my father, it surely is an affair worthy of my time. I am Tracey Wyndell, and I am the president of Grey's Cargo. How might I be of assistance to you today?"

Well, he was smooth. He also spoke with power and conviction—all good qualities. I stood and firmly shook his warm human hand with my cold, dead vampire one.

"It is a pleasure to meet you, Mr. Wyndell. I am Lady Mary Beth Alcott, and I am the owner of the Grey's Cargo Corporation, the one you claim to presently be president of."

Tracey Wyndell's eye dilated full and his mouth gaped a good two inches as I released my grip and returned to my station on the settee. Gregory looked straight down at the floor, a face-wide smirk presented to the carpet.

"Lady Alcott?! I had no idea. I assumed you'd be older. I-I apologize for the otherwise hasty introduction. How may I be of service?"

"Hmm. It's amazing what a simple name will do, isn't it? There was a time in the history of this company when everyone who entered our doors was greeted warmly, whether they be a prince or pauper."

"Um, yes, ma'am."

"Now, I have it on good authority that you are, despite your youth, a good captain of industry." I patted Gregory on the knee. He had finally managed to hide the smirk on his face with my change in tone. My affection for Gregory was not lost on Tracey, and it seemed to give Tracey some unexplainable bit of reassurance.

"I have to say, Lady Alcott, I am very pleased to finally be meeting you."

"That's nice, Tracey, now answer the question."

"Yes, ma'am, I have a firm handle on all aspects of the corporation. The profits and business volume have been stable or better since I took over. We handle as much business as is available from industry at any point in time."

"Profits are grand, but how is our client base? Are they happy?"

"Happy?"

"Yes, happy with the level of service provided to them?"

"Ma'am? They keep coming back."

"Sometimes repeat business is repeat business. And sometimes repeat business is simply the path of least resistance. Grey's Cargo has always cared about our level of service and our customers' opinions. They can always go elsewhere."

"That they can, but they don't."

"True enough. And your profit and cost reports state as much. So, onto more important matters: what is the war response?"

"The war response, ma'am?"

"Tracey Wyndell, if you continue to repeat my questions as if they were not plain enough, I am quickly going to become irritated."

"But—"

"I ask a question. You provide an answer. There are no 'buts.'"

Tracey took in the unimpressed look on both faces before him and thought better of posturing. It would seem that he had never been openly challenged before. Oh well.

"The war response is measured at the moment. With conflict having started on the continent, we have released twelve ships to war service. Some ten crew's worth of men have been recruited by the private marine service. Two ships were sent straight to the admiralty. As of right now, no adverse impact has been sustained because of either the trials of war or requests from the crown. That surely will change as time goes on."

"All of our active clients are comfortable with the service being provided to them?"

"Yes, ma'am."

"And the admiralty?"

"Unknown. They were pleased with the prompt response to date. It is most likely that they will make further requests as the war escalates."

"How many more ships can we part with before it becomes inconvenient?"

"Without running number projections on trade restrictions and hostile water situations, say another dozen."

"And I can assume that the work volume at the shipyards has been increased to compensate for this eventuality?"

"Yes, ma'am. The yards normally work on an eight-ships-a-year merchant vessel schedule. They are currently running at a twelve-ships-a-year pace."

"And the cost of those four extra ships?"

"It is currently being maintained by the extra charges on freight through hostile waters."

"And any recompense from the admiralty?"

"It has been quite reasonable."

"Send it back."

"Ma'am?" Both heads came around in a quizzical fashion.

"Send it back to the admiralty, Tracey. As a businesswoman, I am in business to make a profit. As an earl of the crown, I am obligated to support the crown in times of war. We will be supporting the crown as this company has done since it was founded."

Gregory nodded in understanding. It all was perfectly sensible. Tracey, for his part, was less convinced. He was one of those new capitalists.

"Tracey, the corporation is flush. Both of our families have more money than we will ever spend. The crown needs working capital. Send it back to them."

"Yes, ma'am."

"Good boy. Now, just so you know, I am going to be around to watch over things until I deem them satisfactory. You and I are going to need to get to know each other."

An inappropriate and unlikeable twinkle sparked in Tracey's eye as I spoke. I think he had taken to the powerful, willful young woman at which he was looking. Gregory noticed it as well. I could sense him becoming uncomfortable, even though he made no outward sign of it.

I stood, and Gregory followed suit. Tracey stood and came out from behind his big wooden desk to send us off. He had transitioned into full-on smooth talker. That was no good.

"Lady Alcott, it has been a pleasure to finally meet you. I look forward to the prospect of spending more time with you."

Gregory turned away, as he knew what was coming. I really didn't want to do it, but it needed to be done.

I reached past Tracey's outstretched hand and locked four fingers and a thumb firmly around his throat. Then, as calmly as could be, I squeezed until all his breathing had ceased. With a yank, I pulled the sturdy lad down to his knees, so I could look down into his eyes. Loosening my grip, I allowed just the smallest amount of air back in.

"Tracey Wyndell, our relationship will be one of business. I don't make appointments. I don't knock. You exist here strictly based upon my approval. Now, get that shag-and-a-smoke look out of your eye and make damned sure it never returns."

I released my grip with a flick that sent him tumbling back against the front of his desk. Gregory said nothing but simply turned and followed as I made my exit. Outside, Antwan held the door of the auto for me so I might enter and then he assisted Gregory.

"What do you think, old friend, too much?"

"It was high impact, but he probably did require the hard lessons. The young can be precocious."

"Agreed."

I patted him on the knee again in a sign of acceptance. It had been a bit full-on, but I would bring Tracey around to my way of thinking soon enough. Antwan pulled out into traffic, and we were off.

CHAPTER 18

A half year passed and my relationship with the twenty-two-year-old Tracey Wyndell had come around to what I had enjoyed with the other members of his clan. After he figured out in his mind that I had actually been dead for hundreds of years, he relaxed greatly. Apparently, my being a corpse now put him off somewhat. The power, that wasn't lost on him. I embraced my own power with his desire for more power. Where other men in his family ran the business, he was the first one who really wanted it. I could just tell that he looked upon the corporation as his, or soon to be his.

The Wyndell family had been so wealthy and powerful for so long that they had forgotten where they came from. If Charles could see what his family had progressed to, I wonder if he'd be happy or sad.

On a home note, the war had come on full, just as everyone had expected. The German air machines had appeared over the coast in early December, and by the Yule they were a constant theme. The news of zeppelins spotted to the south at one place or another was almost constant. The lines of the encounter over on the continent had also stabilized into the great trench warfare that World War I was so famous for.

German submarines had sunk a passenger ship called the *Lusitania*, which was loaded with Americans. It seemed that the Germans instantly figured out that that was a mistake, because they promptly backed down their submarine activities.

Italy, always too restless to stand by in a fight, jumped into the fray on the side of the Allies. I'm quite sure the Allies were probably pleased about that!

The Germans, deciding that their war innovations shouldn't be confined to mere submersible ships, used mustard gas on the battlefield for the first time in history. The British troops they used it on didn't enjoy the experience in the least, and the casualty count was quite high. As a personal observation, chemical gas is a hideous way to die. The Germans were not to be commended for this move.

Currently, British troops were working their way around the sea mines and landing at some place called Gallipoli. I do remember thinking at the time that hopefully it all went well.

On a business front, young Tracey had lived up to all his high self-promotion. Despite the war, the corporation hummed along with great efficiency. I made my way around London, meeting with the oldest members of the client list. All of the High Street boys seemed to have high praise for Mr. Wyndell.

I had come to find Tracey to be highly intuitive. He just knew what was coming or what way to approach a specific problem. I finally came to decide that numerous generations of Wyndell street smarts had climaxed in his sound business strategies. It was not just Tracey, but all of his fathers and grandfathers before him who had made strides in this direction. They had given Tracey natural business ability. He was the product of his environment. Where in times past the environment had been the street, now it was the boardroom. Dark alleys had given way to well-lit hallways. He was a child so different from some I'd known, yet the drive was the same. That little epiphany made me wonder if time wasn't leaving me behind. I knew that it probably was.

Once summer had come to the manor, I made a request to see the crown. To my mild surprise, it was met with quick approval. So, on a nice sunny June day, I had a quiet meeting in Westminster Abbey with King George V. He was a secret fan of the grandeur, having relatives buried in the structure. I have always been a fan of the glass. So, the setting worked for both of us.

The current king was a more direct man than other monarchs who had possessed his name. I guess that was the cost of war. He was also more private. His retinue and personal handlers stayed distant and left us in peace. It was nice to have the power of a king after all.

Our conversation was light. He seemed confused by Grey's Cargo's returning of the recompense. I explained that we were doing our part for the lads and we needed no extra. He asked if my new capitalists would release more ships to the cause. I told him merely to ask when he was in need. He inquired about living in New York City. I explained that I liked it all quite well, but it wasn't the Grey Estate. He seemed to understand completely.

Once we were well out of earshot and in a setting where no one was going to come upon us unannounced, the king mentioned to me that when he had taken throne, he had received several items. They were a trunk full of items that passed directly from one monarch to the next. It was an inheritance of sorts—things that were meant to remind the current king or queen of who had come before them. And well, they helped to give guidance. I smiled and nodded my understanding as he spoke but did not interject.

One of the items in his cache of heirlooms was a journal, a journal penned by one Sophie Charlotte, queen of England. It had some enlightening things to say about the state of the country and about the earl of Northwick. What was most of interest to this current king was how every monarch succeeding the queen had taken time to pen to the current name, status, generosity, and description of that specific earl in the back of the journal.

When he finished his explanation, he asked what I thought he should pen in it about me. I told him that since I hadn't written what other rulers had written, it would be hard to say. Though, honesty is always the best policy when dealing with the writing of history. Honesty always lasts longer than lies. The king thought for a moment and then agreed.

He looked quietly at one of the many ornate funeral displays and then asked what it was like to be me. I pondered a large ornate sarcophagus in front of us for several moments and then said that I assumed it was like anything else.

"You do what you do to live, as do I."

He seemed to agree with that as well. The king then asked if we might converse on the topic of eternity when times were better suited for it. I stated that all he need do was request my presence. I was deemed direct but nice, just as all the others had said. I smiled and we casually made our way back toward the others.

As I rode north through town, back toward the Grey Estate, I pondered the problems with the crown having a book detailing my life as a vampire. It didn't make my heart warm, to say the least. It was good to find out that they had all written nice things about me. I would need to stay on the right side of crown. *That was for sure*, as the Yanks say.

The thought of being in a journal led my mind to the thought of Effie's journals. That led me to thoughts of the Enfield Trust. I needed to take time and see the marquis while I was in the city. He was a good man and he kept his word. I liked him.

It took a couple days, but I did manage to send out a correspondence to the marquis. As I predicted, the administrator of the Enfield Trust jumped at the chance to converse. Only days on from my note, I was sitting on my study's terrace, waiting on my casual friend Eugene to arrive. The day was mild for midsummer and not exceedingly hot under the cloudless sun. A gentle breeze whistled its way across the meadow and brought the scent of wild flowers. I sat and inhaled the aroma of summer as I waited. I love summer at the estate. The happiness of summer was one of the things that kept me connected to the world. It was so easy to lose grasp of what nature has to offer and just go with your instincts. Flowers on a breeze kept me in touch with the little human girl somewhere still inside me. She loved summer. I loved summer—and in doing so, her/my humanity was preserved.

I didn't spend long pondering the flowers before the marquis was coming up the drive. Just as well—I didn't want to slip into melancholy. The head housekeeper, who also doubled as butler, escorted Eugene out to the terrace and then drifted off to procure some tea. Her name was Sophia. She was a sturdy woman from somewhere in the Ukraine, and she ran an excellent house. She had taken to teaching me Ukrainian when time allowed. She was Old World and could tell that I was something other than what I appeared. I had let her suspect for a time, before letting her in on the secret. It really was nice to have people at the estate who knew about me. It just made all of life's little moments easier. That was enough for me to be happy.

Eugene Stone took up station in an adjacent chair and settled himself in his academic fashion.

"Good morning, Marquis." I smiled with warmth, as to not set the tone with formality. "Eugene, I hope you are well? You look grand."

"Thank you, Sara. I am quite fine. I have to say that I think you have gotten even younger looking since we last talked."

We both laughed. It was heartwarming to have a decent conversation with someone besides my priest. And, besides, I had left my priest back in New York.

"This is just my natural state, eighteen going on three hundred. However, a lady always appreciates a compliment. Thank you, kind sir. I take it that you received the courier with the return of your journals?"

"Yes, I did. I do appreciate you sending them back to us."

"It seemed the right thing to do. You were kind to me; it would be wrong to be anything but the same in return."

"I have to tell you that that is an old way of thinking. These days everyone is about themselves."

"I find it an unnecessary thing to yield to whimsy. Treat people as you wish to be treated, old-fashioned or not."

"I like your view of things, Sara."

"It's easy to take the long view in my position."

"Yes, I suppose it is. On a more positive note, what brings you back to London?"

"War."

"Well, that wasn't very positive."

We both laughed. It was an icebreaker of sorts. He meant the question in a different way and I had been a bit blunt.

"With the empire embroiled in war over on the continent, I needed to return home and do those things for the crown that an earl is required to do. You know what they say about war: it brings the nobility out of people."

Eugene laughed loudly and then went after his tea cup, which had finally stopped steaming.

"Normally, I cycle between London, Bristol, and New York City. They all mean something special to me. They allow me to stay anchored down in a sea of change. Know what I mean?"

"I do indeed. It's the attachments we make in life that allow us to find our place. That is an extremely human thing."

"I hold onto things that give me peace. They help me to not embrace the darker aspects of my personality."

Eugene smiled a very wry smile. He knew I meant my demonic self.

"Yes, as you have quite notably done in times past."

"True. On a lighter note, how are the pursuits of academia? What new topics are of note? I do enjoy new things."

That was the switch that it all needed. Eugene and I sat for several hours as he regaled me with all things new in the world. I enjoyed his insights and learned many things. It was obvious that he missed his days of being a teacher and playing to an audience.

I let him play and absorbed as much as I could. He was a well-learned man, both on the science of the day and more esoteric matters. Somewhere in the middle of the conversation, I drifted off to days gone by and friends long dead. They, too, had tried to teach me new things.

The day was pleasant and the smell of the wild flowers from the meadow blended with the lessons of the marquis. This was one nice day in the midst of the ugliness of war. Even as it was happening, I hoped it wasn't the only such day.

CHAPTER 19

The war did what war does. And in doing so, it would soon become infamous for two things. First, it would be labeled as the Great War, in the sense that nothing like it had ever been seen before. Second, it would also come to be known as the War to End All Wars. (That moniker would be somewhat premature because World War II was virtually right around the corner.)

WW2 would also outdo WW1 on almost all fronts. Such is the way of history, I think.

I was happy to see the Great War sputter to a stop. It would seem odd for a predator to dislike war, but I'm just not a big fan. War screws everything about, and it takes forever to put things back together when people are done. Yes, it's bad for business. But more than that, it's really not a good type of killing. Nature tends toward killing in an efficient manner. Human wars tend toward body count. The end product isn't evolution; it's politics. The politics don't actually help anything, and the carnage produces large amounts of corpses.

World War I did produce large amounts of corpses. Every country involved in the conflict had scores of bodies to deal with. Across England, journeymen kept busy creating monuments to the fallen. The other empires were no doubt doing the same.

As an armchair historian, I like to look back on what has oft times been overlooked in all the warring. The blinding ugliness of the Great War quite easily overshadowed the Great Pandemic that followed on its heels. In 1918, dead on the tailcoats of the war, the Spanish flu appeared on the besieged countries of Europe and started to decimate the population. Where the war saw many able-bodied men die in combat, the flu pandemic targeted the healthy, young civilian population almost exclusively.

The Spanish flu crossed all territorial and ethnic boundaries. It spread as though Effie's magick were pushing it along. There were even stories of people alone in the Arctic and out on remote islands dying of the disease.

At the current time, June 1920, the pandemic still had some six months to go before it would burn itself out. It would eventually claim between 3 percent and 6 percent of the world's population. I have been fond of thinking that nature is always more destructive than anything else.

I can remember that there were bodies everywhere. For me, it was numbing. To others of my kind, it was a windfall. There were so many bodies that no one cared about them. Memorial crypts, pandemic mass graves, large bone reliquaries, and catacombs made normal body disposal unnecessary. Hell, you didn't even have to dump them anywhere when you were finished. Vampires would just leave them where they were killed and someone would come along and collect them with all the rest. The all-you-can-eat lamp was fully lit and everyone was in on it—well, everyone except me.

I couldn't seem to bring myself to do it. Call it human emotion, call it that lingering female instinct for nurturing, call it whatever you like, I just could not come around to the drain-and-dump theory of vampiring. I like killing fine, and I'm extremely good at it, but when it's just so ugly, it turns me off. I'm a hunter.

While my kin were feasting their way around Europe, I set about to see if I could lighten the loss of the weary. The Grey Estate purchased lands and established new cemeteries for the dead. The bodies needed to go somewhere. After construction, the cemeteries were turned over to the public trust for handling, as is common of such places. Also, seeing the need, a couple of large hospitals were constructed to help with the sick and dying. One was built in South London on land that Grey's Cargo had owned. The other was outside Bristol on Brimme House land. As was the case with both enterprises, neither was really big enough for the task at hand. Both the cemeteries and the hospitals were all but overwhelmed before construction was complete.

I bankrolled that Booth fellow for a fashion and helped his Salvation Army deal with the scores of displaced and hungry Englanders. The people running it were exuberant with praise. Frankly, the nod it brought from the crown kept me in good regard all by itself.

I had been out in Bristol, living in Brimme House and overseeing the construction out there, by the time June came. The damage of the war hadn't really adversely affected the city. It was mostly damage from the flu pandemic out that way. There seemed to be a great number of infected in the area, but not as much mortality. That the number of dying was lower gave me optimism.

I wandered about the fields of Brimme House and tried to think about happier times. I had collected such good memories living at the house of my title. The fortified great house was almost a castle and gave me reassurance that things would get better. It had been around much longer than I, and it was still in fine shape. It was a sturdy, safe haven in the midst of chaos.

A slow, seeping sense of contentment was coming to me from my time at Brimme House. That contentment led me onto thoughts of happier times. I began to think back on all the parties that Father used to host at the Grey Estate. They were grand affairs, especially for a little girl. The galas that I had hosted as a vampire were also lavish spectacles. I did enjoy reconnecting with my kind; it gave me a sense of place. I also did enjoy hosting a grand occasion.

The more time I spent at Brimme House, the more I came to like the idea of having another vampire gala. It had been long enough since the last one had happened. Times around the area had changed. My enemies were fewer than in times past, at least the ones known to me. The whole Enfield Trust was no longer a bother. All things seemed to point toward party time in Bristol.

I did have a few problems to overcome if I was going to invite my kin over for the evening, but there were enough people around to help. I just needed to bring them all together in one place. Yes, yes, a festive occasion in the midst of dreariness would be the dog's bollocks.

It took weeks for this idea to solidify in me. But once it had done so, the whole thing was on. I paced about the finely groomed inner lawns and analyzed my thoughts. I needed to assemble the help. I needed to inform the guests and secure the perimeter. Then there was only the matter of stocking the pantry. Seeing how I had pulled off this stunt a couple times in years past, I didn't see any reason it couldn't be done a third time. I had had as much human help with the last gala as seemed available for this one. The issues at hand should be reasonable. Nowadays, people in general were less believing than in days gone by. That could definitely turn in my favor as things progressed.

The first order of business was to appoint a party planner, or planner intermediary. In this case, I already had one of those on staff. I just needed to locate him.

I sat in my study the next morning and composed a correspondence to my butler/confidant Randolf, who was still residing in New York City. He was a Brimme House boy and could handle all of the oddities with unnoticed ease. He was handy and smart, but more than that he was a good judge of people. He would be a fine choice for a staff recruiter.

As soon as I finished composing the correspondence, I realized I was lost in time again. No one sent correspondence anymore, did they? It was 1920, after all. I put the letter back in the drawer with the parchment and walked over to the house telephone. I had become so used to written messages that I kept forgetting that technology had begun to make them obsolete. I placed a call to the residence in New York City and conversed with Randolf directly. It felt strange.

Notifying the guests proposed itself to be a more interesting endeavor. Normally that job would fall to Tracey. The real problem of the day was that I didn't trust Tracey Wyndell. I really liked him and he ran a strong business, but I didn't trust him on the level that was necessary for this task. We just hadn't gotten there yet. He lacked deep individual reliability.

My fallback for this item was Gregory. He was still just barely young enough to be in the mix. Besides, he was a facilitator, not a partaker. I was the partaker. Gregory would also be an asset with the third issue of high demand: the aforementioned security. Where the real-time perimeter security would be handled by my little crystal friend and her ominous powers, Gregory would be the logistical body. I needed to know what was going on with William Bennett's extended band of blighters.

Things as large in number as a gala were always hard to keep a secret for long. That had been the main reason why each of the preceding galas had been followed quite directly by a large formal party for the Bristol business establishment. It kept egos soothed, and the two parties blended in the news that escaped the local area. I know because the gala had raised unwelcomed attention from the Brenfield Society the last time around. Fortunately, that had turned out to be a problem only for me. If this next one was going to rear up ugliness from the Bennett family, I wanted to know they were coming before they showed up at my doorstep.

I made a second quick telephone call to Gregory's residence and left a message to have him get in contact with me. He would, most likely, be happy to help. Even if he wasn't, he would surely provide sound advice on how to proceed.

I had been hearing rumors about Gregory's daughter Jasmine since I had returned home. By all reports, she was smart and sure, a secretive girl just like her forebears. I potentially could use her services if need be. I didn't really want to overburden the Wyndell family, as they had their own problems to work through. Master Wayne Wyndell, dutiful member of the Fourth Battalion, Royal North Regiment, had died as a member of the Black Watch while fighting in Palestine. It had struck me as odd when hearing the news, since Wayne was never the most religious of people. He was a capitalist. He believed in money and profit. Also, he possessed the wealth and position to be able to avoid combat. I didn't highly approve of the fact that he went and fought. However, he didn't stand behind others; he went and did what needed doing. That was a statement about honor that no sum of money could reproduce.

The problem his death produced for the family was that he had been at the helm of the family accounts for some time. Since he had no children, and no real will to speak of, the lack of direction was consuming the family. It seemed that everyone alive now wanted to be the family controller. I could remember when no one wanted the job—my, how the times had changed. It was like a bad episode of Dallas. Fortunately, the founding family members had been sensible enough to create provisions for such occurrences. I suppose that living with a vampire tends to make people look for contingencies. Those Wyndell boys, they were always smart that way.

The whole thing would work itself out quietly enough. The real options for the family were Robin Wyndell, Gregory's youngest daughter, or Jane Winston Synclare, his great niece. Both women were well educated and young enough to handle the reins for some time. I had met both women and had no issues one way or the other, so I stayed my nose out of family business. It was no longer my place to get involved in their disputes.

I will say that as much as I was trying to turn a blind eye to the whole affair, the crown was not. Wayne Wyndell was a highly respected member of the private cabinet, and the Wyndell fortune was not to be taken lightly. The crown seemed concerned it might pose them a problem. I could see their concern, I guess.

Nevertheless, Gregory, being the senior member of the family, had already voiced his opinions to the family and the crown. He was now otherwise unattached and had spare time to help me figure out my party.

I made my way out of the study and headed for the meadows to walk and think about stocking the pantry. Part of my work with the Salvation Army was forming a small company that helped with blood collection. The blood it dispensed helped the wounded of the war and seemed the new way of medicine. They were doing neat things with blood and blood plasma in those days.

I had no intentions of syphoning off too much of the stock, but I could use a bit. The rest of the pantry, as usual, would come from the local slaughterhouses. They, too, had been sending blood out to medical places for scientific studies. Randolf would need to look into that when he arrived.

Yes, as near as I could tell, things would be just fine. I would have a smashing little party, the Vampire Gala III. The only real question rumbling around in my head was: "Do I invite Antonio?"

CHAPTER 20

I stood in the frost-etched windows of the study on December 29, 1920, and looked out over the uniform blanket of white that the winter had produced. I had returned to London a fortnight back and joined in on the holiday festivities the estate put on for the community. I have always been a big Christmas holiday person, and as of late, even more so. The holiday always brings out the best in people, if only for a short time.

Summer and fall in Bristol had passed by quietly. The gala, for all its intended excitement, did not come off. Gregory said he would be glad to do his part. I drug Randolf back to Bristol from America to help me, and he seemed eager to do so. I think he really wanted to see the other side of life. He always had been the curious type. The problem with it all turned out to be me. I know it was all my idea, but come match time, my heart just really wasn't in it.

I had collected my conspirators and was ready to proper plan, but I just couldn't seem to get started. I let them linger for some time as I pondered it all: a party, loads of vampires, Antonio, a new world, an old house, and all the other complications those things produced. After about a month of Randolf watching me pace about Brimme House, I booked him passage back to America. It wasn't coming off.

I have been a trendsetter on several occasions, and many other times I have just gone with the masses. I had (and have) very fond memories of both galas the house had hosted. They were, by every estimate, grand affairs. The thing that made me procrastinate this time was the real sensation that it had all been done before. It had been done and done with style. It had been long enough from one to the next to now, that

I just shifted into "Let's Have a Party" mode. Truth was, after I really thought about it, I realized I was simply going through the motions.

So the conspirators were dispersed and I returned to what I do best: pacing. I spent the summer and fall pacing. I paced all about Brimme House. I paced all about the meadows and the fields. I paced all the fashionable streets of Bristol. I called on the other titled families in the area and paced about their estates a tad. I spent months pacing before I finally realized what was going on.

I found that it all boiled down to one thing: Sara Anne Grey was lonely. I was lonely. It was almost silly. There were people everywhere. I was constantly surrounded by masses of humanity. Yet, it was still true. All the pacing was just me stewing on the fact that I was lonely.

If you removed the sea of humanity that swirled around me, the truth was all my friends were dead or well on in years. Save the housekeeper, all that knew of my disposition were an ocean away or one foot in the grave. The one priest I could confide in was located on a different continent, and letter writing was not one of my favorite things. I was apparently in good with the crown, but that was of no never mind. On top of all of this, I had not as much as sensed another vampire in many years. I knew they were out there, doing what they do—they just weren't coming my way.

I think that more than anything else was the whole subliminal point of hosting Gala III. I just wanted to see another vampire. Another vampire in the flesh would remind me that I wasn't alone.

There were vampires that made their way through London from time to time, but the western territories of Britain seemed almost devoid of them. I knew that Zoe was still up in Scotland somewhere. There was also a chap named Dwight who lived in Dublin. That was about it for us United Kingdom killers. I hadn't seen my friend Zoe since the last gala. She usually sent a card around the holidays, just to say hi. I always reciprocated. It let us both know we were still living. I had never met the Irish lad, though I heard he was the alright sort. I received the occasional correspondence from others I had met, and that was definitely nice. I responded in kind to all I received. I never sent out any of my own. I don't really know why.

That's just me, I guess.

Another thing that had been bothering me was moderation. I hadn't killed anyone in a fashion, and that was absolutely eating at me. I killed people because I am a killer. It had been some time since I felt the need to kill. I had moderated down to letting the amulet's limitless energy sustain me. It made me docile. I no longer acted like a killer. I no longer analyzed situations like a killer. I was acting much more human than I should have been. That was eating at the demon in me. Yes, there needed to be more killing, much more killing.

All of this I summed up in the thought: Sara Grey is lonely. I did not like this loneliness. I did not like it one bit. In an unexpected twist, the day I voiced my assembled thoughts out loud, the amulet voiced a few of her own.

I was standing on the outer terrace of the study at the manor, looking out on the meadows past the lawn, when it all coalesced in my mind. I spoke the thought that formed in my mind and a luminous blue thump of energy pulsed out of my friend's crystal cage.

"You are never alone," echoed inside my mind as Effie calmed to her former state.

"Oh, Effie, sweetheart, I didn't mean you. I know you're here looking after me."

"You always have a friend in me."

"You have always been good to me. I do appreciate that. I do greatly enjoy our friendship. I just miss the emotional touch of my kind—that and some of my more animalistic intentions. I'm not the person I once was."

"Neither am I. I am who I am, the same way that you are who you are. We choose to be whomever we choose to be. It's the thing that we two have control over: deciding to be who we want to be."

"Effie, I do like your view on things."

"In the numerous millennia that I have been locked in this cage, I have had very few acquaintances that I would call friends. You are one of my best friends yet."

"And you have always been one of mine these many long years."

"I say go, if you want. Embrace that part of you that feels neglected. Do what is going to make you happy."

"I am sorry if I offended you."

"It's quite fine. I, too, feel lonely at times. I understand your position."

"Thank you."

I continued to ponder that exchange for the remainder of the day. Effie was right. I had to just go and do it. Do what makes me happy.

The problem I had now was, in deciding to be me, what did it really mean to be me? What was I missing out on, and what did I want to do first? I knew I wanted to be killing, but what else was there? There was interaction with other vampires. There was blood. The blood of the dying could go a long way to making it all better.

What to do? What to do? The list of things I'd been missing seemed pretty short. There was killing, seeing vampires, and blood. That really didn't seem like enough weight to produce all of this drama. Apparently, I was a more complex creature than was originally intended. I wasn't sure if that was good or bad.

Well, first thing's first, as I like to say. There was a need for someone to converse with. I fashioned a letter to Father Ryan back in New York City and asked him if he knew of another understanding priest that might live over in the British Isles. I imagined that it would be getting to be a small group, clergy that believed in the old ways. I explained that I did like the Anglicans, but that at the end of the day, a priest was a priest. It was the spirit of the conversation that mattered most. I asked that he give me a telephone call at his convenience.

I figured that if the answer he returned to me was no, I could always check in with my new friend at the Vatican. Or I could go out and handle it the old-fashioned way. Any way around, there was a conversationalist out there somewhere. If I really had to, I'd just hop a ship back to the NCY and talk to Father Ryan. Though I did like him well, I was pretty sure it wouldn't come to that. There were priests by the thousands in England. One of them was a talker.

Next on the to-do list seemed to be either vampires or killing. I could do the blood without the killing these days, I just didn't want to. The adrenaline in the blood was the point of the killing. They went together. So it was vampires or it was blood.

As I stated earlier, Bristol really wasn't, and still isn't, vampire central. I could easily go up to Scotland and see Zoe or dodge over to Dublin and track down that Dwight character. I could also head back to London and see if anyone was passing through. There was also all of Europe. Scads of vampires resided over on the continent. There were at least a half dozen in Paris alone. Paris really was a strange city.

Nope, London made the most immediate sense. I could hunt there quite confidently, and there was a good chance that vampires would move through. If not now, well then they would soon enough. I was also not out of place in my own hometown. I would be semi-anonymous there. Many humans knew me there. I was as natural there as the stevedores on the docks.

It all took some time to make the transition back to London. Brimme House was large and commanding. It was not the same house that could be mothballed like in days of old. I saw to all the business interests and announced to the staff that I would be returning to London. They went about making preparations. Not much changed. It was more just me checking on all the stewards of the surrounding lands to make sure they were all sorted. As I suspected, they were quite fine. The whole operation of Brimme House, and all of its associated lands, was a well-oiled machine.

I packed my trunks with the fashions of the day and had the valet deliver me down to the train station. The ride out of Bristol to Paddington station was quick and comfortable. I was constantly amazed at how the pace of life increased. The first trip I had taken from London to Northwick took days. This trip took hours. It was also somewhat more comfortable. I well-liked the trains of the day. They didn't clank and bang along as the previous systems had, and they were a vast improvement on the horse and coach.

At Paddington Station I was met on the platform by a pleasant young man who collected me and my trunks. The ride from the station north to the estate was also quicker than in days past. The large, black touring car whisked me along the snowy lanes in a blur. Before I could even settle in, the auto was pulling in through the gates of the Grey Estate and onward up the drive. I was home.

I have to say I have always enjoyed London in the winter. The weather is still moderate and the trappings of winter make everything move with purpose, especially down dockside. I spent a bit of time getting on with the locals and blending before striking out. I checked in with Tracey to see how the corporation was faring. I was glad to see that he had finally adjusted to me. I also sat for tea with numerous old business clients. They appreciated my time greatly, the same way I appreciated their money. I even popped down to the palace and checked in with the crown. As always, moving through the court was akin to navigating a maze full of vipers and jaguars. Needless to say, King George received me in a pleasant fashion.

That would be King George V. There did seem to be a long line of Georges. Even so, it was nice to see that the House of Windsor was well intact. Stability of the crown led to stability of Parliament, which led to stability of the empire. It was also always good to have military men at the head of the empire. The king was also the Prince of Wales, which made him my neighbor upon occasion.

The conversation at the crown was cordial and quick. The affairs of the empire are constant. He was pleased that I had come and was glad to see my corporation prospering. He asked on the health of Gregory Wyndell and if a decent successor was coming along. Time passed quickly, and soon enough I was on my way. Having met all my dutiful obligations, it was time to get on with my business.

With the December weather being moderate, London snow was falling as London rain at the outset of my little scouting mission. I had never been a big fan of getting wet, and the rain seemed to push all the coal smoke from the stacks straight to the ground, making the air even grimier than normal. At least the snow made things look clean. Yes, snow was much better than rain.

My area of choice was Lambeth. The area around Waterloo Station produced large masses of commuters. It was also a receiving station for people migrating in from the lands to the south. It was a natural spot for people to go missing. The informants of the day said that it harbored a healthy gang situation and that violence was common in the area. The good fellows at Scotland Yard also had no real interest in cleaning the place up. It seemed like the right place to go.

The first to fall was a sturdy gent who looked the dock-working type. I ran into him a couple blocks on from St. George's on Blackfriars. I was standing on the corner, looking about, when he approached with that "all business" smile. I admit my fashion was quite moderate, but I certainly didn't look like the working girls in that area. The fact he couldn't tell the difference was now his problem. We wandered up Webber Street to a darkened alley where some business received its deliveries. Dock worker said something about the spot being quiet. I agreed, took a quick look about, and savagely sank my fangs into his neck. The quick attack stunned him, but he pushed me off with a powerful burst. I planted a full-on kick to the knee, bones shattered, and the big man crashed to the cobbles. I planted fangs a second time and it was over. His adrenaline pushed the blood out so fast that he was empty in no time. I removed him of his valuables and disposed of them in a sewer drain a ways down the street. A small bit of extra knife work and fang marks looked like a throat slashing. The old boy must have gotten mugged and tossed—at least, that's what the bobbies would think.

The second fellow to fall was a thin and wiry chap down by Doorstep Green. He didn't even put up any resistance. After deciding he was the one, I simply walked up and punched him in the side of the head. He hit the ground and I planted enamel spikes into his carotid artery. A stomach full of blood later, he was also transformed into a mugging victim.

Number three met his end on the edge of the Thames under the Southwark Bridge. He was large and streetwise. At first he was sure and thought he was in control, but soon enough he found that he was no more than food. Number four was also found floating in the Thames, but he was put in just upstream of London Bridge. I hadn't actually planned on killing him as I was slowly sliding my way out of Lambeth and into Whitechapel, but the opportunity presented itself. Besides, who am I not to yield to temptation? I also admit that he was tasty. He was in his good years, fit, and well fed—all the things that make for good blood. His family would probably be put out, but it was a rough part of town. He shouldn't have gone off looking for trouble.

Four corpses collected in five days. I was so full of blood that adrenaline still lingered in my veins. I was giddy with it all. I felt back to being completely me. The melancholy of Bristol had fully passed. I could tell the killer in me had been reawakened. The success made me pleased.

By the time the fourth chap had hit the water, the weather had changed rain back into snow. A blanket of white now lay across the city, making it look clean again. That made me pleased.

Now, I stood in my study, looking out over snow-covered lawns. The lads from Scotland Yard had not come to visit, which was good. I was mere days from the eve of the New Year and looking forward to seeing my family come to linger about.

Upon the New Year I would need to find another of my kind. For now, things were pleasant. Sara Grey was happy.

CHAPTER 21

Yule came to the Grey Estate as planned. All of London was fully rejoicing over the many magical things that Christmastime brings. The estate, too, was well decked out and celebrating the joys of the season.

I truly liked Christmas time and all its traditions. Still, for me and some other old families scattered about the city, it was Yule. The ancients had been making the holiday long before the Christians came to our shores. There were families that were still happy to hold onto glimmers of the old ways of log and stone and hearth, even if it was now wrapped in a new religion.

I personally liked the original ways, well, because I'm old. I was vested in the old ways at a younger age. I was like the holiday: an old thing wrapped in a shiny wrapper so I would be seen as something new. I understand the tactic well.

The Grey Estate brought in the evergreen and the Yule log, and then we all went to Mass. Ha, ha, yes, I know I'm Anglican, but once a year it really doesn't matter. After all, they're basically the same thing.

I have to admit I was proper excited on the way home from midnight Mass. I had been embracing the gifts of the holiday season, waiting patiently for Yule to arrive. Yule is one of the primary days when the divide between this world and the next is diminished. Yule is one of the primary pagan sabots. It was picked (so I have read) because of the closeness to the netherworld. It's a moment when the fabric of space-time is thin and one has an easier time reaching through the void. The thinning of the veil is a time of apparitions and allows all manner of ghosts and specters to be seen about the city. It also enhances the depths of Effie's vast magicks as she pulls on the power from the opposing side of the void. The thinning also allows me to spend a few brief moments with some very old friends and some long dead family.

I was excited when I realized what the thinning of the veil could accomplish. I had very much enjoyed meeting my grandfather. He seemed exactly the man one would expect to meet.

It was years back when I finally got the shock I wanted. I had talked with Father on several occasions. He was always pleased to see me and hear what I had to say. It was the inclusion of my mother, several years ago, that almost brought me to tears. She was so beautiful. She was the sheer vision of youth. I had talked to her in the cemetery on countless occasions, but I got to see her at Yule. Seeing her apparition floating in the study next to Father made me recoil into being a little girl once more. Somewhere deep down in my subconscious, I had always missed my mother. Young girls need mothers, I think. They really need them. Father had done the best that he could, and so did my nanny, Ms. Palmer, but a mother would have been better. All the way home from church, all I could think about was seeing mother. It was my real Christmas present.

My company of hearty revelers came crashing through the main doors of the manor and headed off toward the kitchen. It was time to steep the tea and make merry a while longer before the needs of the day needed to be met. I excused myself from the throng and headed off toward the study.

Every house has that place—that spot where things just happen. It's the place that holds the energy of a building. In most modern buildings, that place is the kitchen. It makes sense, since that's where the provisions of a home are stored. In some ways that's also true of the estate, though its real power center is the study. The studies of both Brimme House and the Grey Estate are the places that made everything happen. They were the meeting, work, relax, plot, and plan areas of the buildings. In this way, the study of the estate was the real power center. That is why the ghosts of old came and gathered there. They centered themselves on the energy source of the building, or so Effie had informed me.

I liked that they came out to the study to see me. Not one of them was in any way malevolent. They were not the ghosts of Edgar Allen Poe or Mr. Lovecraft; they were my friends and my family. They used the thinning of the veil to ease out of their earthly plots and look about for a moment. In an age of industrialization and science, they were most welcome friends.

I took up station in my favorite chair and closed my eyes so I might calm my mind. I could feel Effie's energy twitching out in the open spaces of the room. She was slowly drawing out the energy of the void. Fortunately, her recharging seemed to have no effect on the appearance of the ghosts. They just came and went of their own volition. The swirling energy currents of the void seemed to be of little consequence to the spirit world. They were different types of energy, I guess. I really don't understand how it all works. The other side is a strange and mysterious thing to me. It makes me afraid at times, since I will not get to go to the place where they exist. As a demon, I am headed to a different place when I make my transition from this world.

I opened my eyes and focused them on the chair next to mine. It was the place where Charles used to sit. He was usually the first to appear. Upon occasion, he would be joined by his wife, Susan. Susan never really stayed with us. She had been the head housekeeper at both Brimme House and the estate, so she usually wandered off to inspect the state of the manor. Sometimes she would give the staff quite a start as she materialized through the stone walls, moving from room to room.

Charles paid little attention and honed straight in on his overstuffed leather chair. Each time, he seemed contented that things were still in their proper places. Most of the ghosts of Christmas were really just being observant to the passage of time. They wanted to see what was changing around them. I could easily understand their curiosity.

I sat in the quiet of the room for a short time, watching the hearth's warm glow light the space, before the first apparition began to appear. As expected, it was Charles. He always liked to be early. A small startled screech through the wall signaled that Susan had made the trip down from the cemetery with him. It was pleasant to know that she had come down. She was a nice lady.

Charles's image materialized before my eyes and softly smiled at me. He appeared pleased to see me. I was definitely pleased to see him. I smiled and quietly greeted my oldest friend. Quick and quiet, I filled him in on all the recent happenings of his family. It seemed to take longer than expected, seeing that we had not talked since before I left for America. He was pleased for the update and nodded as each new piece of information was added to the story. His little family was large and wealthy and a power of their own these days. He seemed to give off that feeling that things had been accomplished. It was a new sensation for me. Usually, he just seemed pleased by the news. This occasion he seemed pleased and content. That sensation made my spine twitch.

As I finished my dissertation on Charles's family, he calmly folded his hands in his lap, as he had done so often when he was alive. Once situated, he turned his head toward the window. Shimmering in the window was a vision of the most beautiful woman. I caught my breath as she solidified into form. She was never a guaranteed participant in these gatherings, so seeing her always made me very excited. I tried to calm myself as quickly as I could.

"Hello, Mother. You look lovely."

My mother's shimmering image smiled warmly. She always managed to seem happy. Sometimes there was a melancholy in it, but it was still happy. I knew she had been listening, so I started in on what had transpired in my own life. She listened intently, constantly giving off the sensation of love. She always had that sensation, no matter the topic of conversation. She was my mother. I quickly looked about as I finished telling her about my life.

"Did Father not come down the hill with you this year?"

She smiled a strangely giddy smile and pointed her slender finger toward the stacks at the far end of the large room. It was a section of the study that was seldom used in current days. It contained volumes of histories and lineages of different families. It seemed I knew enough about history these days as not to want to venture in there.

Now that I was oriented in that direction, I could sense the rustling. It lasted several seconds before Father appeared. It was Father, and he had Grandfather in tow. They came out of the stacks, two massive, leather-bound books floating in front of them. The men and their books casually floated across the room to where I was seated and paused. My Grandfather smiled broadly at me. My father pointed down at the books as they settled on the floor by my feet. Grandfather had a great, mischievous smile, and Father had that look that said, "This is the business." Or was that, "this is the answer to the business?"

I turned my gaze to the books at my feet. The title of the top book was *The Great Dukes of Britain: Alliances, Wealth, and Family Condition with the Crown.* I smiled broadly, thick enamel fangs glinting in the hearth light. These two long-dead codgers knew exactly what was going on in my world. I could only assume that the answer to my situation with the Bennett family lay in those books. I looked back up at my two ghostly conspirators, both still holding their original expressions, and nodded thankfully. They both looked appreciative and then mellowed.

I looked about the room at each of my guests and then settled into my chair to explain the situation at hand to those not in the know. Mother seemed very happy that I had found a peace with the Enfield Trust. Charles seemed very unhappy that I had been gunned down in Central Park. Everyone seemed pleased that Effie had remedied the situation. She glowed a bit brighter as I regaled my guests with her part of the story.

Then, as long as I had waited, and as grand as it had been, it was done. Each one in turn smiled, nodded, and shimmered off into the mist. Father gave me that strong look that said, "You are my daughter," and pointed toward the books once more. For some strange reason I could feel Grandfather's mischief in the room for another good half hour or so. It seemed that he was both a businessman and a prankster. I guess you just never know about people.

I didn't see how the solution to my problems with the Bennett family could really be in those books, but the ghosts that brought them would not steer me wrong. Somewhere in their passages was a weapon, a piece of information that would do damage to the Bennetts. I could sense that I had some reading to do in the coming days. Things had been nicely quiet lately, so there was time for reading.

I relaxed into the chair and looked out on the hearth. The crackling fire in its chamber sent shimmers of light throughout the entire study. In the open space of the great room I could see streams of colored energy swirling about a point in the air. The wisps of the void coalesced into a small current of power. I could feel the tingle of a primal energy run down my breast bone as Effie twisted things about.

"Effie, you aren't planning on blowing up the study, are you?"

The words, "No, I'm just making pretty lights" ran through my mind, and I calmed. I sat and pondered how the books were going to help me away from my deep seated desire to just be about killing all of the Bennetts. It would all become clearer later on, I guessed. For now, I was just happy.

CHAPTER 22

Spring came to the Grey Estate and I decided to put off for a time both my new reading assignment and the quest to find another vampire. The Bennetts hadn't reared their ugly heads in a time, and I knew Zoe was up north somewhere, so it seemed a time for other things.

I had taken to spending time with Patrick Wyndell since I had come home to London. The younger of the current Wyndell generation, and by far the most streetwise, he had come to be a nice change of pace for me. Patrick was younger than Tracey and possessed the stamina of youth. I did enjoy his vigorous nature greatly. He made me want other things out of existence. That hadn't happened to me in quite some time.

As men go, he was tall and possessed the rugged features of his long-removed grandfather, Charles. He was sturdy and sure on his feet. Dark hair and shadowy eyes set above a square jaw made him quite easy to look at. I fancied in just taking him at surface sexiness, because when I looked deeper, I could see so many of his predecessors in him.

He possessed most all of the good qualities of his lineage. They were all of the qualities that his brother Tracey lacked. Tracey was a fine businessman and helmed the corporation in good fashion, but Patrick was Gregory's real successor.

My time out in public with Patrick was casual enough. We did what the rich people do. I strolled with him about town and he bought me pretty things. We took tea on High Street, as was always the fashion of London society. We looked upon the works of long dead people that hung in the galleries scattered across the city. We took in the symphony. He really was good company.

Patrick Wyndell had married very early in life and the couple had produced three children. They were two girls and a boy: Wendy, May, and Steven. They were quite well behaved. Each of them possessed that indescribable "it" factor that successful Wyndells possessed. Patrick's wife had succumbed to a fever several years back, leaving him to be a single father. Initially it distracted him, but as Wyndell men do, he overcame it.

I think it might have been that lone father image that initially drew me to him. He had the unshakable perseverance of my own father. His children were well-adjusted and showed none of the dysfunction of a broken household. I could feel all of the similarities of my own childhood in them. It was somehow emotionally quieting.

Effie had taken to Patrick in a way she had not done with other humans. I didn't know why, but I just assumed it was a good thing at the time. (Forgetting about my little friend's ability to transcend the normal threads of time and space, I didn't take the omen for what it was. I have not since made that misstep.)

Patrick and I had been in the sack with each other for the better part of a year, and I had taken to him in a way that I had taken to no one, save Antonio. The swelling sensation that his presence produced in me was at odds with my demonic nature. I knew that I hadn't known him long enough to have fallen in love with him, but there it was. Somehow, I had mistakenly fallen in love with a human.

I didn't think that I was any longer capable of love. When I had fallen in love with Antonio, I was still a silly human girl. I was young and looking for a man to sweep me off my feet. Brother, was that a mistake! I fell madly in love and received the gift of demonic eternity. Now, I was apparently falling in love once again. What gift could this possibly bring me? History seemed to be yelling that nothing good was coming.

For his part in this little romance story, Patrick was not naïve. He knew that I was a vampire. He had expounded to his father one evening about the wonderful young woman he had met, and my old cagey friend Gregory set him straight in rapid fashion. Strangely, the information didn't put Patrick out in the least. Somehow he seemed to embrace the whole thing. Seeing the immediate acceptance, Gregory led Patrick to the seldom-used section of his library and set him to reading. His education came on quickly and he was up to speed in no time.

What I found to be the strangest of it all was that as he learned, his opinion devolved. The more he learned about my condition, the more that he seemed to see me as just anyone else in the world. I wasn't a vampire, or an heiress, or a noble lady … I was just Sara. The more that I became Sara, the more I fell in love with Patrick.

Deep down in the dark places of our minds, we both knew that nothing was to come of the relationship. There was simply no way that a human and a vampire could have any kind of emotional relationship that wasn't bound to end terribly. However, in both of our frontal lobes, neither one of us cared much.

I was a 288-year-old vampire who was in love with a 25-year-old father of three. Not only that, but he was a member of the family that I had spent my entire demonic existence looking out for. There really was something Shakespearean about it all.

It was easy to tell from Patrick's actions that he was in it for the long haul. He, too, had become lost in the situation. He spent his time with me as if it was the end and nothing was to ever come again when it was over. It was his Wyndell street smarts turned inward toward the topic of emotion.

Patrick had taken to spending the weekends at the Grey Estate. He would bring out his children and let them loose to do what children do. His children would cause mischief, and we would spend our time wrapped up in each other. The Grey Estate had always been a playground for Wyndell children, and Patrick embraced that the same as the rest had done. It was easy to keep them occupied, which left ample time for Patrick and me. My time with Patrick was intoxicating. When each weekend would come to an end, it would seem as if it had only lasted minutes.

Those misguided days in the spring of 1921 were some of the happiest days I have ever had. It was affirmation that anything was truly possible in this world. One just needed to be open to the possibilities for good things to happen. They were happy days but also short-lived.

Unlike most problems that come to me wrapped in shadows and darkness, my newest problem came to me in public on a sunny afternoon. In retrospect, it seemed so utterly out of place that I should have been prepared for it, but no vampire expects trouble in the middle of a sunshiny spring day. Once again, I let my guard down and it cost me dearly.

Patrick's nanny had the children preoccupied, so the two of us snuck off to the city for the afternoon. Mayfair was always quite nice in the spring. That area of London sandwiched between Hyde Park and Green Park is a well-heeled piece of ground. On this particular day we had landed ourselves at the Dorchester. I enjoyed the opulence of the establishment. The Dorchester had a lovely view of Hyde Park and a fabulous afternoon tea service. Discerning people from the upper crust of society could often be seen partaking in the tea. Patrick and I had been there on several occasions.

On days when the weather wasn't on the dreary side, as many in London tend to be, we would stroll down Park Lane and walk the gardens at Buckingham Palace. Using the back gates to the secluded gardens was one of the perks of nobility. It was one of the very few parts of being at court that I actually didn't despise. Patrick always acted like we had just broken into the place. He could be shifty. I found it all somewhat amusing. Being from a wealthy family that happened to have a member on the king's private council, the crown knew exactly when he came and went. From the crown's point of view, money was to be watched over.

The plan on this particular day was to do the same as we had in the past. We were going to partake in the tea and then casually stroll down the street to the palace for some quiet time. It had all gone to plan through the end of tea. Patrick had been in an especially giddy mood and set out taking the mickey out of our attendant. It was all in jest. Our young attendant was the good-spirited sort. The whole tea interval was laughter and lighthearted banter.

We had paused in the salon and decided that the sun over Hyde Park looked too inviting to pass. We would first make a quick loop around the Reformer's Tree and up to Speaker's Corner. I had always liked that Speaker's Corner existed. For a little corner in a big lawn, in a single city on earth, Speaker's Corner would see the likes of Karl Marx, Lenin, Kwame Nkrumah, and Mr. Orwell. They all took their turn on the soap box, sputtering out what they considered to be the truth of things. As we exited the Dorchester, I was sure that the Corner would be a whirlwind of activity on such a nice day.

Patrick and I crossed Park Lane, Patrick on the outside to shield me from the rush of oncoming motorists, as gentlemen did in those days, and we headed for the park. Once across, we made our way down Park Lane and entered the park by the fountain. The day was bright and the park was quite pleasant in the spring splendor.

Numerous couples roamed about the park, conversing and taking in the views. Other couples could be seen lounging on blankets or seated on the scattered, shaded benches. I drew a deep breath and pulled the scent of spring into my lungs. Patrick smiled broadly as he adjusted his arm in mine. The day was perfect, everything in the city was wonderful, and life had finally become blissful. In that specific moment, I wanted nothing. I could have stayed that way forever and I would have been happy with every second that would come.

We had no more than crossed the broad walk that led to the path leading toward the Reformer's Tree when a man casually wandered up next to us. He was no different than anyone else out, taking in the views and in a pleasant mood. As he reached us, he tipped his hat to say hello as gentlemen are taught to do. Patrick reciprocated and I said hello.

Without missing stride or altering expression, the man pulled a pistol from his pocket and fired twice. A large, tin-can-shaped sound suppressor attached to the end of the barrel deadened the revolver's retort all but completely. Two bullets expelled from the weapon and thudded into Patrick's chest. The rounds punched through his chest and exited out his back without fanfare.

"An early birthday present from the Bennett family," the man said with a measured tone. Patrick's body collapsed onto the path as the gunman turned on his heels and headed back the way he had come.

I could literally feel the life leaving Patrick as his body hit the grassy lawn next to the path. I was shell-shocked. I couldn't seem to move. I really didn't even know what had just happened. I couldn't think. All I could do was stand there and feel the life as it left Patrick's body.

They had blindsided me! They had caught me out of my wits again. I had let the damned Bennett family get the better of me a second time. And this time, they had done it well. They had attacked me, out in public, with loads of bystanders. How could I react? What could I do? How in the world could I explain what had just happened?

I should have been reacting, fighting back, but I couldn't. I couldn't form a solid thought. All I could do was feel Patrick shuffling off his mortal coil. I was so completely beyond reaction. I was vapor locked, but the amulet was not. She had also missed the whole thing coming, and I think she was embarrassed. A blue thump of light emanated from the jewel, which was mostly concealed by my dress. The gunman clutched his chest and began to twitch and shake as he hit the ground. People in the park seemed to notice the gunman's throes of pain and ignore Patrick lying by the path. The numerous couples in the park headed toward the gunman to see what had befallen him.

About that time, Patrick stood and turned toward the park entrance. My eyes went wide as I saw blood still flowing from the holes in his chest. I do remember a loud, clear, young voice talking in my head.

"You need to walk out of the park now. I am not going to kill the man with the gun until the two of you are away. But Patrick only has moments of life left in him. You need to leave now. Now!"

I did as Effie instructed without thinking. Effie animated Patrick's body along next to me as if he were perfectly fine. The blood that had been flowing from the large caliber holes in his body had reversed its flow. What blood he had available was now basically all back in his body, though I could still feel his life force draining away.

We walked straight for the front of the Dorchester, where the valet saw us approaching and retrieved our car. Effie smoothly walked Patrick around and sat him in the car as I thanked the valet and climbed behind the wheel. I made my way through the traffic as Effie held onto Patrick and made the gunman suffer. I pulled my car into a secluded spot I knew of around the backside of Wigmore Hall. I had been to the playhouse several times and remembered its well-secluded back area.

Pulling the park break on the roadster, I turned my attention to Patrick. He was turning ashen. I could feel that he had all but given up the fight for life. He was now well -on toward the world of the dead. I couldn't lose Patrick. I didn't know how I would exist without him in my life. I didn't know how to fix humans. I knew how to kill them well enough, but healing them was beyond me. I had read numerous medical texts, but I'd never thought I would need to use the information. I didn't know how to be a surgeon. But—I did know—how to save him.

"Patrick, can you hear me?"

"Yes." The word came out weak and low, but it was there.

"Do you want to stay here with me, Patrick?"

There was a long pause before he responded. I thought for a split second that he had passed on.

"Yes, please."

"Patrick, are you sure that you want to stay with me?"

"Yes, please."

And it was done.

I slammed my fangs down into the inside of his wrist and took a long pull of blood. Patrick's blood came out thick and pungent. It tasted like death. I swallowed it as best as I could. It was foul. Without missing a beat I drew a fang across my own wrist and let my blood fall into Patrick's semi-open mouth. I ramped up my heartbeat as the blood gushed out of the gash in my wrist. Several seconds on, with blood full in his mouth and spilling over the sides of his lips, he swallowed.

As close as Patrick has been to death, it took only seconds before the demonic spark of lightning flashed. Both eyes rolled full back into his head. He was truly on his way to a new and different land now.

I shook off my blood flow and reached over to hold my lover as he transcended death. Holding Patrick as he moved on, I wondered if that was how I had looked as I made my way past death's door. Had I taken it as gracefully as he had? As Antonio was both my maker and my lover, was I now the same to Patrick?

"What have I done, Effie?"

"You did what needed doing," Effie said in a calm and reassuring tone. "Now, you need to get him to the estate before the change takes hold."

She was definitely right about that. I knew she was right. I let Patrick's head rest on the seat and adjusted myself back into a driving position. Brake off, ignition on, gas applied, and we were off. I drove north in a blur. What had I done?

CHAPTER 23

We had solidly moved into day four of waiting before Patrick started to stir. From every sensation that I could pull through the walls of the dungeon, he appeared to be in the same state of confusion that I had been in when I was turned. His great apprehension was almost soaking through the walls of the whole estate.

I had been worried after the initial encounter that I had once again done something wrong. One needs to get the initial mental connection quite sound or the victim will not move past the fact that they have just died. It is best that they do not grasp onto the fact that they have died until after they have moved past death. A current realization will usually send them mental in a way you can't fix. A couple times before I have tried this stunt, so I know of what I speak. Those episodes didn't end well, and I have no intentions of discussing them here.

It took Patrick some time to actually get to his feet, wander about the cell, realize the door was open, and start down the hallway toward the lone candle burning in the distance. I have to say that even though I could tell he was boiling inside, he looked very calm as he approached the coach at the end of the hall. His lingering human emotions were still trying to keep him in control of the situation. Oh, how sadly he was mistaken this time.

I gave the man a quick visual inspection from where I sat. His eyes were wild, but otherwise he looked pretty good. His hair was all about the place and his clothes were about half on as well. He had ripped his shirt open at some point, probably to look at the bullet holes. The two slug holes in his chest had healed nicely during the transition. He looked sturdy, solid in an almost unnatural way. It was the way Antonio had first looked to me so many long years ago. Some long dead memories started to stir in the depths of my heart, but I quickly put a stop to them.

Knowing Patrick well, I would think he looked a good five years younger than he really was. That was nice. It was good that he got a little something out of his deal with the devil. Patrick stood pensively for several moments; the ache had to be all-consuming from the look in his eyes. It was probably time to start.

"Good morning, love. You look like you've had a long night." I spoke in words so quiet that even the dead could barely hear me. Patrick heard me fine. The initial change of senses leaves everything acutely adjusted.

"How long did I … sleep?" It came out as a low growl. That wasn't good, yet it wasn't unexpected.

"Just on four days now. I was beginning to wonder if you were going to stir."

"What happened to me? What am I now? Why do I feel this way?"

"Right now, you are at the beginning of a transitory phase in your existence. You are—"

"YES! WHAT AM I?!"

"The word I was searching for was revenant."

He stared at me.

"It means a reanimated corpse."

"I KNOW WHAT IT MEANS!" He looked like he really wanted to kill someone, and I was the only one in the room. That certainly wasn't good.

"Relax just a bit, Patrick. Have a drink." I pointed at the large goblets on the table next to where he was standing. He scooped up the first one and drank it like he had been lost in the desert, which in a sense wasn't far off the mark. I had been a bit kinder to him than my maker had been to me. My graciousness showed immediately on his face as he pulled the cup back.

Patrick emptied the large vessel and then ran his finger around the inside to inspect its contents. Apparently, his pain had ebbed just enough to make him sensible.

"All right, the thick part was blood. It tasted like human blood, not that I know what human blood tastes like. What was the other?"

I smiled broadly. If I ever make another vampire, I am going to remember that it pays to teach them about themselves first. He had remembered all his teachings well. Now, he was utilizing that knowledge in a very personal way.

I pointed at the second large vessel on the table and he snatched it. As he drank, I quietly explained that his body was changing to become more demon and less human. His bones were stiffening, his trademark fangs were growing out, and all his organs were shifting and adjusting as needed. All of these alterations required basic human building blocks; the most important of them was calcium. The very deep-seated pain he was feeling was his body changing. The relief he sensed was calcium from the milk that was mixed with the blood. The calcium was like opium for the pain.

I could tell Patrick was taking everything in. Even with the gulping sound of liquid from the goblet, he was intently listening. So, I continued to speak.

I explained to him that way back deep in time our ancestors used to eat animal bones to get their fix. That and actions ten times more gruesome were used. At some point, some thinking vampire realized what was happening and attempted to solve the problem with milk. It was a magnificent solution for the transition step. The pain and loss created by the transition step drove many of our kind to do horrid things. The stories of old had truth in them, as he could now tell.

The more he drank and listened, the more he calmed. As the pain momentarily ebbed, the growl changed into speech. His natural tone had deepened with death. It gave him a menacing presence. I could just tell that if he survived, he was going to be a great killer.

I pointed toward a bunched-up cloth on the table that hid another pitcher. He reached for this one in a calmer fashion. He was learning.

"How well can you see?"

"I can see everything in the room as if it were midday. From the dust in the corners to the worn upholstery of your settee, I see quite well."

"How well can you hear?"

"Considering you are making all but no noise, I'd say I can hear fine as well. I have been listening to the conversations of your staff at the other end of the manor."

"Hmm, good. When I was in your position, I listened to a mouse that scurried about in a wall at the far end of Antonio's mansion. It, too, was disconcerting at first."

"I agree."

I smiled broadly again. He had come back around to his senses. He had realized that the blood was blood in as quick a time as I had. He had listened to instruction well. There was only one thing left for the first day's testing.

"Before we finish up with day one, I need to know one thing: what are you?"

"What do you mean? You made me."

"You need to say it, out loud. It takes saying it for some to really have it hit home."

"I am a vampire."

He said it so matter-of-factly that we could have been discussing tapestries in the hall upstairs. That was good but odd. Anyway, he had passed the tests. I let him finish his drink and escorted him back to bed.

With his huge blood belly to calm him, Patrick slept for another two days. That was a good thing. I hadn't been able to manage that much time when I made the transition. He would come out of it better if he adjusted fast.

Those two days and the four days before them had given me time to deal with some unpleasant business—namely, the sticky business of killing off Patrick Wyndell for real. That was much more of a challenge than it had been back in the day. The dirty, downtrodden, rat-infested London of the 1650s lost people on a daily basis and no one really cared. This cleaner, modernized, industrial London of the 1920s was a different animal. Scotland Yard had come of age. Dead people needed to be accounted for. Stories needed to be checked and confirmed to be true. All the people involved needed to be questioned. What that really meant was that people needed to be paid off. Lies needed to be told.

Said lies then needed to be confirmed. Constables and families needed to be placated and sent off grieving.

I found it good at this point that I still kept up quiet relations with one or two unsavory characters from down dockside way. Master Robert James was an unsavory sort that could have given any of the rest a merry run for their silver. He was as untrustworthy a sort as money could acquire, and I paid out a lot of money. He was also known to the bobbies of the day, which made his word acceptable.

Master Robert loosened himself up a section of bridge rail over the Thames and waited for just the right moment. Opportunity right, he launched a human-sized sack over the side. A grand performance for the passersby and numerous shouts for the bobbies produced a scene worthy of the stage. The Scotland Yard lads appeared after the street patrols had done the beginning investigation and went about questioning everyone again. Master Robert earned his money.

Since bodies seldom ever wash back up from the river, not finding a body for Patrick was of no consequence to the officers of the day. The suspects were none. The whole affair seemed a simple matter of bad luck. A wallet was found on the bank a day later, confirming Patrick's identity. A much grieving family was notified of the affair. The children were gratefully accepted in by one of their aunts and smothered with attention. A grieving Lady Alcott, the woman he had been seeing for some months, took the news as expected. It was all a tragic loss.

On or around day five of the whole performance, I received a visit from a now very-aged Gregory Wyndell. He really seemed put-out with me this time. I couldn't really blame him; he had the right to be. We sat, and I explained the whole thing to Patrick's father in a straightforward manner. I explained the shootout with the mysterious representative of the Bennett family. Then I more cautiously explained what came after. Gregory absorbed the whole affair and seemed to gain strength from it. He asked what was to become of Patrick. I told him that he would have the same opportunity to survive that I had been granted. If he was meant to survive, then he would survive. The same as if he were still a human man.

Gregory changed tack and asked what was to become of this mystery man. I explained that the mystery man was deceased, and at some point in the very near future, when Patrick was not consuming my time, I was going to expend every effort to destroying that whole family. That, as much as anything else, seemed to bring the old man peace. He asked where Patrick was to be sent. I told Gregory that America was a new land of plenty, and one could do very well there.

We discussed some friendlier things for a time. We had traveled many roads together. Then, feeling finished, Gregory headed back to his mansion toward the south. Somehow I could sense that that was the last time I would see my old friend. As I watched him depart, I desperately hoped he wasn't disappointed in me here at the end of our friendship.

With the family officially handled, I returned my attention to the fledgling vampire in my dungeon. When Patrick rose for the second time, he was much more human. That made me happy. The transition could be so hard to handle. A great many didn't handle it as well as he was.

We sat and discussed many things during our second meeting. He was great at absorbing knowledge. I gave him the same intensely painful experience with the cross that Antonio had given me. The searing sound of his dead skin from its impact with the crucifix took me all the way back to my own beginnings. I wondered if it had done the same thing to Antonio.

Unhappy, but otherwise informed, Patrick took the lesson for what it was. He needed to know the boundaries before he reached them. I explained that he could go to church; he just couldn't touch anything while he was there. It was a mandatory lesson for a demon to learn.

Being a well-built, streetwise man, I didn't see the need to actually teach Patrick how to kill people. Men took naturally to that type of business. I did explain how to do it though, how to cut across the jugular of the neck with a knife until his fangs came in full. Since the actual act of killing was different for every vampire, I explained to him that he would simply figure it out as he went.

To make sure that he survived long enough to learn the initial lessons, I told him that he would be leaving England. He would go somewhere where no one knew him and where he could become whoever he was to become. To help him on his way, he would be given some assistance. A man named Randolph would meet him in America and teach him the remainder of his lessons. It was expressly stated that Randolph was his teacher and never ever to be considered expendable. If Randolph was expendable, then so was Patrick. He vowed not to kill him. He was so much like Antonio. It had to be a male thing.

When all the lessons were parceled out and Patrick had absorbed all that he would learn from the House of Grey, he was given an old pair of glasses and escorted out the back door of the manor and into the meadows. The fresh air of the back meadows was as good a reprieve from the dankness of the dungeon as anything to date. We walked for a while and discussed the end of things.

"How do you like your new, gray world?"

"I always wondered how you saw the world. I guess that now I have my answer."

"When you settle in America, you will need to find a pair of spectacles that aren't so old-fashioned. Don't lose them, or you will lose your night vision. Your night vision is a tool you will most definitely need."

"I will be diligent in holding onto them."

"That's a good boy. Trust me, after a century or so, it won't look so bad."

"If you say so. By the way, how am I going to get to America?"

"When we return to the manor, you will be introduced to a fellow named Cliff Stedman. He will escort you to America and make sure that you arrive at Randolph's door in serviceable condition."

"He knows that I am a vampire?"

"Yes. I know, you know, he knows, Randolph knows, and your father, Gregory, knows. That is the sum total of humans and vampires that know Patrick Wyndell still walks this earth. By the time that you reach America, Patrick Wyndell will no longer exist. You will become someone new. It is the way of things."

"I understand. Why does my father know?"

"Because he is my very old and dear friend. I don't mislead my friends."

"That is good to know."

"It's a lesson that you might want to learn when you get back to the having friends stage."

"I'll consider it."

"There is one more thing for you to seriously consider during your boat ride. The only two vampires who know that a vampire can walk around during the day are standing right here, right now. It is, in my opinion, the penultimate piece of camouflage that we possess. The humans don't know, the vampires don't know, and we two are safer because of it. If I even remotely hear of gossip that this information is spreading, I will kill YOU as sure as you are standing here right now. If it comes down to you or me, YOU are a dead man! Am I perfectly clear?"

"Yes."

"Are you very sure about that?"

"Yes, ma'am."

"Good boy."

We turned and made our way back to the manor. Once at the back door, I introduced Patrick to Cliff, and the two of them promptly disappeared in a motor coach. I made my way into the house and up to my bedchamber. I was exhausted. I needed to sleep for a while to put things right.

Patrick had been my love. He was not the great love of my life, but he was definitely the next one in line for the job. Sadly, once he was shot he ceased to be that. Well, kind of. He was still one of my very special loves. That would always be so. But, the transition into a demon made him something else complete. Now, he was a predator. Now he was more ruthless. No less Patrick, but also somehow more. That required the same standoffishness that I had received from Antonio when I was turned. It was the way it was. The newly transformed need time. They needed time to come back to themselves. Patrick would be fine. I could just sense it.

CHAPTER 24

Time passed by. I slept a great deal. It wasn't that making new vampires was particularly exhausting; I was more emotionally than physically spent. I had been dealing with so many new things that I was emotionally at ends. Normally, I would compartmentalize things and deal with them one by one. Vampires are extremely good at compartmentalizing. We seem to just develop a knack for dealing with the most important things first. It's a survival trait, I think.

I had been handling things the human way for a while, before and after Patrick's run of bad luck, and it had taken a toll on me. So, stress led to melancholy, and melancholy led to sleep.

Even in my nocturnal funk, I could hear the whispers about the manor. The staff seemed concerned about my constant withdrawal. I could see their point, I guess. It was odd behavior for a human. It was odd behavior for a vampire, too. They even called in a physician at one point, but I dismissed him immediately. It would have been problematic to let him do his examination.

Looking back upon it now, I can see where 1929 was one of those times in history that would draw me away from complete lucidity. The truth is that I wasn't completely out of it, I just slept a lot. I was passing time. I had been very active in the years leading up to 1929, and I was just taking some time off. That was a good thing for everyone concerned, especially me.

America had been whirling along like a dervish for years now. Its economy was growing bigger and stronger with every passing year. Business sprang up seemingly out of the weeds. There was prosperity everywhere one looked. It was just oozing out of the cracks of the whole country.

It was also flash. It didn't really exist. All of the money hedgers kept telling me and the Wyndell boys that it wasn't real and it surely couldn't last. We all agreed, but no one could put a finger on what the timeline might be. The hedgers seemed to predict it would go the way of a ship caught in a gale. I tended to agree. You could just smell it coming at you, like a foul salt tide. One thing that Father had taught me right from the beginning was DO NOT work on credit. Credit was your sure downfall. Being responsible to others left them in charge. Credit was evil. Credit was even more evil than me. That one lesson had worked to make me wealthy beyond measure. I pounded that thinking into the Wyndell family until it became their standard as well. With it, they also became wealthy to the fullest.

In the mid-1920s, everyone and their brother was chasing after the illusion of easy credit. Businesses were beginning from nothing and expanding to unrealistic heights as quickly as was possible. The great economic illusion seemed to have all in its grasp—well, all save for Grey's Cargo.

I had started having long conversations with Tracey back in 1924. It took a little work to get him to see beyond the curtain, but once he did, he was fully on board. In a series of moves that left most of the corporation confused, Grey's Cargo began to consolidate. When every other business in the first world was expanding, we were pulling back. This drew major flak from the business world and much attention from places like the crown.

Our very first move was to notify every business that utilized our services that we were not a credit-granting agency. One would need to pay for service when it was rendered, or go elsewhere. That did not sit well with a great many clients. That was too bad. We weren't working for nothing.

Next we began to look at the structure of the corporation as a whole. Somehow, Grey's Cargo had become the 1920s version of the East India Company. I mean, we were everywhere. We had developed a foothold in so many little local routes that we did almost everything for almost everyone. If you added in my private railroad holdings in America and the corporate railroad holdings in Europe, our company probably did everything.

The reality of a good profitable company is thus: core markets produce core profits, external markets produce auxiliary profits, and no business can exist by modeling auxiliary profit as core profit. If you confused your wheat from your chaff, you were all done in business. I didn't want to survive in whatever this new landscape was to be, I wanted to thrive. So next came an eye to all the extemporaneous parts of the corporation. Tracey laid down a plan to the board to quietly dispose of some of the corporation's smaller pieces at a profit. I helped him with a plan to vastly increase the corporation's liquid assets, which was quietly implemented by Tracey's masterful business hands.

Over these years I had come to like Tracey Wyndell greatly. I decided that my original vision of him was misplaced. He had proven himself to be a supreme leader of the corporation. He possessed the *"it"* thing that all of the great Wyndell men possessed. I think it was street smarts mixed with generations of education that made him such a lethal business administrator. The smooth, casual demeanor that had annoyed me so greatly upon our first meeting was a thing of beauty when applied to business clients or a skeptical corporate board. He was the Cheshire cat of shipping, and he knew how to go about getting exactly what he wanted.

The two of us had managed to streamline the massive corporation into an agile, sturdy thing of beauty. I was so pleased by the end result that I stepped back to consider other things. All the work led to all the sleeping, I think. I used to sleep a great deal when I personally ran the business. That return to work took something out of me. I was pretty rested and the corporation was looking in fine form. I stopped to look around a bit and found that many things were transpiring in the world.

In January a telephone connection had been made between the Netherlands and the West Indies. It hardly seemed possible to me that such a thing could even happen. The world was getting more interconnected all the time. A pact was signed between Romania,

Poland, Latvia, Estonia, and Russia. That little piece of paper would come to raise its ugly head in years to come.

Out in Chicago, where Patrick was now residing, the St. Valentine's Day massacre killed off a bunch of gangsters. That was fine with me. America had a lot of gangsters.

The year 1929 saw the first telephone installed in the White House. Herbert Hoover would get to be the first telephoning president.

In March the first direct England-to-India plane flight took place. It took almost two days to get there. It seemed a feat that would go unmatched at the time. I still hadn't boarded an airplane at that point. I had wanted to several times, but I didn't really have anywhere that I needed to go. I was greatly enjoying driving, so the airplane seemed like it could wait. However, the idea of flying halfway around the world did definitely appeal to me. Oh, yes it did.

My friends down at the Vatican saw their land become a sovereign state. I received a pleasant correspondence from the newest cardinal to take over the reins of the historical and secret archives after they internalized. He stated that I was still welcome. That was always good news. Shortly after that, Russia signed an accord with the Vatican. Apparently they were full ready to act as their own country. Shortly after that, they signed another with Mexico.

Germany decided to renege on paying its World War I debt. I wasn't shocked; their economy was still all bollixed up. However, they did manage to get the Graf zeppelin up on an around-the- world flight.

Turkey and Persia decided to get along. That was nice, since they border each other. On September 3, the New York Dow Jones Stock Exchange hits a record high of 381.17. The country of Yugoslavia was founded out of the kingdoms of Serbs, Croats, and Slovenes.

On October 24, Black Thursday hit the American economy. The Dow plummeted 13 percent down to 260.64, and all of the illusion of good times officially ended. This was just the start of a worldwide economic downturn that would crash industrial fortunes and national economies alike. In '29 it just seemed like a disaster. The true devastation was to follow.

Tracey sat at the head of a full board meeting with complete vindication on his face. The board members nodded their heads like automatons as he outlined the cuts that were still to come. We both could see the winds of change blowing our way, but I looked upon them much more personally.

For some eighteen years of human life, I had been a semi-normal human girl. My father had money, but we lived in line with the other families of the day. He was never a person to show off his means, unless there was something to be gained from it. From the point where I died and came into my title, I have lived my life as an earl should. I have been enjoying my wealth for almost three centuries. I really had no interest in going back to the modest way of living I had grown up with. I mean none at all. I could see that we had put the corporation in a good place to survive and even thrive during the downturn that was to come, but that was only if it wasn't severe and long lasting. Unlike other corporations in 1929, Grey's Cargo had generated a vast cash reserve to exist on. What was better yet was that the corporation was actually designed to be compartmentalized. We had mothballed all of the less profitable pieces well before the downturn. Tracey had outlined to the board how the residual pieces would continue to be mothballed one at a time as the depressed economy lingered on, slowly pulling the corporation into the core business. He also explained that as the cash reserves became exhausted and exterior sections of the corporation were shut down, we would need less and less cash to survive.

Tracey's strategizing was most pleasing, but somehow it was also uncomforting. I had some comfort in the fact that a great deal of my personal wealth was liquid. My land holdings in England were titled lands granted by the crown, and they would continue to do what they do. If they stopped being fruitful, it would mean that everyone else's lands had also gone downhill. That was a situation that I would deal with when it came to be. I had to stay in good graces with the crown. As long as I did, I would be fine on that front. That didn't really seem an issue, as I had a better in with the crown than most other nobles.

As far as personal interests, there was the Grey Estate and my residence in New York City, along with a scattering of investment land parcels. I could easily dump all the peripheral pieces. That would work toward lightening the load, but at the same time, land barons were land barons for a reason. Land has an inherent value associated with it, because, as they say, they aren't making any more of it these days. That's as true a statement today as it was in 1929.

The thing I really needed to do was stay calm. I also needed to hope that Antonio's people kept hold of their good business senses. The original evil deal was still at the core of my business model. Our current European routes had all but been established around his needs. I had been made eternal so my business could see to the needs of his businesses. That was the original pact; since the day I died I have been doing this.

It was obvious to both Tracey and I that Antonio's businesses would need to significantly downsize to survive. It was the same thing that we had done to compete. The move would reduce the need for our services. Less shipping meant fewer ships, and we were already planning on part of the fleet going into hibernation. Once again, we fortunately already possessed space to pull up the fleet. For some it would be retrofit, and for some it would be the breaker's yard. The newer vessels would run strong.

Our plan basically hinged on the world economy not completely collapsing and Antonio's companies surviving at a 50 percent working load, at least. Both things seemed plausible to Tracey and me, though we would need to keep an iron grip on the rest of it. I had every intention of staying and doing just that.

This time of crisis was one of those things that led me to wondering if my time had passed. For centuries, I had wandered in and out of my little kingdom. I appeared and inserted my two cents worth of hot air and then let the Wyndells steer the kite wherever the winds were going to blow it. In the beginning I had had my hands tightly wrapped around the helm of the company. Now, in our corporate days, I was not really the director of affairs.

By the time that 1929 had come to the planet, it seemed that the business had outlived me. I came back to a place, almost unfamiliar, where the only person who knew of me was Tracey. I no longer possessed the command that my mere presence had generated in years past. Tracey occupied that position. It seemed that it really was his corporation now. I still owned all but complete interest in it, but it was definitely his entity.

I could see the writing on the wall at this point. This had been what I had wanted so many years ago when I had stepped away from the business. I had gotten what I wanted, but my human sense of need didn't like it now. I had taken my father's company, built an empire, and then handed it off to the Wyndell family to run. Now, they were running it just as if they owned it. As this realization sank into me, I thought that maybe it really was theirs at this point. It reawakened a seed deep down inside of me that wanted to part ways with the whole affair. If I sold out to the Wyndells, no one save the crown would be the wiser. I was obviously no longer an integral part of the management team.

As I rolled the thought around in my head, I decided to push it back down where it had come from. It wasn't the selling, it was the timing. Another lesson my father had taught me well: never sell at a loss.

Giving things away was for weaker people than the Grey family. Business is about one thing: making a profit. I would make a profit if I needed to kill off the whole of my competition to do it. That idea also surfaced. I rejected that quickly as well. That thought seemed to have been what had gotten all of Effie's other companions in trouble. I mean, she could crush them all, but how was that any different than warring or empire building? No, I would survive of my own accord. That was the way that things needed to be.

CHAPTER 25

The evening of September 7, 1940, I stood on the widow's walk above the high tower at the estate and watched the Surrey docks burn in the distance. I wanted to go inspect the damage personally, but the bombs falling from German planes were just too thick to be ignored. Operations Loge and Seeschlange had officially brought the blitz to London and the other industrialized cities of England.

The lads in the Royal Air Force were behind the ball in island defense. German Messerschmitt's were wreaking havoc as far as my demonic eyes could see. Word filtering out of the city said that the Thames had been turned into a path of burning and sunken ships. The docks of the London harbor were faring no better.

The German high command would go on to bomb old London town nonstop for some fifty-seven days. They assumed that they could break us. The British Empire doesn't fold that easily.

The bombs rained down on London. The bombs rained down on Bristol. The bombs rained down all across the aisle. It seemed that they would continue to fall like the winter rain drops in the meadows. It was all quite exasperating.

Just beforehand, it seemed that things were almost getting back to normal. The House of Grey, Grey's Cargo Corporation, and the Wyndell Family Group had all managed to ride out the Great Depression without significant trauma. To the contrary, when the world economy finally did take off again, there was a lack of competition that allowed the corporation to flourish. Being solvent left us all with the ability to take full advantage of a new global land of plenty. And, as would be expected, Tracey Wyndell attacked it.

The corporation was full sails when the turmoil over on the continent started. As was good business in times past, Grey's Cargo quickly turned arms transporter to respond to needs over on mainland Europe. Many countries needed arms to fend off the advance of Nazi Germany.

In a much undocumented piece of history, we were also now the primary arms transporter for our own country. The arms and munitions bought, begged, borrowed, and just given to England by a most generous American government were quietly transported across the Atlantic on Grey's vessels. Those shipments were made for free. Call it a gesture of good faith toward the crown. It's what the nobility does during times of war.

Now, we also moved materials for America. Those shipments were not as cheap as the above mentioned arrangement—for us or them. Grey's Cargo lost numerous ships during the great buildup of World War II. All of the shipping done for my longtime second home was done for a substantially reduced fee. We had to charge something, as cost needed to be covered.

The "Sleeping Giant," as Stalin had referred to America, literally came to life at the start of WWII. What would become the world's greatest economy sprang from its internalized slumber and began to produce goods on a truly massive scale. This meant great things for Sara Grey and her investments in the American business machine.

It is an almost universally agreed upon statement that war is good for business. That being said, world wars are definitely great for business. There are also definitely losses to be sustained along the way. Losing ships to the perils of the sea increases substantially as the perils in the seas increase. Cargo destroyed in the ports is also a problem to be dealt with. All situations that arise out of conflict are not for the weak to survive but to produce measureable profits for the strong. We at Grey's Cargo were a strong lot. The profits flowed in. The mothballed fleet came back to the black water, and the great company that my father had started charged forward. Much like her two countries of origin, the corporation's will was determined and unyielding. King George and the lads, along with some help from the colonies, were also taking it to the Germans. They were keeping the British end up.

As I stood that night and watched the dockside burn, illuminated on all sides by the flash of exploding bombs, I knew in my gut that it was only a temporary thing. With very limited exceptions, the people waging the war on both sides lacked the depth of history that I had. They had not sat through the numerous tides of war, or had been a side seat watcher to epic moments between countries. I could still remember the stink of death that came from World War I. I could remember the treaties of my youth that ended the Hundred Years' War. War was an inevitable piece of the social mechanism. The House of Grey had seen many wars. I was sure that there would be more wars to come after this great war was finished.

Being unable to move about freely due to the relentless stream of bombs falling from the sky, I stayed to my estate and did the best I could to spread my arms wide. Brimme House had been transformed into a way house for the displaced and injured citizens of the area. The corporation was doing all that it could to be patriotic. The Grey Estate poured out help to the people wherever it could find a need.

Though the damage to the city of London was extensive, and Grey's cargo all but needed a new place to conduct its affairs, the Grey Estate somehow managed to come away unbothered. This was completely due to the dark powers swirling around the amulet that hung from my neck. Effie and her limitless energy lay over the Grey Estate like a warm and comforting blanket. She would let the occasional bomb land in one of the far meadows—it kept up appearances. But no real harm came to the estate's many hectares. We sheltered many under her bomb-proof roof.

Effie really enjoyed the war. All of the energy from Hitler's explosives that poured down from the sky only made her stronger. She absorbed all the energy of the explosions around her and spilled it back out over the lands of the estate. Her crystal prison gave off such a radiant glow that I had been forced to wrap it in a heavy cloth—that way she wouldn't hurt my vision. I was amazed. She was giddy.

Effie's influence continuously spiraling around me kept me at peak level. I spent longer hours in my study, reaching out to needy and helping those in harm's way. It was like a blood overload, but all the time sleep was unnecessary, as was feeding. In current terms, it was like being on an ephedra buzz. It left me jittery.

At some point in all of it, Effie had pointed my mind toward the volumes that Father and Grandfather had laid at my feet many Christmases back. I had not forgotten about the Bennett family. I just hadn't had any time to deal with them. With bombs raining down all over and Effie pumping out the power, I could sense that it might just be the right time to invest myself in the affairs of the long-dead grand duke's family situation. My desire to cause them pain had not waned in the slightest degree. Why was it that people needed to keep after me? Why couldn't they just leave me be? I did more good than bad—wasn't that enough?

I made my way over to the large study table where the books still rested and moved them to my desk. Yes, it was time to turn an eye in that direction. So, the next morning, in the midst of temporary quiet, I made myself comfortable at my desk and proceeded to inspect my homework. The oversized leather chair that I was lounging in was a favorite of the many generations of Wyndell men who had used the desk for conducting business. I liked it because it reminded me of them. I was much more accustomed to the overstuffed leather chairs stationed at the front of the stacks, as the reading chairs were my natural place. But work requires a workspace, and big work requires a desk. This task was definitely a desk job. I liked work at times. I was good at puzzling out facts buried in reams of excess information. It's what had made me a formidable businesswoman back in the day.

One of the staff had appeared and deposited a large tea service on the other end of the desk at about the time I had finished adjusting myself in the chair. I have always liked tea. I find it soothing. It helps me to remain calm and view things in the right frame of mind. It's also inherently English. I don't really know why; it just is. I never really cared for tea that much when I was human, but I was so young then. I didn't take to it until I was about one hundred or so. Everyone in business seemed to drink tea. The crown drank tea. Hence, I learned to drink tea. I blend in as best as I can. Now, it's just one of those things that define me as still being English.

It's kind of funny, but there really aren't that many things that do define me anymore. I have traveled so much that I have lost most of my natural British character. I have spent so much time in America that I fully talk like an American. The London accent is still there a bit, but all the words are Yankee. The London girl seems to only come out when I swear. And I swear more than a lady should. I still wear my title like a warm coat, but I would say that's about that. Over the years I have blended into many societies and cultures and mellowed into just being a person. I'm not British. I'm not American. I'm not whatever. I'm just me. I like that.

Upon this particular morning, I was a focused me. There was steamy tea, bright sunshine through the windows, a good-sized study surface, and the smell of ancient knowledge. I pulled the first of the big tomes off the top and positioned it in front of me. *The Great Dukes of Britain: Alliances, Wealth, and Family Condition with the Crown* was a big and smelly old affair. Big, smelly, and old were usually good signs. Someone had written something important down and then left it to be forgotten about—or I was hoping that that was the case.

I flopped the big cover over and inspected the rich script. No calligraphy—that was very nice. At least it would be an easy read. The text was the thick, rolling script of the 1700s. The thing smelled much older than that. The cover also mentioned the 1700s. Maybe it just aged differently than other books.

I pulled up my tea and began to read the stories of the grand dukes. A great many of them were quite noble figures. All great fighting men, with their families going back to the Norman founding's. I read the stories, one after another. They were all fascinating. They were great men who had been given large responsibilities by the king, thanks to blood spilled in battle. It was a tale as old as time itself. The true and the brave reaped the rewards of their deeds. I could find great comfort in these men.

I read some eight or nine lineages before I came to the Bennett family. It seemed that in the beginning they were just earls, like I was.

That was interesting. The original Grand Duke Bennett, a crafty fellow named Percival Bennett, started out as Earl Bennett over in the outskirts of Lowestoft, down Peydon way.

This turned out to be exactly what I had been looking for. Young Percival was a boyhood friend of the king. They had attended military training together. Apparently, Percival's family was quite well-to-do in those days because of the fields of plenty that they controlled.

Somewhere along the way, it seems that Percival and his chum the king had struck a bargain. The actual grand duke presiding over their lands died and left behind no heir. The king, needing to appoint someone to the position, deeded to make a new duke. However, even in those days, earls did not become grand dukes. A new grand duke would come from a regular duke, or the son of a grand duke who had performed some exemplary service. Someone who had proved themselves to the crown would be rewarded. That was always the way— except in this case.

Our boy Percival struck a deal with the king. He would produce wealth for the crown equal to that of the old grand duke. They would assume the title, as long as they continued to produce for the crown on a set basis. A little more reading and that set basis turned out to be every twenty-five years.

So, crafty old Percival had bought himself a title. There was no great harm in that. It had happened on numerous occasions. As long as the family paid off the crown at the same rate as the other grand dukes, then they got to be grand dukes. It was an interesting point but hardly helpful information.

They occupied all the lands they needed to be out in front of the other families, even in today's money. They could continue their farming and harvesting and little town ways for some time before modern industrialization got the better of them. They were land barons, and land always produced.

I sat back in my big chair and pulled my legs up underneath me. The tea steamed away in my hand and worked at the edges of my mind. Being a land baron wasn't a new concept. I was a land baron. I had many tracts of land stretched out around the Northwich estate. It was what produced my own noble wealth. Well, to some degree it was.

I looked up and scanned the interior of the study as I pondered. The answer was in here, somewhere. Father was not wrong about such things. It really was too bad that ghosts couldn't talk. It would have made it all a lot simpler. Oh well, I would just keep at it.

It took about three minutes for my eyes to float over and inspect the second large volume they had brought me. I hadn't looked at it, as it was on the bottom. It was slightly larger and half again the thickness of the one in front of me. It possessed the industrial title *Land Grants and Acquisitions of the Noble Families.*

I pondered the title of this second behemoth for a bit. Percival was a land baron. Land barons needed large amounts of land to be prosperous. The book that Father had brought me was one of land grants and acquisitions. That was the thing with the tool. I just had to find it.

I grabbed the big monster and drug it over on top of the first. This time I didn't sit and study it; I went straight to the House of Bennett. I read it all feverishly, two complete times through, and then sat back and smiled as I drank my tea. The glint of my fangs could be seen in the black shiny surface of the liquid.

It turned out that old Percival was a right dodgy one after all— clever, I guess, but definitely dodgy. He had made his deal with the king and backed it with leased land. The original earl had apparently leased all of his lands from the reigning grand duke's family that Percival was now trying to replace. That was why he wanted to be duke, to get rid of the land leases. But he had struck a bad deal, because the land leases didn't go away. The original duke had registered the leases with the crown, apparently not completely trusting the arrangement.

So, as the big book said, after the king had granted the Bennett family *use* of the title, he made them come good on their land leases. Seems they weren't as good of boyhood friends as Percival had thought. The king had really stuck it to them. That I enjoyed greatly. The leases for the land needed to keep up the charade were also on a twenty-five-year cycle.

At this point, I snatched up pen and paper. I did the math three times to be sure. Even at modern prices, the land leases were cheap. They were collectively somewhere around a million pounds due the crown each cycle. That was quite low, even by the standards of the time. It was a lot of land.

The true genius in it all was the timing. After checking math another three times, it turned out that all the land leases came due in just over a year's time. The year after that, the allotment for the title was due.

The Bennett family had to buy their position in life from the crown in one year's time. Hmm. The Bennett family was old, but they were not as wealthy now as they were in Percival's day. Without those land leases to buoy them up, they would not survive. They would simply dissolve away.

The smile on my face broadened until it almost hurt. They had such a massive Achilles' heel that it was just hard to believe. I would crush their little fake family the truly old-fashioned way. I would simply take all of their lands and watch them turn to dust. I definitely had a better stance with the crown than they did.

Yes, that was the answer. It was so simple that it took the dead to figure it out. I was pleased. I was oh so pleased. I sat down my tea and turned my head toward the path that ran up toward the cemetery. The sun was shining through the windows and made the path look warm and inviting. I could almost hear the two schemers laughing in their caskets.

"Thank you, Father. And you, too, Grandfather. Thank you very much."

CHAPTER 26

It turns out that it was good to have a year to make my deal with the crown, because the war with Germany was really making things inconvenient. Troops spread all about the continent, German planes dropping bombs all across the island, and ships dragging all kinds of whatnot out of America. I was surrounded by things to contend with. After reading Father's little present, I ramped up my noble visibility. The earl, and Brimme House, could be found everywhere. I was a friend to the troops, giving graciously in any way that was possible.

True, it was equal parts patriotism and ploy. I did want to help the lads in any way that I could. War is just such a dirty business. I also wanted to put myself front and center with his highness, king of the United Kingdom and the British Dominions, George VI. I wanted to be top notch with him before I attempted to strike a blow at the Bennetts.

Fortunately, since George (or Albert, to his friends) wasn't supposed to be king, that role went to his brother Edward. We were rather well acquainted. He had made all of the usual social rounds after his service in WWI, and we were of good regard. I hadn't actually spoken with him since he had taken up the thrown, but I was sure that that wouldn't be a bother.

The year 1941 was no different than 1641 when it came to getting an audience with the king. It was all about what you had done for the king. The earl did her part for the king, so audiences would definitely be granted. Then there was the matter of that pesky royal journal that I was sure he had read by now. That would help me get my way, though it was a blessing and a curse. Every time I thought about that journal, I thought that I needed to be more secretive about who I was. One day, being loose-lipped was going to be my undoing.

I was doing my best to be a picture perfect earl. I will say that one of the best things about being able to do as I pleased was the fashion. You can't even understand the happiness that comes from getting rid of the bustle. It was physically and emotionally liberating to do so.

In those days, I tended to follow the trends of the Paris fashion houses and the pages of *Vogue*. The young and prominent earl cut a striking line in knee-length skirts and coats of similar color. I enjoyed the return of gloves, as they hid my cooler skin. Simple layers were also quite welcome, and I reveled in the fashion of the day. Accessories changed my mood as much as the removal of bulk from my garments. Hats, bags, and shoes in striking colors set off natural fashions nicely. The introduction of man-made fibers also came along and produced that ultra-female fashion item: the nylon stocking.

Because of war-time sanctions, silks were hard to come by. Nylon and cotton quickly became the trademarks of the day. Most women worked the production lines in factories to serve the needs of the war and, as such, wore trousers as a rule. I, too, wore trousers whenever possible. Most people assumed that I was presenting myself as part of the people. I really just wanted to wear the trousers. I love pants! Pants are the number one fashion choice of a predator. All respectable army troops chose pants. I chose pants.

Now, it should be stated that all of this glamorizing did take some work. The Paris fashion houses were under German occupation. Clothing all across the British Isles was strictly rationed, utilizing a system of points. Even in America, where I acquired most of my items, there were big restrictions on women's fashions. Green and brown dyes were needed for military uniforms and were not allowed to be used in civilian clothing. And stockings were all but a luxury.

As an importer of military goods for the crown and a transporter of arms for America, smuggling war-banned women's fashions wasn't really an issue. No one wanted to stop and inspect the cargo on my vessels. Extra boxes marked "Machine Parts" were just that, extra boxes.

As the war settled in for the long haul, I had once again done my utmost to build support for the local inhabitants around Brimme House. More hospitals and shelters were made, along with buildings used to warehouse items in need by the populous. Rubble-ridden pieces of ground around London that had been bombed flat were re-envisioned into aid stations and soup kitchens. The displaced in the cities needed to be helped, as they lacked the resources of the country folk. And, as such, a young and fashionable champion of the people would do just that. I was an earl of the people, helping the people whenever and wherever able and utilizing my fortune for the best of a nation. It was PR that movie moguls couldn't buy.

But let it not be said that no good deed goes unpunished. This is as true a statement today as it was in 1941, or in 1641 for that matter. The biggest problem with being a vampire and being out in the limelight is that you're out in the limelight. Even in the middle of a war zone, escaping the gaze of snap-happy photographers and cameramen was a constant problem. I turned down numerous requests from different offices of the crown to appear in motivational film clips or to have my photo taken for magazine articles about the good works being done. Avoiding camera lenses was a constant issue.

General note … I have numerous high-quality photographs of myself in the estate collection. Taking a picture of a vampire is as easy as taking a picture of a human being. Vampires possess the same image quality that any other three-dimensional object possesses. The major problem is that vampire lack a reflection. Having no reflection means you do not appear on film where the image was gathered through a lens and mirror system. In the days of film cameras, that was a considerable problem. With the invention of direct image capture in CCD systems and the use of solid-state camera technology, that problem, by and large, disappeared. You still really need to pay attention to what is behind you in an image. You don't want secondhand reflections from wall mirrors to go missing. But, it's definitely better today than it was then. I actually quite enjoy having my photo taken; the same way that I enjoyed having my portrait painted in centuries past.

I got a little sidetracked there. Not surprising, I tend to obsess about fashion. Don't get me started on the pants again.

On the evening that I made my way to Windsor Castle to see the king, I wore a simple, yet stylish, full-length, blue cotton, pleated skirt with a sensible flat shoe and small belt. A white blouse under a blue sweater was covered by a gray-blue Eisenhower jacket. Simple black lace gloves and the family pearls completed my look. Effie was tucked down in her usual spot between the waps and was content. I did a once-over with my chamber maid, a middle-aged lady named Millicent, who knew of my condition. With a little makeup and a touch from the French stink bottle, I was bang tidy. Millie gave me the official nod of approval and I was off to see the king. It was time for let's make a deal.

With the war botching up travel, the trip south to the castle was a slower affair than I had come to enjoy. I thought back on the days when the carriage ride could take the better part of the afternoon. They seemed like simpler times back then. Well, they were slower maybe, but probably not simpler.

The sentry for the Grenadier Guards was firmly standing at his station, but the remainder of the people hustling about were no longer male. Apparently, the lads going off to war had also depleted the king's court. That simply had to be a good thing. We all know what I think about the court and its intrigues.

A properly attired lady met us at our vehicle and directed me to the auxiliary entrance utilized by members of the nobility. I knew where I was going quite well enough, but formality is formality. I went inside, through the outer corridors, and down the hall to a second properly dressed lady who checked to make sure that I was me. How she did this I am not sure, since all she did was ask my name and title.

After checking the box on her form, she informed me that I would be allowed a strict fifteen-minute audience. I was informed that I should be very pleased, as all recent visitors had only been granted five minutes. I nodded my understanding of the situation and my mind started whirling with what to say first. The secretary at the desk waved her hand toward the guards stationed by the door, and the doors were opened slowly so that I might pass.

The king's receiving room was dimly lit. The large, ornate draperies that normally covered the gilded windows were all drawn back full. The carnage of the blitz and its prolonged bombing was evident from all views. The king stood off center of the window's middle arc, hands clasped behind his back as if he were inspecting a suspect racehorse. A second appraisal showed that the naturally upbeat man I had known was now dark-eyed and worn.

I stopped on my imaginary mark out in the center of the floor and proper curtsied. The king didn't turn around but waved his hand in that "come up here" motion. I stood and walked to where he was standing at the windows. A closer inspection showed that the trials of his people had been wearing on him heavily. The toll was written on his face. He looked older than when I had seen him last.

"Lady Sara Anne Grey, fifth Earl of Northwick, how are you this evening? Yes, I've read the journal."

"I am as well as can be expected, Majesty. If I may inquire, how is your state?"

"I am ... tired."

We stood and watched the city of London for several minutes. The searchlights overhead left streaks in the night sky. The silence that came between the shouts from the air raid sirens was all but deafening.

"You have a different view on things than men do. What do you see this whole affair coming to?"

"Highness?"

"Do we win? Is it all worthwhile? Is there a greater meaning to war than dying, or is it all just folly? Am I simply destroying everything my family has built?"

"Hmmm." I stared out the window for a moment or two. How to answer such an inquiry.

"Your Highness, whether the country wins or loses is up to the lads and our allies. For one, I say we come out on top. As for folly, that's hard to say. War and death are things humans do as a matter of course; whether or not its folly is more philosophy than fact."

"Interesting. And what about the legacy of Britain lying in rubble all around us?"

"Britain is people, not things. It's thoughts and ideas, not roads and bridges. Since you know my backstory, let me tell you of a time when the mighty Thames had few bridges and everything from St. Paul's to the Tower was bars and brothels. There was a time when the great ministry of defense didn't exist. That time, at some point, will also come again. I remember the bell towers at Westminster Abbey actually being constructed. These are mere stacks of stone. Things come and go. Buildings, bridges, are just buildings and bridges. When this is over—and you are victorious—the monarchy will set about rebuilding Britain, the same way it has for the better part of a thousand years. I am sure there will be many monuments erected as well."

The king smiled broadly, and then he began to laugh. He laughed nonstop for a good minute. If it was possible, he seemed to get younger-looking as he went along. I smiled but stayed silent.

"Oh, my young-looking friend, I do like the way you think. I like it very much. I haven't laughed since the start of the blitz. I can't tell you what you've just done for my spirits."

"I am happy to help wherever possible, Highness."

"And you have done so on all fronts. Now, what did you come to discuss? Whatever it is, let's make it so."

"Majesty, my inquiry involves the Grand Duke Bennett's family, or more to the point, their land grants."

As we watched the searchlights, I explained to the king all about the deal Percival Bennett had struck with his predecessor. I laid out how he had bought his way into such a high station and the tenuous way that his family held onto it. The king nodded and rubbed his chin but didn't interrupt.

Once we were level pegging on the situation, I explained that I wanted to buy those land grants. I would pay the crown whatever value they thought reasonable for them. But I had come south to make a deal, and I hoped a deal was what we were making.

The king looked off toward the searchlights and pondered it all for several minutes. A small knock came from the outside of the door. The king did not respond but continued to ponder.

"Lady Grey, I have no problem handling the transaction you request, but there are three things you should keep in mind. First, the land leases are surely worth considerably more now than when they were originally granted, so a new number would need to be agreed upon. Second, taking control of the land would functionally strip the Bennett family of both wealth and title. I suspect that this is your plan, but I would also suspect that they won't take it lightly. Third, and most important, doing what Percival did doesn't by proxy make you a grand duke."

I smiled broadly. The king was a gambler, too. That was good in a king.

"Your Highness, my math puts the real world value of those leases at approximately a million pounds. I will give you ten million pounds for them, set on the same twenty-five-year cycle."

"You, Lady Sara Grey, have a bargain." The king turned and extended his hand. I took it and shook it soundly. He smiled.

"As for your second suggestion, it is my full intention to break him and his conniving little family. Once they are broken, I plan to remove them from the planet. I'm tired of their meddling in my affairs. And for number three, I was offered the opportunity to be a grand duke once. I didn't want it then, and I certainly don't want it now."

"That last bit probably makes you the smartest one of the lot, I think."

I smiled and gave the king a quick curtsy. He laughed and nodded his approval. Another more persistent knock came from the door. The king scowled a little and looked back at the large wooden slab sealing off the entrance.

"It would seem that my secretary fancies me to be about other business. I think she secretly runs the place."

"The second-in-command usually always makes the place what it is going to be, be they generals or secretaries. I have already taken up too much of your time, Highness."

"I will have the land leases forwarded to your estate in the morning."

"I will have payment forwarded to the crown when the banking houses open for business, Highness."

The king smiled and gestured toward the door. I curtsied and headed to leave. I had just put my hand on the large round metal handle when he spoke again.

"Sara, I can't fathom that you are all the things that the journal says you are, but I do like your view of things. I find your candor refreshing. May I ask you one last question tonight?"

"Yes, Highness." I turned to face the king once more as he spoke.

"You have known several generations of my family. How do I fare compared to previous rulers?"

"If I'm permitted to answer without seeming too bold, I will do so."

The king nodded.

"I have known kings and queens before you. They all possessed great strengths and great weaknesses. You may use them as reference, but they are not you and you are not them. I think that you are doing a right fine job being the king right now."

The king smiled warmly, as if he had just needed a nudge in the right direction.

"Lady Grey, your years have made you wise beyond your youthful shell. At some point, I may call upon you for more of your frankness."

"As stated, I am happy to serve the crown in whatever capacity is required. May I ask a favor of the crown?"

"Please do."

"Could you burn the queen's journal, thank you very much?"

The king rubbed his chin a second time and smiled coyly.

"Probably not, Lady Grey. It has much useful information in it."

I nodded and curtsied. "Highness."

The king smiled and said good evening as he gestured toward the door a second time. I responded in kind and left the receiving room. His secretary gave me a stern look as I departed. Apparently, forty-five minutes was too much time for an earl to converse with a king. Whatever.

I made my way back to my auto and headed north. I had managed to get what I wanted. It was a good night. Even Effie seemed pleased by the proceedings. The king knowing I was a vampire was as problematic as it was beneficial. At least it simplified some communication issues.

I sat back in my seat and pondered. I had just stuck a deep knife in the Bennett family. When they found out, there would definitely be war. I would need to prepare for that.

CHAPTER 27

It all took a little longer than expected for the fallout to begin. I had really expected something to happen immediately. Apparently, both the war and the crown slowed the pace of things. It had taken the crown the next morning, as promised, to deliver my new land leases to my door. It had taken me just hours longer to provide adequate compensation for said leases. Transaction completed as suggested. Fallout—none of note.

For some reason that I cannot explain, but motives I could guess at, His Highness had the crown wait some six weeks before notifying the grand duke of his new situation. I suppose that because of the war, no one from the grand duke's people had been paying proper attention to their bottom line. They really should have, because when they received official notification of their eviction, they had been working some six weeks without any revenue stream. Just so you know, when old man Silverton read the official notification from the crown, he was one right pissed bugger.

I was quite happy to give them the financial stick. It felt quite rewarding. I had no use for the money stream, so I just let it dump into a setup fund for a while. I used the six weeks of peace to establish the Lowestoft Charitable Disposition Group. The little endeavor was the business end of my property takeover. Lowestoft and its surrounding communities were in keen location to be a profitable place for industry. I wanted to transform the farming area out on the coast to an industrial port that Suffolk could prosper from.

All right, I wanted to stomp my boot heel on the grand duke's forehead and make him suffer and watch. Yes, that was exactly the plan.

At the same time, there was no reason that the locals couldn't gain from the exchange.

What turned out to be convenient for me, and not so convenient for the soon-to-be ex-grand duke, was the timing of war. Already being in possession of a port on the coast, the area took a right pounding from the Germans. I had been granted ample, freshly demolished space in which to build my new industrial fiefdom. The timing of the Germans was just perfect.

Once the not-so-grand duke realized what had happened to him, he did attempt to rally a defense. Sadly, he was way behind the proverbial ball. They had somehow failed to notify him, but they had not failed to notify everyone else involved. By the time the family had thought about reacting to the coup, it was way too late.

Now, if this had transpired back in Percival's day, it wouldn't have been nearly as much of a blow. The family had the resources to drive on and attack. With the current grand duke, Lord Silverton, the family was not nearly as flush. Unknowingly running six weeks with drying coffers had pushed the family into the pinch.

They had been displaced, they had been stripped of the majority of their money-making ability, and thanks to the crown, they couldn't do jack about it. The Disposition Group had settled in and taken a firm hold in the area. They had developed a quick rapport with all the landlords and business people of the area, and they had already reached out to all of those displaced by the war. The family of the duke was now literally no more than a tenant along with the rest. They had lost pretty much every ounce of power they once possessed, and the country folk were just as content without them. They had been fully usurped—and were fully pissed!

I heard a rumor that the official notification had come with a correspondence. It basically said not to waste time objecting to the notice, as it wasn't up for discussion. Yes, sir, I bet that little extra really chaffed their collective arses.

The whole affair produced exactly what I thought it would: a piece of poorly planned retaliation from the ex-grand duke. Humans are a fairly predictable lot. Frankly, as long as I had been dealing with the

Bennett family, they had all but become easily planned for. I had stung them, and now they wanted to sting back. It was human nature to want to retaliate. It all made perfect sense to me, but I couldn't really understand why they didn't stop to think about it. Why wouldn't I see it coming from them? They just never thought. It all came out like water color on canvas. They should have thought first and considered their losses. Besides, it was only the start of it all.

Henry Monroe Silverton, first cousin to the preceding member of the Bennett family and mediocre businessman, decided he would come at me head on. Of course, he was too lazy or cowardly to actually do it himself. The first attack came in the form of two lower-level members of the family. Two youthful fellows named Barnesby, both nephews of Silverton, decided that just sneaking onto the estate and killing me would solve the problem. Without stopping to research dates, I would say it took them about a week to cook up their cockamamie plan. Needless to say, it was all a bad idea.

The two hoodlums approached the estate from the south. It was the shortest way from outer border to the buildings. They picked a cloud-covered evening in the rain, thinking it would hide their approach. I at least compliment them on using the weather to their advantage. They were supposed to know all about me. They should have known that I'm usually a little edgy during bad weather. It really backfired this time, I mean we were at war and all. The bombers also came when it was dark and stormy. My little friend picked them up when they hopped the first hedgerow, way out by the boundary meadows.

For their part, they made an adequate approach to the manor, utilizing all the natural cover provided by the property. I waited on them patiently until they committed themselves to making an entrance. Once they settled on the delivery entrance at the rear of the manor house, I made my own move. In proper English fashion, I waited until they had actually entered the main estate before I dispatched them. I try to stay inside the law, you know. I could have happily killed them as soon as the crossed the boundary fences, but I wanted there to be no doubt about it.

The two young Barnesby men slid through the rear entrance and closed the large wooden slab of a door quietly behind them. They dropped their rain-soaked jackets next to the door and slowly proceeded into the residence. Manners, that was nice to see. The first Barnesby turned the corner just past the entrance threshold and ran directly into the business end of my Webley British Bull Dog. The solid-frame revolver thundered in the stone hallway as the .450 Adams slug removed most of Barnesby No. 1's head in a nice pink mist. The heavy lead projectile carried on and punched a small chunk of stone out of the wall. Hmmph! Even though Father would approve, I needed to be more careful. It was an old house; I probably shouldn't beat it up like that.

I adjusted my focus on to Barnesby No. 2 and found him covered in bloody gray matter with a rivulet of urine working its way down one trouser leg. His look of horrific shock was undeniable. He was obviously not the true fighting type. I leveled the Webley's barrel center mass and smiled as I pulled the trigger. A second thunderous crack came out of the revolver as the young man's chest folded in on itself. The bullet punched a fist-sized hole through the second man before embedding itself in the solid oak planks of the door behind him. Damn it! I did it again. Well, at least the door took it well.

The two bodies lay on the stone floor of the hall entrance, oozing blood. Neither one of them as much as twitched while I inspected the scene. I gazed in satisfaction for a moment or two before deciding it was over and done. I had initially considered letting Effie dispense with body disposal, but that would have been problematic. Too many people in the estate would hear the gun shots, and that needed to be compensated for. I simply walked back to the salon, sat the revolver down, and notified Scotland Yard on the telephone that I had two dead intruders that needed handling. As expected, the bobbies and the detectives were quite accommodating.

That was the start of it. There were the Barnesby boys, and then about six months later, there was a threesome of cousins that tried it again. They had no more success than the first lads. A year on from that, two young men and a young lady named James had a go while I was down in London for the evening. I let Effie amuse herself with them. No muss, no fuss, no cleanup with Effie on the case.

A man named Montrose put a slug in the windscreen of my 1936 Aston Martin MK II. The nutter dropped another in the bonnet before I introduced his kneecaps to the front bumper. He was a tough one. I actually had to get out and slam my calfskin boot heel down on his neck. Needless to say, after a quick and audible snap, he was done, too.

There were two more random attempts in 1946 and a pretty stealthy try in 1947 before it had run its course. Ex-Grand Duke Silverton was exhausting his relatives at a rapid rate. Apparently, he finally decided it wasn't working. It was just as well. By the end of WWII, I had killed as many members of his family as the Jerries had. His staff must have been running low.

By the end of World War II, I had full control of all their lands and wealth-producing entities. I had killed off all the stupid members of the family, and the Grand Duke Silverton was now just Silverton. Good bit of business done, in my opinion.

CHAPTER 28

The summer of 1952 was pleasant enough, as I remember. Mr. Silverton had somewhat faded from my everyday concerns. I had planted one of his kin in the ground, back in 1950, but that was about it for the last couple of years.

On the quiet nights it left me something to ponder; he had been a grand duke, after all. He had come from a family long known for scheming and manipulation. It wasn't like his kind to stop, actually realize he was beaten, and accept it. No, sir, he was cut from the same cloth as Brutus. That would be Marcus Junius Brutus, the chap who planted a knife into Caesar. Yup, he was the knife-in-the-back sort.

Still, things were quiet enough. The earl of the people had been kept quite busy helping to rebuild the better part of Britain. I had numerous enterprises engaged in the reconstruction of the empire. I also kept an eye on the Disposition Group, which was building a whole new industrial zone out to the northeast. And, on top of it all, I had my dealings with Grey's Cargo.

All right, even to me that last bit sounded disingenuous. Anyone you might find who was around at the time would definitely say the same. I had not been bothering with my corporation at all. I hadn't dealt with the running of the company or its concerns for some time. I stopped to talk with Tracey upon occasion, or his handsome son, Steven, but I didn't provide any necessary direction. The truth was they had run the corporation for so long that there wasn't any need for me to show my face. No one working in the corporate offices, save the small group of board members, even knew I was involved. I was just a wealthy woman who stopped by from time to time. That young earl who was always in the tabloids.

It really was nice that way. I didn't tread on the Wyndells, and they made me scads of money. What was it that Julian had said back in New York City? 'They ran their company well." Well, that they did.

I was busy being an earl and the Wyndells were busy running corporate affairs. Those two things had run along nicely untangled until now. I believe it was the later part of June when Tracey Wyndell came knocking on my door. Unlike almost every other generation of his family, Tracey and his siblings had not grown up at the Grey Estate. He had only been to my residence one previous time, for a ball I had hosted. Of course, Tracey felt obligated to attend, since there had been numerous business clients present, along with most of British society. As I remember, he did enjoy himself well enough; it just wasn't his natural setting. Seeing him that morning, waiting in the manor's elegant entryway as opposed to the study, made it clear to me that times had definitely changed.

The housekeeper escorted him to the study and fetched up a tea service. I showed him to a chair and took up station in an adjacent one. He looked all business, which was uncharacteristic of him. He usually possessed a somewhat more carefree manner around me. It seemed he was here to deal with issues. Oh well, to the issues then.

"Good morning, Lady Alcott. Thank you for receiving me this morning."

I rolled up my face a little and gave him an oddly disapproving look. He retrieved a cup of tea and repositioned himself in the large leather chair.

"Tracey, you're a smart chap, why don't you just use my real name? You have always seemed old enough as to have no need for mincing words."

"Fine, Lady Sara, no minced words. There is an issue at corporate level that you should be aware of."

My focus narrowed on Tracey as he took a sip of his tea. He seemed calm, which made me less so.

"Proceed."

"There is an investment group, of sorts, buying up our stock. Normally, this wouldn't be an issue, but we decided to do a little digging since they have some volume. We like to know who is investing in our concerns. The group I mention is actually just a storefront for a larger banking interest. Take a guess who owns the larger banking interest?"

My internal radar suddenly went haywire. I could even feel Effie twitch under my blouse.

"Hmmm, I'm going to say one Mr. Silverton?"

"Correct, ma'am. Apparently, your attempts to cripple him several years ago were only semi-successful. His banking interests made it through his downfall intact. They have done quite well for themselves in the years since the war. Mr. Silverton once again has a good wealth at his disposal. It would seem that this time he is going to try economics over gunmen."

I threw my tea cup across the study. The fine china cup impacted the heavier leaded-glass picture window and shattered. Tracey raised an eyebrow but said nothing.

"How much stock are we talking about?"

"Right now, not a lot. It's also all common stock. You own the vast majority of the voting stock, and the remainder of voting owners have no desire to be selling."

"Is he still buying?"

"Yes. And if he buys enough, he gains common control."

"That can be a problem."

"Maybe, maybe not. He has little wealth compared to either of our families. Simply buying out what he's using to buy them with would solve our problem."

"I see your point. Sadly, that would just give him more wealth to work with."

"True. But actions have consequences."

"That they do, Tracey, that they do. How long do I have to think about this before something needs doing?"

"I should think you have a bit of time, but don't wait too long."

Tracey gave me a workup on the state of the corporation, what stock was where and whatnot, and then casually departed back to London. I sat in my study and began to brood.

There needed to be a way out of the situation that didn't add fuel to the smoldering fire. I couldn't just buy out his bank and give him more needed capital to use against me later on. He obviously needed to die, but that didn't solve the stock problem. No, the economic problem would persist long after he was cold in the ground.

The more I thought about old man Silverton, the more I wanted my stock back. Until one day I thought, what if I don't. Silverton meddling in the Grey's Cargo Corporation only mattered because it was my corporation. But what if—it wasn't? What if it was just some other corporation in the business system? Why would I care about that? Why would the Wyndells care, for that matter? They would just have another investor of means. This whole affair was personal to me and Silverton. It had nothing to do with the Wyndell family. Besides, they also had enough money to crush Silverton. They were now a family not to be trifled with.

I smiled a wicked awful smile. My large ivory fangs glinted in the light streaming through the study's grand windows. It was the optimum solution to my problem. It worked for me on so many levels. It was bloody perfect.

Father would certainly never let me talk to him again once he found out. No, that's not right, father was a businessman. He would understand good business. Charles would certainly have no objections, as long as it was for my greater survival. No, it was definitely the right move.

The next morning I made myself up in businesslike attire and headed off for the East End. The corporate offices were a whirlwind of activity when I arrived. All slips dockside were full and the stevedores were busy shuffling bulk containers of all sorts. I made my way directly past reception and straight on to Tracey's private secretary. She appeared unpleasant as always but spoke nicely enough. I informed her that I didn't have a meeting but was completely expected and Tracey could meet me in my office. The old bat stared in disbelief as I continued on past her to an unused office at the end of the hall. As I slid the key into the door labeled "Owner," the old girl jumped into action.

I had managed to settle myself into Father's stiff wooden office chair and run my finger across the dust-covered desktop before Tracey came bulling in with a semi-shocked expression on his face. Steven, a vice president at this point, and the receptionist lady stuffed the space in the doorframe as Tracey slid to a stop.

I frowned at the dust and then looked up at Tracey and smiled. I pointed to one of the leather chairs on the other side of the desk and he got the point.

"Good morning, Tracey. If you happen to have some time in your schedule, I would like to share some thoughts about our discussion topic. Oh, Steven, do close the door. This is an owner/CEO conversation. Thank you."

Steven looked miffed as he disappeared behind the door. Tracey smiled broadly and settled himself into one of the leather chairs. I frowned at the dust again.

"The maid on holiday?"

"You haven't spent two minutes in this office since I've known you. It didn't really seem necessary."

"I suppose you're right. Still, it does show a lack of concern for the management."

Tracey looked around the office and inspected the thick layer of dust, and then looked back at me and smiled his playful smile.

"I'll have the janitorial staff come through once we're finished. Now, get to it."

I laughed loudly. He was in his mid-sixties but still the same man I had met so many decades back. I liked that about his family: they were a well-grounded bunch. I looked for a moment at an old dock painting from the Bristol Mooring and smiled a faraway smile.

"A very long time ago, I came to work every day and, with some help, turned my father's small business into an empire. That was back in the day when we were located farther down the Thames. They were quieter times. However, a century or so ago, the corporation really required an on-top type of leader. The earlier Wyndell boys wanted to do it, and as such, really started coming into their own at that point. They did so well that I relinquished a great amount of daily control to them and just faded from view. And in doing so, I left your family to run an empire."

Tracey rubbed his chin and wiped some dust from his suit sleeve.

"Yes, ma'am, I know the family history. Father made it a mandatory piece of education after our first meeting."

"Back in days gone by, I used to make each of them swear an oath to do their best or die. You managed to escape that somehow. Times do change, I guess."

"Once I fully understood the situation, I assumed that it was implied."

I smiled to lighten the mood. It made Tracey calm.

"Yes, you and your family have done a masterful job here."

"Thank you, ma'am. If I may ask, where are we headed with this?"

"We are headed to a solution to my latest issue."

"Proceed."

"When I left New York City back before the war, a very nice man named Julian told me that you did a great job running your corporation. I'm curious—would you do it any different if it was—your corporation?"

Tracey's eyes dilated so fast that I would have sworn he'd been bitten.

"You mean, you want us to—take over the corporation?"

"No, silly boy, I want you to buy it from me. Silverton has no interest in the company, or you for that matter. He is after me. If I have nothing to do with the company, he will quickly lose interest in it. And you will own that which you have so long only ran for someone else."

"I see your point," Tracey said, actually rubbing his hands together.

"Now, as near as I can figure, my percentage of the corporation is worth approximately 3.6 billion pounds. Since I do love your family greatly, let's set the selling price at an even 3 billion."

"Three billion pounds?"

"That's not a reasonable amount? All of my common and corporate stock, save 5 percent for old time sake, and all of the property it sits on for an even three billion pounds."

"That's an extreme amount to procure. I will need to have some discussions with the family."

"I was pretty sure that you would. I imagine that they will also have some valid concerns."

"I seriously don't think we can liquidate three billion pounds all at one time."

"Okay, fine, we do it in threes. How about three one-billion pound installments? That should solve your banking concerns."

"Yes, ma'am, that would certainly help. I think we can muster that kind of turnaround."

"Good. So, do you want to buy my corporation, or do I put it out on the open market?"

"No, No, no. We will definitely come to an agreement, Lady Sara."

"That's what I've always admired about you Wyndell boys—always quick to see a good opportunity."

We both laughed loudly. I really did like the Wyndell family greatly. I could just sense that the laughter going through the door was causing confusion in the hallway.

"Okay, Tracey, I appreciate that you will need some time to discuss it all with the requisite family members, but if they agree to the buyout, I have a few conditions."

"I would expect that you do. What might you require?"

"The artifacts that were in long-term storage should be shipped out to the estate. I want to keep Father's things. I would also like the contents of this office as well. I really don't care if you change the name. It almost seems appropriate at this point. Please, just choose something respectful of your family. That, and the 5 percent of the voting stock. You can call it a souvenir of days past. Seem doable to you?"

"Yes, ma'am, I'm sure that we can meet your requirements. As you said, I will need to converse with the other senior members of the family. I will let you know as soon as I have a confirmed answer."

"That sounds more than fair, Tracey." I stood and made my way around Father's dusty office desk to Tracey. Being a gentleman, he stood with me. I extended my hand and we shook. It was a solid, personal handshake. It was the way business was supposed to be conducted. I paused at the door and waved my hand about the room. Tracey smiled.

"Yes, ma'am, I'll have the janitorial staff here right quick."

I smiled and proceeded out the door, not bothering with young Steven or the secretary still standing in the hall.

Lady Sara Anne Grey left her corporate office and headed straight for High Street and some shopping. Afternoon tea was taken, as was a leisurely stroll around Mayfair. As the sun tipped, I headed back north to the Grey Estate, comfortable in my own skin for the first time in centuries. I could feel a new world slowly coming up under my feet.

I had been sitting in my usual chair admiring the view through the study windows when Millie entered and informed me I had a call waiting. I stood and walked to the house phone located on a side table adjacent to the desk.

"Good evening, Lady Alcott speaking."

"Good evening, ma'am, Tracey Wyndell."

"Oh, hello, Tracey. How are your meetings going?"

"The conversations were quite fast and are done now. The answer is a firm yes. The bankers are currently at work turning out the first installment. They will develop a schedule for the remainder as well. The corporate lawyers are handling all of the paperwork and will have all the legal issues worked out in a couple days."

"I'm glad, Tracey. It really should have been in your family's hands ages ago. Let me know when the paperwork has been tended to and I will be along to solidify the deal."

"I'll keep you informed, ma'am. Have a lovely evening."

"Cheers, Tracey."

I sat the handset back down in the cradle and looked out the large picture windows toward the path that ran up to the cemetery. Yes, new times were coming. I probably would need to go and explain it all to the others at some point.

CHAPTER 29

Tracey Wyndell was as good as his word. It took the collective group less than a week to work out all the entanglements and produce legal papers for the sale. The corporate lawyers had to dig down through layers of the corporation's history to figure out how Lady Alcott actually owned the corporation. They, along with everyone else save the crown, actually thought the Wyndell family owned it all. I guess no one ever bothered to stop and check.

The Wyndell family bankers needed a longer period of time to accomplish their part. They managed to liquidate the first billion easily enough, but figuring out how to liquate the other two took considerably more effort. The family obviously wanted to do it without taking a big hit. I could sympathize, as I would have done the same. You never want to lose from the gaining.

Three and a half weeks passed, and all was ready. I presented myself at the company of my name at precisely 10:00 a.m. on a dreary Thursday morning to dispose of the thing that I had been turned into a demon to protect. As the song says: The times they were a-changin'.

Tracey and Steven met me at the entrance and ushered me in out of the weather. Tracey made some comment that the weather could have been better. I told him that my father was fond of saying, "As long as the ship are sailing, it's good weather on the Thames." He smiled and nodded his appreciation.

The main corporate boardroom was at absolute capacity. There almost wasn't enough oxygen in the space for the number of business suites it possessed. I had never seen so many bankers and lawyers in one place at one time. It was absolutely crazy. No, change that—it was greedy. That is exactly what it was. The new capitalists were feeding on the sale. I didn't think less of them for it, as I was doing the same.

A man named Hallson led the whole procession. He was Grey's Cargo's senior attorney; he was a nice man of modest years and too many fine meals. The document package that he laid in front of me was akin to the Magna Carta in its scope. The attorneys must have killed a tree printing the thing up. I was in shock. There was no way that I could read all of that! Fortunately, I didn't need to. Mr. Hallson pulled out a second copy and most calmly went through each section for Tracey and me. The education was thorough and of a constant tone. We paused twice during the reading so one lawyer or another could expand on a given point.

Three hours later, Hallson drew a final breath and casually stated, "Does that sound fair to both parties?"

Tracey and I just looked at each other and blinked. I shrugged and Tracey kind of slowly nodded his head. We turned and looked back at Hallson, who was looking less than pleased by our reactions. I said that I thought I was comfortable with the stated arrangement. Tracey followed suit and concurred with my statement. The collective grin that came from the lawyer's gallery was electric. The bankers stayed stoic, as bankers tend to do.

Considering the length of the dissertation, the actual business signature part of the transaction was quite quick. Four signatures did the deal: one to transfer ownership of the stocks, one to accept the terms of sale, one to accept understanding of what was to be considered a corporate asset, and a final one to approve the method, amount, and schedule of the payments.

I signed four blocks, Tracey signed four blocks, and the deal was complete. The Wyndell family now properly owned the Grey's Cargo Corporation. Or, should I say, the Wyndell Group now owned all but total interest in it. Mr. Hallson gave me a copy of the documents and a shiny new leather attaché to house it in. Some lawyers hustled up the other copy of it and exited the room. I assumed that they wanted to record the transaction before someone changed their mind. All of the bankers shook hands and patted each other on the back. All of the lawyers still in the room began to talk about landmark business dealings. I just sat there lost in it all. Nobody even knew I was still in the room. They all congratulated each other as if they had just seemingly accomplished some undertaking. I found it all disheartening.

I looked over at Tracey, who was also still sitting in his chair quietly. He looked pleased in a good business done way. He also looked slightly older than he had at the start of the day. It really is different when it's your money. He had just felt that painful realization. He would be fine. He was a business mogul, after all.

The news of the sale reverberated out across the planet before the ink was even dry. The trade papers of the day lauded over the greatest single business transaction to be struck. I didn't know if it was all of that, though it was a grand sum. Every single paper in Britain carried news of the sale on its front page. The news spread like wildfire. I would have loved to have been in the room when old man Silverton learned that he owned 4 percent of common stock in a corporation that had just been sold. I bet he was fit to be tied. The thought of that made me smile just a little.

When everyone had finally made their way out of the boardroom, I stood and collected my new attaché. I made my own way out of the room and down the hallway, almost unnoticed by the mass of people still milling about. Steven found me at the top of the stairs and quickly came to escort me down. Tracey broke free from a group of like-dressed people and met us at the bottom of the stairs. He seemed to have regained his lost years in the intervening time. The leader of the ship was back to leading once more. Tracey took my arm and escorted me away from the crowds and out into a semi-empty dockside warehouse that was attached directly to the main offices. I set my case on a small wooden shipping container and rubbed his arm in a comforting way. He smiled and touched my cheek softly.

"So, will you change the name?" It came out quietly, as if there was an emotional connection that needed to be broken. Tracey responded in kind.

"No, I think not. Everyone on the planet knows it this way. There's no reason to send another tremor into the business crowd."

"That's nice of you, I think Father would like the thought that his little company is still out there somewhere."

Tracey smiled but didn't respond.

I looked out about the warehouse nostalgically. I was in a new space, but all I could see was that first warehouse back down the Thames. It was always dusty and full of wooden boxes.

"Does Steven know anything about me or my condition?"

"No, Sara. He just thinks you are an heiress of some kind."

"We should keep it that way. It's probably time that the Greys and the Wyndells emotionally part ways, so to speak." Tracey looked over at me the way a student would look to a favored teacher.

"Are you sure that *you* want that? You have been with us for a very long time."

"I have learned an incredible amount from your family over the centuries, and I have tried to give back wherever I could. But I think that it's probably the right time. The Wyndell family is safe and secure, which was the promise that was made so long ago. And I will be fine."

"Then we will … just let it all linger until it goes."

"Thank you, Tracey."

Tracey smiled broadly. For the briefest of seconds I saw Charles looking back at me. It caught my breath in my throat. I hadn't even realized that I was breathing.

"Sara, do you remember our first meeting? It seems quite different times from way back then."

I smiled warmly. There really was a little bit of Charles stuck in there somewhere.

"I do. We have come a long way together, you and I. Time changes us all as it goes along."

"Yes, ma'am, it does do that."

"Well, it would seem that I'm all done here. I wish your family all of the best in your business pursuits. Tracey Wyndell, you be well, my friend."

"Thank you, Sara. I will do my best to make us both happy."

"And please do stop out to the estate when time permits—one person taking tea with another and all that."

"I will make every effort, Sara Grey."

We touched one more time. Not an embrace but an acknowledgement of closeness. I retrieved my case from atop the wooden crate and slowly made my way through the outer warehouse door. Tracey headed back inside the main office to the waiting pool of reporters and business people.

I climbed into the back of my waiting Rolls Royce and sat the attaché next to me on the seat. I had sold a corporation. I had just taken place in the single largest sale in British history. A billion pounds worth of certified bonds had been placed in an extremely secure vault below the crown jewels in the White Tower. (It's a perk of being in with the establishment.)

I sat in my posh car with my big stack of papers, but I didn't actually possess a tenner more than I walked in with. It felt very strange. These new capitalists were an interesting band of buggers, to say the least. I waved my hand and the Rolls pulled out of the corporate auto park for the last time. A small tear began to form in my left eye, but I was having none of it. This was business.

It took several minutes of heavy traffic for me to calm again. History was done; now it was time to contemplate the next thing. Normally, I would need to ponder this for some time, but not this day. There had been an uneasiness lingering in me for some time. I thought that maybe another vampire had made its way to my island. It felt like that, but it was much stronger. It was a solid unease. I had assumed that whatever was producing it was just being amplified by the business transactions. That made good sense to me. I could just tell that something was coming out of the ether.

I looked out the window as the busy London traffic whizzed by. The dreariness of the day had not released its grip on the area. I think it had even managed to get more dismal. Breaking the northern boundary of London, the traffic began to lighten. The Rolls Royce picked up speed, and in no time we were back through the gates of the family estate. Effie upped her glow a bit to warm that spot where my soul should have been.

I smiled a passing smile at the hedges along the drive and tried to push the uneasiness from my mind.

I made my way quickly from the car into the house. Even with the large, covered receiving station at the main entrance to keep me dry, I was not in the mood for foul weather. I had made the top step when the large wooden slab of an entrance door swung open. Millie stood center stage, obviously waiting for me to enter.

"Ma'am, glad to see you back in one piece. The weather is turning foul. You have a visitor waiting for you in the study."

"A visitor, Millie?"

"Yes, ma'am. Said he was one Donovan Tate from Chicago. He did not specify his exact desire to speak with you when I inquired. Just said you were old friends is all."

"Donovan Tate, you say?"

"Yes, ma'am. Something strange about him, too. He seems oddly familiar, like I met him before or some such thing. Moved around like he'd spent time here. Is he a formal acquaintance of yours?"

"Yes, Millie, he is that." I smiled and let my thick enamel fangs slip out a little. Millie turned ashen. I turned and headed down the hallway.

Both large doors swung open as I made an entrance into the study. Donovan Tate stood at the end of one stack, inspecting a first edition copy of *The Inferno*. He looked every inch the man I had known some years back. The vampire in him had made his looks more rugged and had added a bit of mass to his frame, but he was definitely the same man.

"Donovan Tate? You look in excellent form. How has America been treating you?"

The wooden study doors slammed closed behind me. The transformed Patrick Wyndell smiled at me broadly and placed the book back on its shelf.

"Lady Mary Beth Alcott, you look absolutely ravishing—a true picture of beauty if there ever was one."

"Thank you, kind sir. A lady always appreciates a compliment."

"Well, in that case, you also have an excellent book collection."

I laughed. He smiled. We met in the middle of the room and embraced. His large muscular arms wrapped around me, and I was instantly happy. The feeling of being held by a large and powerful man made all of my animalistic libido come to full boil. He had been an excellent lover when he was human. I could only imagine what the night was going to bring me now that he had unlimited stamina.

Millie appeared with a tray of tea and disappeared as quickly. We continued to embrace, Donovan's large hands wandering the curves of my breasts as we did. We skipped the tea and went for the Scotch whisky bottle on the liquor table.

We both found a Scotch and a chair. Once we were both settled like adults, Donovan began to tell me a story about being a young vampire. He had made it to America on the ship without going insane, but apparently it was close. There was a small feeding frenzy in Boston and a journey west to the city of Chicago. I had never been to Chicago, so I listened intently as Donovan told me all about the city by the lake.

He said it was actually a very nice place to live. He had encountered other vampires and wayward demons as they passed through on their way west toward the Pacific. The city was large and had all the usual amenities one would expect of a European city. They had numerous playhouses and social entertainment was the style of the day. The city also held a large immigrant population. There were many Pols and Hungarians, Czechs, Germans, and Italians in the city. It had a healthy European stirring under its completely American exterior. All of it sounded grand. I would need to visit it one day.

It seemed that the massive immigrant population, a seething mass of humanity in close approximation to a lake and rivers, was the right place to study being a predator. He had refined his killing abilities on the city's populous. By his account, he was now an accomplished killer.

We discussed killing strategy for a time. Donovan, being a large individual, tended toward using his mass as a weapon. Where I needed a plan to fight large opponents, because of my light frame, he could merely attack. He was naturally large and the demon in him made him powerful. It kind of reminded me of Antonio. For a split second, I wondered what was currently happening to my old love.

Seeing Donovan excited me. He was still the educated, worldly Wyndell man he had been when he was human. The vampire had just made him more. He was now suave, commanding, and readily desirable. He had always been desirable, but it was now amplified. I imagined that it must have had an overwhelming effect on unsuspecting humans.

We talked for quite some time before retiring to my bedchamber. He ran his rough and ready hands over me in a purely dominant fashion. I submitted quickly, as large sections of my clothing were ripped from my body and cast to the floor. I managed to get Effie free from his unwrapping and lay her on the bedside table before I was summarily planted on my back somewhere near the middle of the bed. Climbing onto the bed like a conquering hero, Donovan took full command of events. In not enough time for talking, my eyes were rolled full back in my skull. The pleasure of being taken so completely seemed fully at odds with the swirling unease of earlier business transactions. I just gave in. What can I say? It had been a strange day.

CHAPTER 30

I had spent about a week happily getting the plugging from Donovan and wasting time on the telephone with different business interests before my lover announced that he needed to be back off to America. Having Donovan would be a short-lived affair. I knew that. It just caught me at side glance when he said it.

He had come to know me well before I turned him, and that knowledge had not escaped his early vampire educations. Like the rest of us, he had never been able to dispel some of his base human emotions. Holding onto them, he was much more a hybrid than he was full demon. Basically, he was more me and less Antonio. He had returned to London to observe the status of his children. Being dead, he wanted to be in and out before he was noticed or recognized. He had learned what he wanted to know over the previous days. The state being that his children were both well and adjusted. He had acquired a good feeding from the London underground population. It was time to be moving on.

I could easily sympathize with him. I had spent decades doing the same thing with his family. The great Wyndell troop had long been my extended family. Being protective was an interestingly comfortable feeling for a vampire to harbor.

I told Donovan that all was quiet and peaceful. The Grey Estate was a secure place to be and our mighty industrial age had made vampires all but myth. I encouraged him to stay a while longer. He finally relented and said he would stay out the month. That would give us another three

224

weeks or so to do whatever we were doing. That made me very happy. In retrospect, he probably should have left when his instincts told him to.

My little friend in the jeweled cage had been all but silent since Donovan's arrival. The diminished conversation inside my brain left me a bit hollow. I filled myself with Donovan, but Effie's absence was noticeable. If she was looking into the future, she could have at least said something to me. She had in the past. But, as a creature of her own designs, she did as she pleased.

The three of us were taking the sun on the far west terrace, discussing Marx's views on society, when the fine lads from Scotland Yard came up the drive. The London detective wanted to personally inform me of some odd occurrences that had been taking place in the city. It seemed that two break-ins had been reported at a warehouse that I owned in the old part of the city. I explained to the detective that the warehouse was of no consequence to me or anyone else for that matter. It was full of old furniture and housewares from a property that I used to possess.

The house, on what used to be Banker's Row, had been as much of a home to me as the Grey Estate had been. When I had liquidated the property almost a century back, I had the contents moved to a nearby warehouse that the company had owned. Tracey had tried to get me to sell it several times, but the emotional connection was still there. (Of course, I didn't tell the detective this last bit.)

The nice detective informed me that the break-ins had occurred seven days apart. Both times, nothing had been taken. He thought it was probably gangs looking for new hangouts. I thought it was more likely a calling card, though I didn't voice the idea. I mentioned that the man who watched over the warehouses in the area had phoned the estate with the news. I would need to do something to secure it better. With that, the detective seemed content that he had done as much of his duty as was really required and thanked me for my time. I thanked him for his effort and then sat and drummed my fingers on the glass tabletop as he drove back out the drive.

"What's the worry, love? The nice fellow said that nothing was taken. You just need to put better locks on the doors. Or maybe go feed on a couple young hoodlums?" He seemed perfectly pleased with himself as he spoke.

He could be right, but he was young and hadn't lived through what I had lived through. It was not hoodlums.

"It could be, but more likely it is an invitation to come out and play."

"An invitation?"

"Yes, an invitation from a fellow named Silverton. Two break-ins, seven days apart, with nothing taken either time? If you wait another three days, there will most likely be a third break-in. Ex-Grand Duke Silverton is saying, 'Come out and play.'"

"So, what do you think you should do?"

"I'm going to accept his offer."

"Then we shall accept his offer together."

I smiled without warmth. If Donovan wanted to kill a few people, I certainly wasn't going to tell him no.

It did seem a strange move for the old man to make. The warehouse he picked was almost in the heart of London. He couldn't mask himself from a conflict there any more than I could. Killing me there, even without a body left for evidence, would most certainly still produce a crime.

Why would he risk the exposure? Why would he assume that I would risk the exposure? I had beaten his family almost to ruin. He obviously had less to lose from a conflict than I did, but still, a live henchman would talk to the police. Henchmen always talked. That's part of why I don't often employ henchmen anymore. Sadly, he used them all the time. Whoever he sent to deal with me would inevitably lead back to him. It was a strange move to make.

I drummed my fingers on the table and stared off toward the woods beyond the meadow. Something was definitely afoot. Whatever it was, it was shadowy at best. Donovan could tell that the general conversation part of the day was over, so he sat quietly. I drummed my fingers on the table.

I woke from my sleep three days on and my radar was on full alert. Even without the window in the tomb-dark bedchamber, I could tell midmorning had come. I certainly hadn't overslept, but it was time to be at it. I reached over in the bed and squeezed Donovan's solid chest. He was still there. Rolling my head over in the heavy down pillow, I blew a lock of blonde hair out of my eyes and focused my gaze on the amulet. She hung quietly on her thick bronze wall hook. She seemed as impassive as always. Why the hell was my radar going off again?

I flipped off the covers and padded over to the wardrobe. I could sense that Donovan was inspecting me as I stood staring into the wad of fashion the wardrobe housed. I reached into the hoard, removed a full-curvature corset, and tossed it on the bed, followed by a pair of Smith's high-waist denim jeans and a stylish black silk blouse. The blouse had elbow-length sleeves and was tight at the waist. It would move well with both the corset and the denim. The load of closely spaced buttons down the front would also hopefully keep it closed once combat started.

"So, from this bunch by the footboard, I can assume that a mid-morning thumping is out of the question?"

"It's time for you to get on your feet."

"Don't get me wrong, I love what corsets do for your bubbly little body, but don't you think that unnecessary seeing how you're headed for some gymnastics?"

"I've done some of my best fighting in a corset and floor-length dress with petticoats. Be happy that you have never had to deal with petticoats. Besides, this one is what I call my combat model. I had all the ivory-bone spines replaced with high-grade steel spines. It's a little harder to twist, but it helps immensely with knives and bats."

"What about bullets?"

"Don't know. Haven't tried it."

"Probably don't want to today, either."

"Probably right."

I tossed one of his big, size-thirteen boots over my shoulder at what I assumed was his head. The boot bounced off the headboard and Donovan got the point. It was officially time to get moving.

We made our way down to my favorite breakfast spot—the terrace outside the study—and planted ourselves at the table. Millie promptly appeared and set the service down in its middle. She took a moment to inspect my attire, from sturdy men's work boots up to the wild blonde mane professionally pulled back into a ponytail, and simply raised one eyebrow.

The morning tea and coffee was enjoyable but not happy. My internal radar was pinging away like I had just located a damned Soviet submarine. I couldn't for the life of me think of any reason it should be doing such a thing. My head was pounding away and Effie just hung there happy as a plum inside my corset.

At just past midday, I strolled into the gun room located down toward the far end of the main hallway. I gave the armory a once-over before retrieving a compact automatic pistol. I shoved a stiletto into my boot top and the automatic in a flat holster at the small of my back. I came out of the gun room to a disapproving Donovan.

"Really? We're vampires not gangsters."

"You're big and strong—me, not so much. Well, I am strong, but that's not the point. I like a weapon as a backup."

"Whatever makes you happy, Lady Grey."

"Don't you forget it. Now, let's get the car and head downtown."

Donovan chauffeured me down into London proper and onto the banks of the Thames. We pulled the Aston Martin into the warehouse and closed the place up so it looked no different than any other day. We clambered up on the roof and found a spot that offered a good view of the open area in front of the main warehouse doors.

The four large warehouses in the area circled around each other and formed a large open central common square in front of their doors. An entry space between each of the buildings gave the central common four access points. The whole thing was backed by a city street to the north and the Thames to the south. It was both a good and bad place to do battle—easy to attack, but no real place to escape to if the fight went badly. The one thing I was sure of was there would be no running. If things really got bad, I had my ace in the hole, so I was standing my ground. We sat on the roof and waited.

The wait on this particular day lasted till the bells at Westminster had struck eleven. Seems the opposition was in no real rush. I was antsy. Donovan was casually leaning against the building's chimney, half asleep.

Three stealthy blokes made their way in around the building to the north by its western opening. They had probably parked out on the street. One stood for watch and the other two headed for my warehouse. I waited for the obvious something else, but it didn't seem to be lingering out there anywhere. They popped the locks on schedule and peaked inside the dark building, and then, as casual as could be, stopped and lit a smoke. What the hell? They were obviously henchmen, but were they stupid, too? Donovan seemed unconcerned. I was antsy. Bollocks on it. I launched myself over the side.

The sturdy work boots landed hard on the surface of the cement courtyard. It broke the silence like a marching band. The noise shook the two would-be burglars into animated action. I hit the first one so hard that he was dead before he hit the ground. The second didn't last any longer. I turned to stare down at their lookout, who seemed unnervingly calm.

"Bird, you realize they wasn't burglars; they was bait."

"I know that. Thank you."

The lookout flicked his cigarette onto the ground and some twenty large men poured out from all four of the avenues. Every one of them went straight into attacking. It was going to be a full-on melee. The group of men possessed a scattering of different weapons, but with so many combatants in the space, they were of little effect.

The gang of men brought Donovan out of his stasis, and he quickly joined the game. His landing in the courtyard wasn't quite as good as mine, and he ended up bowling down a half-dozen men before he righted himself. The introduction of a second vampire shook them for a second. About half of the men focused on Donovan. The two of us fought valiantly. Man after man was quickly dispatched. One of them managed to land a blow with some type of heavy object. The shot soundly broke my right arm. I didn't really notice the pain too much. I was pissed. Besides, it still wasn't more annoying than the damned thumping inside my head.

Donovan stomped solidly down on the last man's neck and ended the conflict with a chilling snap of bone. I looked about quickly, and all that remained was the lookout, who still seemed unnerved. He smiled and lit another smoke.

"Fancy. You two put a right proper beating on them twenty. What say we see how you fare with the next twenty?"

I had time to draw a quick breath and twenty more large men poured out into the courtyard. This whole thing was quickly getting out of hand. We couldn't keep this up indefinitely. It would be ace-in-the-hole time right quick. I wondered how many men the dodgy bugger could have gotten.

It seemed as if this second twenty men had just pooled up in a group before us, when, out of the south, a large shadow came sailing overhead like a rush of crows from an Edger Allen Poe story. A rushing sound swirled over us as the swirling shadow solidified into the shape of a human. The blacker-than-night ethereal shadows pooled up into mass as the hulk of a man came crashing down into the space between us and our opposition, like a beach-landing platoon hitting the shores of France.

The dark hulk stood and flexed his thick shoulders. He rolled his head from side to side and cracked his neck. The image was spine tingling.

He was huge, six-foot-something, and powerfully built, with a mass of wavy black hair pulled back away from his face revealing solid features. A long, leathery trench coat gave him a swashbuckler sort of appearance.

I stood there in shock! It was … it was … IT WAS ANTONIO!

What The Hell!

Not waiting for the surprise to fade, Antonio set into the mass of men without concern. He smashed, beat, and kicked each one as they came within range. The twenty-man group toppled like a group of toy soldiers in a sandbox. It was over before Donovan could even offer any assistance. Antonio slammed the last man's corpse to the ground and then threw his head back and howled. All three of us left in the courtyard just stood there staring at him.

I was transfixed by the man in front of me. It really was Antonio. Sensing that there was still a human being alive in the immediate area, my maker turned and glared at the lookout. This time, the lookout seemed much less sure of himself.

"Well, you're a big one. They didn't say nothing 'bout nothing like you. What say we up the number? Twenty seemed easy. How's forty sound, big fella?"

"How many do you possess?" Antonio asked.

It came out so calmly that it even made me scared.

"Another one hundred. Why?"

"Send them all."

Donovan moved up to assume the right-hand-man position, though he too looked as if he didn't want to get too close. Seeing Donovan move snapped me out of my teenage fixation. A hundred men was way too many, even with Antonio here. Seriously, one hundred to three were bad odds.

"All right, Efuru, it's about time you participate."

The words were no more than out of my mouth and my whole chest under my corset began to glow electric blue. The power emanating from the crystals ramped up so quickly that it literally made my spine shake.

"Gentlemen, you may want to hold onto your rage a moment. There's a big boom coming!"

The speed of sound propelled the words to their ears about the time a thunderous electric blue arc of energy burst out from the crystal in all directions. Every combatant before us and around us transitioned from shock to dead to vapor so quickly it was as if they had never been there. The rush of energy stunned both of my companions and knocked the lookout to the ground. Overhead lights blew out, windows shattered in on themselves, and blackness consumed an entire ten-block circle around us.

The only remaining human, the lookout, lay on the concrete shaking. Antonio and Donovan rubbed their eyes back into action. I drew in a lungful of crackling, electric air and quietly walked over to where the lookout was quivering.

"Effie, are there any more humans hiding around here?"

A calm and collected "No" went wafting through my brain, so I turned my attention to the human.

"Did Silverton send you?"

"Yes, ma'am." His voice shook in a way that it hadn't all night. I planted the heel of my boot several inches into his skull and held it there until the twitching stopped.

"Effie, we're done with this whole thing! This time I've finally had enough. Would you please kill every single remaining member of that wretched family, save Silverton? I don't care how old they are or where they are, just make them go away."

"Consider it done."

Efuru reached down deep into the void and summed a dark force that made my whole being cower in fear. I could feel the blackness of death spread out in all directions from us. It consumed the very light from the stars in the sky as it spread.

Effie's natural electric blue was completely replaced by a black so black that nothing could come out of it. It radiated out of her jeweled case for what seemed like an hour but was closer to a minute. It froze the very air around us before finally fading out and being replaced by a mild yellow glow. A very breathy "It's done" lingered through my head as the blackness relented. I could sense an intense satisfaction leaking out of the jeweled prison on the golden chain.

"Efuru? Why in the name of all that is holy didn't you tell me any of this was going to happen? I mean, not even Antonio? Really?"

Effie shimmered into existence in front of me and smiled. Her young face still beaming with the energy of the void. Both of my vampire companions stood with mouths agape, eyes locked on her presence.

"Let's be realistic, Sara. If I had told you what the last weeks were to have brought you, you wouldn't have believed me. And, anyway, didn't you enjoy the surprises?" She smiled and shimmered out of view. I smiled. She was right.

I turned on my heels to face the lads, who were both still trying to compose themselves, and walked straight to Antonio so I could look up into his large dark eyes. He looked down at me and smiled the way he had smiled when we had first met. I was instantly eighteen again.

"I was at my villa in Madrid and heard about your sale. I was already headed this way, so I quickened my pace to see what was going on. I will say I hadn't planned on combat."

I leapt up and wrapped both my arms and legs around his massive chest. He secured one sturdy arm around me and we embraced. I couldn't really feel any pain from my broken arm, but I didn't really care about that anymore. My love, the love of my life, had finally shaken off his funk and come to find me. Whatever happened next, no matter how horrific it might be, it wouldn't be that bad. No, sir, things were looking up!

CHAPTER 31

We all made it back to the Grey Estate well before the sun came up in the east. Antonio promptly shuffled off to my bedchamber for the day. He was still very old school and liked to sleep his way through the daylight hours. I had to have a quick but frank discussion with Donovan. Mr. Wyndell, er, Tate, took it all in stride. He knew he was my lover and not my love. Antonio was the great love of my life and always would remain so. Donovan was not a passing fancy, but he was definitely not Antonio.

I snuck into my bedchamber and snuggled up tight to my love for a few hours around midday. I really needed a nap. The surety that the touch of his body gave me, even after hundreds of years, was so comforting that I didn't want to part from him. Yet, as always, business needed to come before pleasure.

I was up and dressed like a proper lady by the time the sun dimmed over London. Antonio rose at the same time and appeared ready for anything. Donovan was his usual self, sitting in the study, reading a choice volume from the stacks.

I explained to the boys that I had a stop to make, but it was of no consequence. I would be off alone. Antonio said that he needed to make a stop at his estate and check on the place, so he would skulk off for the evening. I said something else about returning in a fashion more in line with his station. Donovan stated that since I was obviously in good hands, he would be heading back to Chicago. I gave him a long embrace and thanked him for all of his assistance over the last days. I told him to not be a stranger at my door. He smiled warmly. Everyone was getting along—how nice.

I separated myself from the lads and headed for the garage as they began to discuss all things vampire. I could just imagine the things Donovan was about to learn from the old man. In the garage, I found the Aston Martin right where I had left it.

The run from outer London up to Kessingland was a little slow after I exited the A-14 onto the A-12 main road, but it whizzed by calmly enough. I parked the auto by the side of the road, outside the boundary of Silverton's property, just down Church Road a piece. It was a quiet road, and the car probably wouldn't be bothered for the amount of time I planned on being gone. It was next to the outer wall on a wide piece of shoulder, so no one should pay it any mind.

The old manor house of the Bennett family occupied a grand location just off the edge of the sea. It sat high on a small point and commanded a good view of the area. As family houses go, it was modest for a grand duke's family, maybe twenty rooms or so.

I found a gate in the fence line not far from the car and made my way across the grounds and up to the manor itself. A Gothic stone affair, it looked as moody as its owners had proven themselves to be. Fortunately, luck was with me that night. I had hoped that, like most old noble homes, the original grand duke had fashioned it in the church style. If he had, there would be a blessing to travelers somewhere about the entrance. That was what I really needed: a way into the house. I didn't want to knock on the door and ask to see him. That just wouldn't do.

It turned out that old Percival hadn't done any scrollwork on the manor, but in a happy bit of providence, I was still given a pass. The Silverton's had placed a finely crafted entrance mat at their door. The word "Welcome" was scrolled across the mat in large letters. Welcome indeed! Thank you, Lady Silverton, or whoever had handled such things.

I slid through the main door of Silverton's manor without sound. I was a wraith unto his soul that night. Moving without as much as stirring the air, I made my way around his dwelling. I found old man Silverton sitting before a hearth with a heavy blanket drawn across his lap. A pair of English setters lay at his feet, halfway between him and the hearth. They were obviously more house dog than hunting at this point. One of them noticed me entering but made no mention of it. Good doggy.

"Good evening, Mr. Silverton, you look all warm and snuggly tucked into your chair."

You could tell the sound of my even-toned voice put the shake in his spine, though he didn't show it. He was a staunch old bugger. I casually sat in another chair situated off angle to his and smiled at him coldly.

"When I heard the news of last evening, I concluded that it was only a matter of time before you came to darken my door."

"Darken my door? Hmm, you darkened my door first as I remember."

"You wronged my family. That insult could not stand."

"I wronged a member of your family who, by the by, wronged me first. I evened an account and moved on. I cared not about your family then, nor do I now. But you people just can't seem to let go of a feud, can you?"

"Done us no wrong? You have attacked every generation of our great family."

"After they attacked me, sir. And let's be realistic, your family isn't nearly as noble as they appear. There's always a dark secret or two floating around, isn't there?"

"You are a ghoul!"

Old man Silverton glared at me with all of the contempt that he could muster. He was too frail to fight, so he just decided to go out with the verbal attack. No worries, I have pretty thick skin.

"Yes. By the definition of the word, I am just that."

"You may kill me and the rest of my family, but you will always be just that, a ghoul."

"Well, 'long is the way, and hard, that out of hell leads up to light.' Or so said Mr. Milton. He did seem well versed to talk on the topic."

"You will never stop me from coming after you. You can kill me, yes, but you can't stop me or my family. We will always hunt you!"

"That, broken old man, is where you are wrong. I have already killed every single member of the whole extended Bennett family. There is no one to carry on your stupid vendetta. And, to be clear, I can do far worse things to you than kill you, but I won't. I, unlike you, have no deep-seated hatred to be quelled. I simply want to exist in as much peace as I can."

"I hate every fiber of your being, vampire."

"And that is why you are living your last day on this earth. Sad, really."

"You will not kill me in my own house! Not while I have breath in me!"

The dogs stirred but didn't come to attention.

"I have no intention of killing you, old man. Your blood would be foul in my mouth. But, be sure, you will not see the sun rise in the east."

"Hmmph!"

I stood and turned to leave; the conversation was obviously complete. The old man had no nobility in him. He deserved less than a quiet death, but that was not the way of things.

As I made my way from the room, Effie gave his heart a nice little squeeze and the heart attack did the rest. He was dead in his chair, dogs at his feet, before I had casually walked back to my flash car. I paused to look back up the low rise to the house, which was about to become an entrusted part of the crown's property. Why did people need to be so miserable? Why was it necessary to not let go of things? Was it all just bad blood? I shrugged. Whatever the answers were, they mattered no longer. My long battle with Grand Duke Bennett was over. Good deed done.

"Effie, thank you for all of your help. I feel as if I have become one of those men you despise so much. I will do my best not to call on your services again."

I could feel my body get all warm as Effie infused me with her power. A subtle yellow glow began to emanate through my dress.

"Yes, you will. It's all right, as we are friends, and friends help each other."

The words ran through my head as I slipped the Aston into gear. She was content, so it must be fine.

I made my way back down the A-12 main road and onto the Grey Estate. I had rid myself of the last bit of trouble in my life and found the path that would lead me back to happiness. I was sure that Antonio returning to London was a sign of good things for me. Yes, I was sure. Effie was not giving off the slightest bit of sensation that bad things were coming. I had spent the better part of a century battling with the Bennett family. The feud had forced me to make some hard decisions regarding my existence. It was almost like one nation fighting another, just not as bloody.

I parked the Aston in its space and made my way back into my manor. As expected, Antonio was in the study. He was reading the tales of English grand nobility, which was still lying on my desk. He seemed perfectly content with himself. He seemed the same man I had taken walks with when I was human. He was a tiny bit larger than life and oozed a quiet charm that was intoxicating. He was a creature fully different than the one I had talked with in Constantinople. He had found himself.

I sat in my favorite chair and inspected my maker. He was calm and handsome for sure; that made my blood hot. He really was the thing that I would always want in life. Maybe I could never have a family, but that now seemed okay. Maybe I could find a family, as I had done with the Wyndells. Maybe I could never find true love? No, that wasn't true - I had found true love long ago. Maybe I could never have a traditional relationship with a man and grow old with someone, but I had eternity to share with this man who made me so happy and so miserable. Little bits stuck together could be enough. Maybe, just maybe, that was the real secret of it all. It's not meant to be pretty or easy, or well-adjusted. It's really meant to be chaotic and haphazard. Well, if that was the case, I would now be content and take the couple days a century that came my way.

Antonio closed the big book on the desk and came to sit next to me. He told me how he had continued west after our meeting in Istanbul. He had pulled up in Markopoulon, outside Athens, for a short time before continuing on to Zadar in Croatia. The area of the Eastern European sect had always sat well with him, so he stayed for a time. Finally deciding to go home, he continued west, eventually stopping for a time in Malta. Finding Mellieha to his liking, he stayed. He just chilled out in the middle of the Mediterranean for decades. He fasted and considered his ways for a time. He sat there and thought about life until he decided that he didn't need to think about it any longer. So, he hopped a local fishing boat to the coast and headed home to Madrid.

Once he had made it home, he decided that he liked this new Madrid as much as he had liked the one of his birth. He spent many nights comparing one particular area to what it had been in centuries past.

His brooding days were past him. He was going to be happy for a time. He decided that he needed to do something about the way he had left things in Istanbul. He was readying to leave for England when he heard about the sale of the corporation. The news had sent a small tremor through his companies. He knew it was all probably inevitable, but he wanted to come see what was going on for himself. That was how he ended up stumbling into the middle of my melee with the Bennetts. Donovan had been good enough to fill him in on the broad strokes of the affair before he departed. He seemed indifferent to the overall outcome, as I was a survivor and would obviously prevail.

I filled in the parts that Donovan had not. Antonio listened to it all. We moved on to talk about all manner of things before the sun rose in the east. With the rising sun, we retired to my bedchamber for the daylight hours. It had been a long interval since I had shared my bedchamber with someone of Antonio's caliber. We did many things, none of which I will discuss here.

He stayed in London for about a week and then quietly headed off. It was his way. He was an old-school predator. He moved on as to not disturb his food source. He killed to live; something I had not done in a long time. I killed one here and there, mostly for sport. Antonio still used blood to get by, like the rest of our kind.

He promised to return one day and stay a while longer. I loved him for just exactly who he was. I was happy to see him happy. I watched him go and started counting the days until his return. Hope springs eternal, especially for vampires. Yes, things were good.

CHAPTER 32

Being rich and unbothered, life passed me by in an unexpectedly calm sort of way for the next couple decades. Having offed a couple hundred Bennetts, there seemed to be no one out there any longer wanting to bother me; and with the sale of the corporation, there was nothing much that needed looking after. There was no work needed doing, and no money needed making; it was just smashing.

I kind of went back to doing what rich people do. I decided to enjoy myself for a time. I had no illusions that things wouldn't change, but right now, at this time, they were fine.

A couple years on, I sent out a cordial correspondence to Jeremy Black, PhD, the newest administrator of the Enfield Trust. He had sent me a note when he had assumed the position from Eugene. He seemed the nice sort, like Eugene, so I decided to be nice to him. The Trust had kept their word and not bothered me, which required some level of gratitude in return.

Doctor Black was the first member of the whole ancient institution who was not a nobleman. He had made his way in straight out of academia. He was pleasant and friendly, and we talked together for some long hours. I forwarded the Trust a healthy donation, suitably sized for an Earl, to help with their archiving. They were quite appreciative of the gesture.

I finally managed to make it up to Scotland and track down Zoe. Okay, it wasn't that difficult. I called her and asked her what her address was. The trip north in the Land Rover was quiet and comfortable. It was also not nearly as long as expected. It was grand. The highlands of

Scotland are a vast and beautiful, windswept place. I could easily see William Wallace riding down out of the crags, claymore strapped to his side.

I spent a few weeks with Zoe, just doing what vampires do. We hunted a little and talked for hours, mostly about female topics. She was an excellent host and it was all quite fine. I liked hunting up there very much. The nights were "black as the Earl of Hell's waistcoat!" as Zoe would say. And pitch black they were. The stars came out in numbers I could never count. I had never seen so many stars.

Sometime in the middle of the 1970s, I headed down Vatican way and had a quiet audience with the newest cardinal in charge of the History and Archives Department. He, like so many that came before him, was a man with much broader views than most of his contemporaries. They had obviously been keeping informed of me as they went along, because he greeted me with my given name. He was Catholic but instantly likeable.

I stopped on the way home and spent a bit of time wandering around Monte Carlo. The French Rivera really was the ultra-fashionable destination that the Sun's travel section had made it out to be. I liked it so much that I bought a cliff-side bungalow, just outside of the principality. I know, I hate the French—call it a hedge investment.

All of my milling about Europe gave me a great amount of time to observe the actions of my little friend. She appeared to be content with everything and was never put out by my wonderings. She simply moved along with me—no fuss, no muss. She never asked anything of me. She never wanted to go anywhere or see anything. She just gave me energy and traveled with me quietly. I found it all a little odd. She had been on this earth since before there was a written language and longer than most civilizations. You would think that there would be some place that she might like to visit, some spot on the globe she would find comfort in. Maybe she had seen so much that she no longer distinguished one thing from the next? I doubted that. She was on top of her surroundings, and normally on top of mine as well. If she wanted something specific, she would definitely go get it.

Maybe, she didn't know she wanted something. Maybe, she had been traveling for so long that she assumed that was all there was. It made me wonder if she had ever returned to her home. Had she ever made it back to the lands of her human life, sometime later in years, to see what time had made of it? She could easily manipulate men to do whatever she wanted; she must have gone home at some point. But, what if she hadn't?

I pondered this thought, deep down in my mind, and then I decided to do something nice for my magickal friend. She had done countless deeds for me; it would be nice to give her something. I would take her home and let her see her youth. Interestingly, it also would require little work. I was one of maybe three people on the planet that basically knew where she came from. It took a bit of shifty side reading to further narrow it down to a spot on the map but required little study. One needed to be ultra-careful, as it was quite easy to raise her suspicions. But covert I was. Lessons learned; now all put to good use.

In 1981 I purchased my first private plane. It was a white Learjet 31A and could comfortably carry eight people. It was new and gleamy, and so very flash. I was officially a jetsetter.

My new tall ship was white with a blue stripe down both sides. She had five small windows per side and two large jet engines toward the tail. Sleek and nimble, she could take me and my pilot some 1,400 miles before needing more fuel. She gave me the same feeling of home that *The Summer Storm* had given me so many years ago.

My pilot's name was James, and he was ex-SAS. He was large and commanding, a man not to be trifled with. He was also a very good pilot.

I climbed aboard my shiny new airplane on the first of July, and we made our way from London down to Nice. I did a little shopping, and then we continued on. The sun was just breaking past the horizon on its way to the underworld when our wheels touched down on a sketchy, packed-dirt stretch of runway in Djelfa, Algeria. Not much more than a crossroads, in the midst of nothing, the city was a fuel dump surrounded by a scattering of mud-brick huts and a spring. The place lacked a definable smell, but the feeling of nothingness could not be overlooked. Tuaregs could be seen coming and going in the distance as Bedouins kept about the local.

We were met at our plane by a dozen interested locals and a fat Bedouin named Omar. Omar was a warm and happy fellow. He took command of me and escorted me off to the local hotel as James secured the Lear.

'The desert was empty but not quiet, and large but not comforting.' Those words, wherever they originally came from, where definitely true of this place. A sleepless night was to be found in the mud made town, as Effie twitched and pulsed with energy. I think she already suspected where we were headed, but she said nothing.

In the morning sunrise, we were met by a weathered Tuareg man named Samir. He climbed into a ramshackle truck that Omar had acquired, and the four of us headed south. James had had dealings with both men on previous occasions and was quickly asleep in the back. I stared out of the dusty, sand-pounded windows at the endless dunes stretching out before us in amazement. The power of the sun in the desert was formidable, forcing its way through my Wayfarer sunglasses as if they weren't even there. The completely opaque lenses were no match for the power of the sun as it reflected off the dunes. Effie could sense my headache coming on and haloed up my eyes for me. The mystical reprieve was greatly appreciated.

Sometime past midday, we all stopped on the western outskirts of the Tassili-n-Ajjer area and transitioned to camels. The sun was all but relentless and the numerous coverings that the Tuareg suggested I wear were a definite savior. Effie became very calm as we made our way out into the wadi. That made me apprehensive. She had still not uttered a thought to me.

We came to our destination of Tin Taradjeli by the time the sun was tipping. There were still numerous hours of daylight left in the day as we disembarked our smelly transportation at the small Tuareg encampment. Samir talked with several old men, who obviously were in charge. Omar took charge of the camels. James came to my side, and we waited.

The old men of the desert looked at me, as if they were looking at the Ginn. It gave me a bad feeling. I didn't know if they had ever seen white people or if it was something else. Memory is long in the desert, so they say. They looked at me as if they were looking at a demon, which was true to the case. I began to get nervous. The more I became nervous, the calmer Effie became, if that was even possible. She was so calm that she wasn't even there anymore. No, I mean she had left her crystal cage completely. The power of the amulet was dead. She was gone. I didn't know where she had gone to, but I was sure it was bad.

As the old men talked, a high wind began in the distance that made the dunes to the north come to life and smoke. Soon after, a low-pitched drumming could be heard. All the Tuareg men pulled their veils across their faces and began to murmur to each other. After several more minutes of drumming, they collectively pointed off in a direction past the dunes, toward some stone outcroppings. Samir nodded and came over to where we were standing.

Samir spoke with Omar for a moment and then he returned to the others. Omar looked ashen. That certainly couldn't be good. He tried to compose himself as best as he could.

"The elders say you are Ginn, that you bring Raoul, the Drummer of Death, with you. Raoul has not been seen in the Tassili for countless centuries. You are bad spirits."

James and I looked at each other in amazement. He was insulted and confused; I certainly wasn't. I had done a bad, bad thing. Efuru had come home, and she apparently had different rules at home.

"They say what you come to see is in that direction, past the dunes. Head for the stone cliffs. They want you to go see and then leave. Leave very soon."

I tapped James on the arm in a reassuring manner, letting him know I'd be fine on my own. Then, I headed out into the dunes. The walk out away from the camp was peaceful and easy. Some twenty minutes on, I was looking at a mystery.

Basically, the Tin Tarabine is a big chunk of rock in the middle of dune land. Call it a billboard for times gone by. Rock paintings of what appeared to be shamanistic rituals were surrounded by pictograms of cattle, giraffe, and water buffalo. It was amazing. It was ancient. It was possibly as old as Effie was. I inspected the curious imprints that looked akin to human footprints as Effie swirled around me.

The dust storm that she was whipping up was dense to the point of being opaque. It swirled around me like an on-land hurricane. Where I stood in the middle was almost dead calm, while all else was a raging sandstorm.

Off to the opposite edge of the circulating mass, a human form emerged from the maelstrom. It was Efuru. I don't mean an aberration of Efuru, like when she shimmers into light, but it was an actual human. It was Efuru. She walked the dunes with a large, happy smile on her face. A child out in the midst of nothing, clad in naught but animal skins. Her hair was knotted and gnarled but looked somehow in place with her manner of dress.

She walked about as if she was looking at a completely different scene than the one before me. She would stop and inspect some invisible object and then move along quietly. To me it was all just shifting sand. She moved along as a child looking at flowers until she made her way to me. She stopped, looked up at me, and smiled warmly.

"There was no sand in my day. The great Sahara had not migrated into my home yet. Originally, it was an oasis of beauty. Now, it still is, you just need to look harder to see it."

She spoke in an unintelligible mix of grunting that translated into English in my mind. It was her. It was definitely Effie speaking. She reached up and touched her fingers to the side of my temple, and like Dorthy going to Oz, I was transported there.

The new scene before me was of a lush, grass-covered land. A lake in the distance had boats out on it, and streams fed meadows full of animals. Numerous structures were scattered about the scene as I panned my vision from left to right. It was amazing. It was a truly different setting to the one we were actually standing in. I was in awe.

Effie pulled back her fingers and the swirling sand reemerged. She smiled and went back to what she was doing. I sat down in the sand and watched as she explored her lost world. She seemed completely happy here. I wondered why she had never come back to her home. She obviously had the power to escape her imprisonment. I could tell that she enjoyed her home. It seemed odd.

Effie made her way here and there for about another hour before slowly coming back around to where I was sitting. She sat down in the dunes next to me and smiled.

"I have been back here a handful of times since my confinement. I do enjoy it all very much, as you seem to think, but it is just an illusion. My time passed this place by many millennia ago. Now, it's a new place, and it should be allowed to be that place. Though, walking about this illusion does make me greatly happy."

"I am greatly relieved that you are greatly happy. At first I thought I had done a bad thing, with the drumming and all; but now that I know you're pleased, I'm pleased."

"The appearance of Raoul does give the Tuareg quite a start. It's good for them to have a fit now and again."

"So, you're happy?"

"Happy? I'm giddy. You, Sara Grey, never cease to amaze me. Of all the creatures that I have met in my time, I really do like you best."

"You are also tops with me."

Effie laughed. She was such an old soul trapped in a child's body.

"Thank you for this, Sara. Now, I am going to take another walk around, and then we should be on our way. Don't worry about the old men in the encampment. They know you travel with me, so they will be of no bother. Thank you very much, Sara Grey."

I nodded as she stood. As per plan, she wandered about for say another forty minutes and then shimmered back into the dust from whence she had appeared. As she faded from view, the sandstorm began to blow itself out. Only minutes more, and no one could even tell that anything had happened. The desert looked pristine.

I walked quietly back to the encampment and climbed onto my camel with little fanfare. No Tuaregs were to be seen. Omar escorted James and I back to our transport, and we departed Algeria without incident. I could tell that my name would be spoken with hushed tones among the Tuareg for centuries to come. That was fine with me. It was comforting to me that, somewhere on the planet, they still embraced the old ways.

CHAPTER 33

Today was a pretty good day, by my standards. Effie and I have been up to our usual trickery since coming back from Africa. Things have also been quiet on the opposition front since we dispatched old man Silverton. No more bad blood. It's been all-quiet, all-glorious.

About four days ago I sent the jet to Chicago to fetch Donovan. He had sent me an e-mail saying that he would probably be paying London a visit. I didn't see any reason that he needed to be flying commercial to do it.

I had been seeing Antonio quite regularly since he had come back to his senses. His presence in my life has been a great stabilizing force. He is still solidly a night creature. I think he is still under the impression that the amulet allows me to move about during the day. I'm not about to break his illusions. It's just superb camouflage.

Over the years I had my wealth moved around a bit. Investments in currencies other than British Sterling helped me suffer through that downturn in the market. I currently own currencies in some half-dozen countries. I did own a big chunk of euros, but they proved to be a bad investment, so I dumped them. At least having all of the European economies tied together helps to reduce all the infighting on the continent. As countries go; that was then and this is now, I guess.

I rose with the sun this morning to find a text from Antonio, telling me to have a fine day. He was apparently off to bed. I replied to his text and said that he should meet me at that bar out King's Cross way once the sun tipped again.

I wandered into the bath and took a nice hot, soapy shower. The waterfall showerhead rained down hot water on me and brought me back to existence. Shuffling back into my bedchamber, I pulled my favorite Catholic schoolgirl uniform out of the wardrobe. The blouse was one size too small, as was the fashion of the day, and my natural curves strained the buttons. Both of the lads liked the outfit exceptionally well. They were both old hound dogs, as my Yankee friends back in the NYC say.

I collected up my long, naturally blonde hair into a bunch at the back of my head, fixed it with my favorite ivory chopsticks, and left it to tumble down my back. A little splash of Dior, and I was good to go. I grabbed my Ray-Bans and headed for the terrace. Upon arrival, my just-more-than-middle-aged house master James (Yes, he's a Wyndell, but please, don't ask. It would take too long to explain here.) gave me his customary disapproving look.

"Good morning, Sara. Ladies shouldn't dress in such fashion, ma'am."

"Yes, James, I know. Thank you for your concern. I'll be more ladylike tomorrow."

He finished planting the tea service in the middle of the table, and I took up my usual station. He was sweet and knew full well about my alternative lifestyle. He also made me happy. He was an accomplished conversationalist. He held a law degree from Cambridge. What he found to be exceptional about being my housekeeper I really couldn't tell you.

After tea I was in the Aston and down to the city. I spent most of the morning padding in and out of the High Street shops. Decidedly done shopping, I made my way over to Mayfair for a long leisurely lunch. It was a light lunch of course, since I certainly didn't need the calories. I sat and read the business pages in the salon of the Park Lane Mews with a nice glass of single malt. The numerous male patrons didn't really know what to make of me, but the barman had been serving me for some time and liked the way I tipped. I was happy to see that the Wyndell boys were moving full-forward and that Grey's Cargo stock was at an all-time high. That bit of news made me especially happy. I thought that tomorrow I should walk up the hill and tell Father and Charles that things were going grand.

Homework done for the day, I sent Donovan a text and headed out into the city. I have recently discovered that people-watching on the steps of the British Museum is quite enjoyable during the warm summer months. The scene taking place about the wide, cascading steps and lawn is constantly in motion with passersby of every type. Many people from London just come to hangout on the steps and watch the people. It is a fine way to waste an afternoon. I retrieved a Coke from one of the ubiquitous snack carts and did just that. The day was warm and the traffic on the steps was heavy.

Soon enough it seemed, the day was winding down. I directed the Aston to a private garage a couple blocks off Euston Road and walked to the corner of Euston and Midland Road. There was a local on the corner that had outside seats, where one could watch the traffic shoot past. I had stopped there numerous times over the decades that it had been open. There was something rewarding about hunting King's Cross. I think it is all the backpackers that pass through. It's a transient crowd, like in olden days.

I retrieved a pint of bitters from the barman and a dozen inspecting glances from the crowd, and then I wandered outside and found a seat at one of the empty tables. I quickly dispatched a couple different inquiring chaps and waved to some random honking cars. The late afternoon was warm, and I sat for only a short time before Donovan came strolling around the corner to entertain me. He had no more than retrieved a pint from the barman, when Antonio appeared as well. He treated himself, refilled my glass, and took a seat across the table with Donovan.

The three of us sat and discussed different facets of the world as twilight slowly transitioned to streetlights. I looked past the two sturdy killers and focused on the buildings across the way. The new and architecturally current one was the British Library. It sat on the opposing street corner to the old, imposing, heavy stone of the Saint Pancras train station. The two contrasting buildings were a perfect example of the passage of time. They reminded me that I was like them:

I was both old and new. I was both strong and sturdy, made from stone, yet current and trendy as all things new.

I rolled this thought around in my mind happily, until Antonio said something that pulled me back to the conversation. That was the way of things with me: drifting here and there with the tides, sometimes blown off course by the storms but face always toward the sun.

The three of us had another pint and we were done. Donovan was off to the airport, Antonio was headed out to find his dinner, and I was on my way home. The Aston made good time getting north, and in no time at all I was walking through my front door. I retrieved a Scotch from the liquor table in the study and ambled into one of the salons, where James was quietly watching a James Bond movie on the tele. It was a Sean Connery, so I flopped down on the settee and shuffled around till I was comfy.

That's pretty much the way of things right now. I enjoy the lads when they stop by. I enjoy the quiet time watching tele with James when it's there. The remainder of the time I fill with whatever it happens to get filled with. Sometimes I do earl stuff. Sometimes I do rich-girl stuff. And sometimes I hang out on the settee, nuzzled up against James.

I swirled my glass and dumped the Scotch down my throat. Sadly, the demonic part of my metabolism slowly counteracted the alcohol in the Scotch, but it tasted nice. A commercial for *Top Gear* came on. James tilted his head and smiled at me. I smiled back. And Effie just hung there, unaffected by it all.

I don't know how long this will last. Change in the world is inevitable, and my enemies seem to come from the strangest places at the strangest times. But for right now, my life is just fine.